IN A
HOLDING
HOUSE

Emma-Jane Dempsey

ORIGINAL WRITING

In A Holding House © 2012 by Emma-Jane Dempsey

Edited by Emma Sherry

All rights reserved. No part of this publication may be reproduced in any form or by any means—graphic, electronic or mechanical, including photocopying, recording, taping or information storage and retrieval systems—without the prior written permission of the author.

This book is a work of fiction. The characters, names, series of events and places are either thought of at random or are used fictitiously. Any resemblance to true events, names and characters is purely coincidental.

ISBN : 978-1-909007-28-4

A CIP catalogue for this book is available from the National Library.

Published by ORIGINAL WRITING LTD., Dublin, 2012.

Printed by CLONDALKIN GROUP, Glasnevin, Dublin 11

This book is dedicated to my sisters

Jennifer Connolly,

Johanne Connolly

and, of course, Alison Mulhare.

Acknowledgements

Thank you to all my friends and family who kept me sane when I was being a hermit. Thank you to the wise people who put me on the right path and gave me answers to a million annoying questions. I appreciate everything you have done. You know who you are. Thank you to the people who shared their experiences with me. Your stories will inspire me forever and hopefully will inspire other people to intervene unashamedly when they see the signs that a child might be in distress.

And most of all I want to acknowledge the Social Workers in Ireland. I have heard some of your stories and I now know you are the real true super hero's of our time.

Contents

1	1
2	24
3	46
4	65
5	76
6	93
7	104
8	114
9	127
10	141
11	157
12	173
13	187
14	202
15	214
16	226
Epilogue	244

I

Orla wedged the receiver between her neck and shoulder, and in a bit of a struggle took a packet of strong painkillers from the stiff top drawer of her worn-out desk. It was only mid morning Tuesday and already she could feel the golf ball of stress thumping behind her eyes. That particular annoyance usually only came on a Friday afternoon or in the evenings if she worked too late. Its unexpected arrival had thrown her a bit. Maybe she needed a day off.

In a voice that was monotone – to say the least – Orla repeated herself for the fifth time in three minutes.

"Miss Kelly, you have two hours with her at two o'clock on Saturday in the usual place. That's all we can do. I'm sorry but that's just how it is. We can't change appointments, you know that." Orla hated dealing with people who refused to accept what she was saying. Unfortunately, she had found it to be a massive part of her career. She had to repeat herself over and over until stubborn parents got tired and gave up trying to bend the court-ordered terms of their visitation; there was no bending of the rules in Orla's job, not when it came to the people she dealt with. Most of the time Orla had to take a barrage of crap talk before they got the message and gave up. It didn't bother her any more, once she managed to get off the phone while still holding some level of professional composure.

She popped the painkillers through the foil on their plastic tray and let them fall out straight into her mouth. She chased them down with a swig of sweet tea that hadn't been warm in some time, from a cup that ironically read 'WORK ROCKS'.

"But I can't get the bus. That's what I'm trying to tell ya! We can't all be drivin' around in BMWs, us regular people have to use the public transport and… " It was at this point that Orla stopped listening. What was the point?

The office number had been a free phone number until her supervisor Mark realised that parents stayed on the phone for long periods because it was free, and they got more nonsense calls when it didn't cost the 'clients' anything. They had also gotten a shitload of prank calls and drunken threats at all hours of the day, even late at night when the security guard Marcus acted as receptionist for the night staff. Marcus was a master at dealing with angry drunk callers by the time the phones were changed. A lot of parents had only bothered calling the office because it didn't cost them anything. It was a sad fact. In Orla's job you got used to sad facts.

"Look Eileen," she started again, even more direct in her approach to the young mother. "You have been getting the bus every Saturday for the past three Saturdays. Why this week is any different you have still failed to tell me. I know it costs €1.20 to get there and €1.20 back. You get your dole every week so there is no excuse that will work at all. Now, you are only in your first month of visitation with Nicole and already you're saying you can't make it. It's a slippery slope and if you start down it this early on you will keep going down it. I'm telling you that you will regret it when you have sorted your situation out and you're looking to reinstate full custody. So are you coming or not? Because I will not make Nicole wait for you when you're not going to show up."

"Tell her I'm not well and I'll see her when I see her." Eileen slammed down the phone. For such a young woman she spoke like she was much older then her years. It annoyed Orla a bit but she didn't really know why.

She exhaled patiently and put down the receiver. Of course, after working in this area for six years she knew when a parent had no intention of making their visit with their kids. She just hated the song and dance they went through in an attempt to make her believe their bullshit, face-saving excuses. Orla had heard more lies and excuses from parents in her career than she had had hot dinners growing up in Laois. Why they always had to be so ridiculous she would never know; she had heard it all though, that was for sure. There was the odd occasion when a dedicated parent with a good visitation record might have a genuine reason like death, natural disaster or being involved in a traffic accident on the way to the visit but these people were at what Orla called 'stage three' and there really weren't many parents in stage three in Orla's jurisdiction. A lot of parents in stage one though. Stage one is the anger and stand-offishness directly after the initial point of contact between Orla's department and questionable parents. Stage ones rarely made much of an effort, especially in the first weeks or months. Their noses were disjointed at the interference of a state body into something as personal as their family life. They usually expressed their anger in a totally counterproductive way. They would be rude to the social workers, not show up for visitation, and go on benders. If the children are still in their care, stage ones can be very dangerous.

Stage two is a more stable period, when they realise that no amount of shouting or threatening is going to get them what they want and they start to communicate with the social workers in a more positive, receptive way – well, a less aggressive way anyway.

Then there's stage three, the best stage. Stage three is when action happens, when the parents actually make substantial improvements. They make an effort to correct their behaviour and to develop a more stable relationship with their offspring in different ways. Stage two is usually when lowlifes give up and they lose their children to the system. Only the strong get to stage three. Generally most parents make a huge effort in the beginning, only to fall back to stage one when they get sick of the hard work. This sad fact stung Orla just as badly now as it had when she first experienced a case that looked to be improving, only to fall flat when the mother got sick of the effort it took to keep up the façade.

Eileen Kelly was not yet allowed to be tagged as stage three. She was only just after crossing the line into stage two and in light of what had just happened on the phone, she was seriously threatening to fall back a stage. Eileen didn't have a good track record. She had been heroin dependent for years and was only trying to get off it now. She hadn't been clean long. Her life had revolved more around the drug than around her own daughter. She would rather stick a needle in her arm than feed the bright little girl. She hardly noticed her daughter at all when most of her time was spent using.

Nicole was badly affected by her mother's indifference to her. It broke Orla's heart when she had walked into that filthy, damp flat and found the beautiful little girl hiding under her mother's worn and heavily stained duvet. Eileen was someone that would be happy not to have the burden of a little girl to look after. Orla was amazed Eileen had managed to keep custody of the girl for as long as she did. Nicole was a lovely child. Very smart, but very quiet. Her little eyes had seen so much that her mouth gave up trying to keep up with normal day-to-day conversation. Orla suspected that Nicole kept her voice as a survival tool, only using it when she needed it to have an impact on her mother. Intelligent children learn to be very cunning in bad situations and Eileen certainly put Nicole in some very bad situations. She wasn't beaten as far as Orla could tell but she had definitely seen far too much for such a young girl.

Eileen was in care when she fell pregnant at fifteen. She was moved into an unmarried mother and baby facility then eventually got a flat from Dublin City Council's housing authority. Noelle, who retired four years after Orla started social work, had been over Eileen's case since she was fifteen and pregnant, and had gone to massive extremes to ensure Nicole's wellbeing. She would call over in the evenings and weekends just to keep an eye on the girl, but she never removed her or made any reports of anything negative Eileen Kelly had done. Noelle had had her favourites. She would go to the ends of the earth for one case and wouldn't make a phone call for another, seemingly for no particular reason other than she preferred some of her cases over others. It drove Orla crazy but because the family had been so used to such an active social worker Orla felt she couldn't let the standard drop. Nicole depended on the visits and Orla thought things would have gotten worse if Eileen didn't have to worry about a social worker popping over at any time. She had tried the same tactic at first, only to find that Eileen hated her guts for not turning a blind eye to the things Noelle had never even commented on, and slowly over the next year and eight months Eileen's level of care for Nicole had dropped and dropped until Orla and her supervisor finally had no choice but to remove the skinny, sad little girl.

Nicole had deteriorated massively in the three days it took Orla's supervisor and the offices legal rep, Jean McCaile, to get the green light for a forcible removal. Eileen had a never-ending string of flings and romances so when the Guards broke in the front door and Orla had found Nicole she wasn't at all surprised to discover the child had been left alone for two days while her mother was down the country with some fella. Not surprised but still disgusted. Nicole had been left with two boxes of cereal and a two-litre drum of milk. It isn't particularly hard to be disgusted at behaviour like that.

Orla didn't understand these people. She could not get her head around their choices and fuck ups. Surely if you can be bothered going through nine months of pregnancy and then hours or even days of agonising labour for these children, you can be bothered looking after them. Or even just bathe and feed them! But of course Orla knew that not everyone had the same moral standards as she did. As much as Orla hated the adults she dealt with on a daily basis, her passion to raise the bar for the children whose files and stories were brought to her attention more than made up for it. But telling a child their parent would be missing a highly anticipated visit, especially for the first missed visit, tugged at her heart more than she would like to admit, being a professional and all.

She picked up the receiver again and punched in the number of the youth care centre where Nicole was now happily housed. After three rings a sweet, sing-song voice tickled Orla's eardrum.

"Hello, Annabelle speaking. How can I help you?" Orla smiled widely. She knew Annabelle well and knew that despite the calm in her voice, chances were that Annabelle was covered in finger paint and spew-up with at least one toddler on her hip and more tugging at her clothes.

"Hey Annabelle. How are things going down there?" Orla heard a small child start to cry in the back ground but she didn't recognise the cry. "Sorry, are you too busy to talk? I can call back in a few minutes if you want?" Sometimes when Orla needed to talk to Annabelle she would have to call back after Annabelle had the children set up with a game with the assistants or a movie in the den so the flowing-haired, usually barefooted carer could have a few minutes to get down to business.

"Hi Orla. No, we're grand to talk. Most of them are in school. We are absolutely tip top here. Happy out. We have a new little girl, Penny, who arrived today so we are having a little welcome party. She is a doll and a half. We have three empty places at the moment too but I don't think they'll be free for too long."

"Oh don't worry, I'm not calling for a bed. How's Nicole?" Orla asked, not wanting to keep Annabelle any longer than she had to.

"She's in school now but she's okay. Much better but still a way to go yet. Still quiet, but not nearly as quiet." Annabelle giggled but then sensed what was coming; her voice fell grave. "I'm guessing this Saturday is off then?"

Orla sighed loudly.

"They are always great in the beginning. Eileen says she can't afford the bus but she wants us to tell Nicole that she is sick. I think that's a bit traumatising. The poor girl will be picturing her mother all by herself and sick to boot. What do you think?"

Annabelle tutted loudly three times.

"Yeah you're right. Not seeing her mam for a little while might not be too bad an idea. Nicole has been doing great but when she comes back from a visit it's like she comes back worse off. It takes a few hours and a lot of coaxing to get her to come back around and if we didn't we wouldn't hear a peep from her." It wasn't hard to find the note of annoyance in Annabelle's response. She hated "wishy-washy" parents; her words, not Orla's.

More dots in the case of Eileen and Nicole Kelly were joining together in Orla's mind. She was getting a far clearer picture of the pair.

"I know. The supervisor said their meetings are awkward and strained. All three visit reports said that Nicole was eager to please her mother and wanted more physical affection from Eileen but she just ignores her. She sets Nicole up drawing or playing a game then she reads magazines."

Annabelle tutted loudly again.

"That's what it is so. Anyway, don't worry about telling her. I'll do that. I'll stick it in the staff email too. Yvette and Louise are with me today; I'll make sure we give her some extra-special attention."

Orla felt the pressure between her shoulder blades ease up a bit. Annabelle was a godsend. She knew exactly what to do for each child to make them more comfortable and still she ran the home like clockwork. Annabelle was a perfect combination of easygoing calm, total organisation and efficiency. She gave that home her all, and at times like this Orla wished they were closer so she could express her utter gratitude for Annabelle's kindness. Knowing that once a child walked in through Annabelle's gate they would be perfectly safe and lovingly cared for was something that Orla did not take for granted. Instead she settled for

"You're one in a million Annabelle. Thank you so much."

Annabelle's smile rang down the phone in her voice.

"Anytime. Anyway, I hope you'll be down to visit us soon? A few of the little monkeys would be delighted with a visit."

"Of course. I might see you by the end of the week. I'll give you a buzz and let you know when I'm on my way. Thanks again Annabelle."

"Great! Not a worry at all. I'll have tea and bickies ready. Bye!"

Before the line went dead Orla could hear Annabelle go straight into another conversation with a little someone who wasn't allowed to pour more red paint... .

No time to dawdle of course. As soon as the conversation with Annabelle was over Orla noticed her supervisor Mark hovering over her shoulder, with a definite hint of distress on his face.

"What's up Mark?" Orla swivelled to face the pale little man. Mark always looked sick, or 'under the weather' one might say. For a weak-looking man he had a strong voice. It was a funny sort of combination.

"We got a call from a teacher in a national school," he began as he walked around Orla and perched himself on the edge of her desk. Orla hated when people did that. Their butts on her work space, like it was nothing. She always managed to stop herself from showing her displeasure.

"It's pretty worrying really. I would go myself only I have my whole day blocked with those bloody things." Mark gestured across the room to a stack of files on the floor beside his cubicle; it must have been as high as Orla's hip, and that was pretty high. She could just see it through the alleys between the desks of her colleagues. Orla turned back to her desk and flipped open her diary.

"Okay, no problemo. Who am I meeting? Where am I going?"

Mark looked visibly relieved.

"Her name is Grainne Hopkins. She is a High Infant's teacher in The Divine Trinity. Dinny Thomas went there."

Orla thought for a second. Yes there was a vague memory of the small school in Swords.

"I remember it. So does she know I'm coming?"

"Yeah of course. The claims she is making could be down to a few things. Basically, a young girl in her class, who only moved to the school this year, seems to have lost weight throughout the school year. A lot of weight. The teacher seems to think she is at the point of being malnourished. Every day she has a packed lunch and perfect uniform but supposedly the child hardly touches her food and even though the uniform is perfect, she has poor personal hygiene and falls asleep in class. Sounds like a domestic issue but it could be an illness or something the family haven't informed the school about yet. I need you to check out the school then the home."

Orla went into autopilot instantly.

"We need a reason for contact. Has she missed many days at all?"

Mark pinched his lips together and nodded silently.

"At least two days a week since the start of the year."

Orla finished scribbling down her notes.

"Well we have our reason for contact so! That makes life easier." She knew the steps of this particular dance all too well at this point in her career and Mark knew that Orla would give the case as much attention as he would give if he had the time to take it on himself. Happy that she had it under control he gave her a Post-it with the teacher's name, the name of the school and the name of the student, Tina Madden. Orla would visit the teacher and get more of the little girl's details before she would call out to the home address to get a feel for the family environment, using the absences as an excuse to initiate contact. It was pretty practical stuff and the system came so naturally to Orla that she often ended up with more files on her desk than she would have agreed to if she had a choice.

An hour and a half later, with rain beating down on her windscreen, Orla swung into the staff car park of The Divine Trinity National school. She had driven straight there from her office. Obviously she remembered the small school better than she had realised. It was well over three years since she had been there and Orla was pleased with her memory. David, her ex, had always said she had a crap memory and a terrible sense of direction.

"Well fuck you now mister," Orla muttered out loud.

The car park was pretty full and the only parking spaces left were at the furthest point away from the glass entrance. Typical. Orla grabbed her handbag and made a run for it. As soon as she was through the entrance the smell of school hit her like a smack in the face. Suddenly she was six years' old again. Wearing itchy navy socks and feeling like some sort of gaudy-looking giant. She shook it off and strode confidently in the direction indicated by a sign that read 'Principal's Office'. The heels of her black work boots made a terrible noise on the tiled flood. Horrified at her own indiscretion she put her weight on her toes as much as she could and kept going. By the time she had passed artwork from every single class blu-tacked up on the yellow walls and what seemed like twenty doors, Orla thought she might be close. She was right. The office had a red glossy door that was shut tight. She hesitated for a moment then knocked lightly and waited.

"*Tar isteach*," a nasal, older female's voice called after what seemed to be a deliberate delay.

Orla popped her head around the door.

"Hi there. Sorry to bother you but my name is Orla Flynn. I have a meeting with a Mrs Hopkins?"

"Miss Flynn. Come in! Come in! You probably don't remember me but I was Dinny's teacher, Mrs Gray. I was appointed principal after Sister May. She was the nun you dealt with all those years ago." The small, frail-looking woman had rushed over to the door and pulled Orla in by the sleeve of her jacket before manoeuvring her into the vacant chair across the desk. Orla could not shake the feeling that she was about to get told off, or at least scrutinised to the last. She could sense it. Mrs Gray was perched back behind the table, chin propped up on her hands, staring intensely into Orla's eyes.

"So Mrs Hopkins….?" Orla hinted, only to be cut off.

"So tell me about Dinny. How is he doing?"

And it begins, thought Orla. The woman's smile could not hide the nosy curiosity beaming through her eyes from the back of her skull. Orla decided she was not a big fan of this little crow of a woman.

"I am very sorry but I can't discuss the details of any case with anyone without getting authorisation first."

Mrs Gray smiled, half-patronisingly and half-pleading.

"Oh now. I am just wondering about a past pupil of mine. Where is the harm in that? Who would I be telling about Dinny Thomas?"

Orla looked the woman dead in the eyes but kept her mouth smiling.

"That's the point Mrs Gray. I don't know. I am very sorry but my time is needed in a few places today. Could you please contact Mrs Hopkins for me? I would hate for her to think I am late." She was being snippy and she knew it but there was no way she was going to be stuck in that office for any longer than she absolutely had to and if that meant pulling rank, then fine; that's exactly what she would do. But Mrs Gray was more cunning than Orla could ever have imagined. She was so bad that Orla couldn't help but see the funny side. Mrs Gray's face shadowed over as her brain comprehended Orla's words and tone. Eventually she screwed up her face and replied with one unexpected word:

"Miss."

"Excuse me?" Orla asked, slightly confused.

Mrs Gray stood. "It's *Missss* Hopkins." She glared at Orla for a moment before going in for the kill. "You were engaged the last time I saw you, or am I wrong? I noticed you're not even wearing your engagement ring this time. Hope things didn't go badly for you." She was already out of her *cathaoir* and was heading for the *doras*. The bird woman hadn't even given the stunned younger woman an opportunity to respond, she disappeared out the door as her spite melted out across the room into Orla's ears.

Orla was so shocked that she giggled to herself, ruining her snippy façade for the few moments she was alone. *Wow. And that woman is in charge of a primary school?* she thought, looking around at the bird woman's choice of office décor. Not exactly child friendly. Orla shuddered to think of all the children who had been in trouble in that badly lit, wallpapered room with crosses of all varieties (two Saint Bridget's, three regular wooden crosses and two full-on crucifixes with the bleeding tortured Jesus hanging off them) and the giant picture of Jesus with bloody hands reaching out to the room. Minutes later the prick of a principal returned, followed closely by an average-looking blonde girl. Mrs Gray made the appropriate introductions.

"Miss Flynn meet Miss Hopkins. Miss Hopkins, Miss Flynn."

After receiving a limp, disappointing handshake and a weak smile Orla took the bull by the horns.

"Is there somewhere quiet we can go to have a little chat Miss Hopkins?"

Grainne Hopkins turned red and replied quietly,

"Oh yes of course. Please follow me Miss Flynn."

As the two young women headed out of the office with Mrs Gray staring hard at their backs, they exchanged small smiles, leaving her hissing that she knew where she wasn't wanted. Orla was glad to see the young teacher ignore the passive-aggressive old cow. As the pair started down the corridor Mrs Gray, not surprisingly, appeared at the door of the office again and called Grainne back to her. Grainne hurriedly obliged. Orla couldn't make out what Mrs Gray was saying but she didn't have to wonder for long. As soon as Grainne had caught up with her, Orla heard her tiny voice say,

"She wants me to come back to the office as soon as you're gone."

Orla chuckled.

"She wants to pick your brain."

Grainne scoffed surprisingly loudly.

"She has a better chance of picking my nose."

Orla chuckled louder.

Soon Grainne and Orla were sitting on a comfortable couch in a little room with a sign that read 'Sick Bay' with two cups of tea Grainne had gotten from the staff room. Neither woman brought up Mrs Gray's conduct; neither wanted to look unprofessional in front of the other. After some general pleasantries about the artwork on the walls and the joys of working with kids the conversation settled on the more sombre topic at hand.

"She is under an unnatural amount of stress for a child, that is obvious, but it's not over school work. She has never completed one piece of homework since she came into my class."

"Have you made contact with the parents at all? Parent-teacher meeting? Phone calls?" Orla asked, leaning forward.

"Well yes. I tried calling but the number seems to be cut off. I asked for a mobile number and I was told the mother didn't teach Tina the number. Mrs Gray has tried to contact them on a number of occasions but to no avail unfortunately. I have a log book where I keep a record of all notes sent home to parents and phone calls made to parents if you'd like to see it?"

"Oh yes please, that would be very helpful. But maybe we'll just continue our chat for now and sort out anything else we need to get sorted after?"

"No problem," Grainne continued. "Well the parents are just non-existent from the looks of things really. They didn't show up on sports day or at the parent-teacher meeting. The last the school has seen of the mother was on Tina's registration day and at that only Mrs Gray met her. We know nothing about her dad other than his name, Kevin." Grainne looked relieved to let all the information that had been whizzing around her head fly out into someone else's ear; someone far better equipped to deal with the situation and get to the bottom of it.

"My supervisor mentioned the girl is suffering from poor hygiene?" probed Orla.

Grainne paused for a moment. Only a moment, but just enough time for Orla to read the wave of anxiety that crossed her bare face. It was hard for this young teacher to talk about a student's personal hygiene.

"Well, I hate to say it but there is a definite smell. I don't want to be cruel but it's a smell... of urine. I mean a strong smell. I don't think it's from her uniform, that's always fine, but her hair is greasy and her skin looks... clammy. She isn't taking regular baths, for sure. The other children have noticed and I just don't think it's fair that any child has to put up with that. We try our best to deal with it but you know how kids are when they know they are out of earshot. I try my best to manage it but it is still hard on Tina."

Orla was nodding her understanding. She was impressed by the teacher's genuine worry. *There are a lot of bad teachers out there, but this is not one of them*, she thought. Noticing Grainne had again fallen silent, Orla realised she would have to guide the younger woman though the entire interview.

"That's awful and you're one hundred per cent right. It is totally unfair. God knows school is hard enough without having to deal with that. And she has lost weight since the start of the school year?"

Grainne's head moved purposefully up and down in exaggerated confirmation.

"She is thin as a whippet now and she really wasn't big to begin with. At the start of the year her uniform fit her beautifully; now her shoulders are stooped and her socks keep falling down. Her legs are too skinny to hold them up anymore. Even her face is gone so... sunken looking. I used to check that she had a lunch every day but she always did. Then I watched to see if she would eat it and I realised that she would never eat her sandwich but ate the apple and carrot that are in her lunchbox every day. I mean, she has never ever eaten any more than the apple and carrot in front of me unless I bring in treats, in which case she nearly has a stroke with excitement. That has to be the most animated I ever see her, on treat days. Usually she is sluggish and much removed from the goings on in the classroom. She has dark circles under her eyes all the time and she's always falling asleep in class. It's extreme. For example, once when the kids had come in after lunch I noticed she hadn't come back from the little yard with everyone else so I went out to have a look before reporting it to Mrs Gray." Grainne rolled her eyes dramatically. "No point in rattling her cage until all other avenues have been explored. I found her fast asleep on the grass between the tree in the yard and the wall of the car park. It was pure luck that I managed to spot her. She was curled up in a ball. It was heartbreaking. Really. I brought her down here and tucked her up on the couch for a few hours. I lied to Mrs Gray. I told her Tina was poorly and surprisingly she said it was best to let her sleep. The woman can be rotten, but she really cares about these children."

But Orla didn't hear what Grainne had to say about Mrs Gray. Her mind was racing with a general note of *Oh shit, this is bad.*

"Would you mind if I take notes Miss Hopkins? Only I have a feeling you might have been right to call us. I definitely want to check in on Tina at home."

The panic on Grainne's face melted away before Orla's eyes.

"Please call me Grainne. I thought you might agree. I really waited until I was sure. I didn't want everyone to think I was kicking up a fuss. The only other thing is, despite Tina knowing some things here and there, I don't think she has been in a school before this year. On her file her mother said she was in a small Catholic school in the city centre but when I asked Mrs Gray she said Tina's mother was not the kind of woman we can hound."

Grainne shook her head in a defeat that Orla understood. She really knew the horrors this young teacher went through during her months of concerned observation. Most people felt that contacting Social Services was being too intrusive. Nosey even. Grainne had struggled with these feelings too and Orla was thankful she had managed to overcome them. This was a little girl who needed to be checked up on. The fact that Grainne didn't think Tina had been in school before was a worry. Why would parents lie about something like that? Maybe she had been in a school that was much more informal than The Divine Trinity? Maybe she just didn't know how to act in a school like this? Maybe Grainne was just wrong.

"You did really, really well Grainne. If there were more teachers like you out there, there would be less need for people like me. Have you ever noticed any marks or bruising on Tina? Has she ever shown signs that she is in pain or has been hurt in any way?"

Grainne thought for a moment.

"Well not that I have seen but Tina is not one for physical contact or excursions. So I haven't really been able to tell. There have been a few times when I catch her moving like she is in pain but then she is fine again and I wonder if she just moves like that sometimes. I couldn't be sure." She looked at the social worker with desperation.

"That's alright. Every little detail matters, no matter how small. Is there anything else you can think of or that you want to tell me?" Orla needed to hear everything. Then she needed to go and find this poor child. Grainne was not wasting their time; Orla knew that Tina's parents would have to explain the situation their child was in. There were definitely questions that needed to be asked but Orla would have to be smart about how she went about her preliminary investigations.

Grainne broke through her train of thought.

"Yes there is something else I've noticed about Tina's packed lunch. I think she has the same sandwiches every day for a week at a time. Remember I said the way she never eats her sandwiches? I don't think she is allowed to eat them. I think they are for show. And every day the same note from her mother. *Have a great day, Love Mommy.* It's laminated and it's always there. Tina doesn't even notice it but I do. The carrot and apple reappear everyday though, sometimes worse for wear."

Orla was still scribbling all the little details in her refill pad.

"Okay now can we get the parents' details from the school files? Or would you prefer I get them myself?"

Grainne stood immediately.

"I'll get them for you right now. We even have a photo of her. We take security photos of every child at the start of the year in case something ever happens. Mrs Gray knows why I contacted you. Even though she didn't think it was my place, she couldn't stop me or reprimand me for it so I have full access."

Orla put her refill pad and pen back into her oversized handbag and got to her feet.

"That would be great. Is there any way Mrs Gray would have a quick word with me about how Tina's mam was on registration day?"

Grainne's eyebrows pulled together in doubt.

"You can try. She might not be as receptive as you might like."

A small smile played across Orla's lips.

"Don't worry. I can take her."

Grainne smiled.

"Right I'll lead you to your demise. I'll get the information you're looking for and drop it into the office when I have it. Feel free to give me a wink if you need an excuse to leave."

The two women made their way back down the long, low corridors to the principal's office.

That night Orla was lying on her couch in her echoing apartment in the leafy suburbs of Ranelagh. A photograph of a six-year-old was propped up against a cup on the coffee table in front of her.

Tina Madden is a beautiful child, she thought, but she is in a bad way. The girl looked so thin in the photograph. And that was at the start of the school year before Grainne noticed the drastic downward spiral. Orla was terrified about what state she would find the child in when she finally met her. In the past she had dealt with some pretty bad cases. Some had begun even more horrendously than this, but for some reason Orla had a feeling in the pit of her stomach that this was not something to put on the back burner. Mrs Gray had been as much help as a rubber screwdriver. One-word answers and really saying nothing other than that Patricia Madden seemed a bit rough around the edges but that she seemed like a good woman.

The worst part was that the school had no idea where Tina had been the year before other than the vague description of the small, un-named, Catholic school in the city. Grainne mentioned that Tina never spoke or answered questions about her old school and she didn't know you had to put up your hand to comment or ask questions or that you had to ask to go to the bathroom. Grainne had had a terrible time trying to explain how Tina had to put up her hand, wait to be noticed, and ask permission to go to the bathroom before she could go. Tina had hated the attention of asking to go to the bathroom and had wet herself repeatedly. Thankfully the school had a washer/dryer for the bathroom towels so Grainne had been able to straighten her up before she went home each time. If there was an accident too late in the day, Grainne would rinse out the uniform, pants and socks and stick them in the drier for as long as she dared before the bell would ring and it was home time.

Orla picked up the picture and popped it back into the new file. Then she picked up the remote and turned up the nine o'clock news. Tomorrow she would look up Tina Madden as soon as she got into the office.

Stephanie was bored, and hungry. But mainly bored. The window had a big board over it so she couldn't even look out at the back gardens. How many hours was she here? She had no idea. She couldn't even guess. Ten weeks? A month? It could have been a year for all Stephanie knew! She had been at home, then she was taken and brought here for a day, then she was sent to live with Mister Tom, then she came back here. Now what? How long would she be left here? Would she have to go to another house after here or could she go home?

Her hopes had been so high when Mister Tom put her in the wheelie case and wheeled her out to the back seat of his car. Stephanie knew she was being put in the car because she had felt every stone on the way across the gravel in the front of his house. Then she heard the car *bleep bleep* when Mister Tom was rattling keys. He was whistling. Stephanie hated that he whistled. Then the car door opening. Stephanie had thought that they were done with her. Finally she would be brought home to her nan. But no. She was taken here again. Better than Mister Tom's, not as good as Nan's.

When she was brought back to the first smelly house again, Stephanie expected it to be like Mister Tom's; lots of horrible stuff happening all around her and to her, but here she was left alone. She had only been in this house for one day before she was sent away again so she had no idea what it would be like to spend time here when she got back. No one had bothered her. No one made her do anything other than stay in this room. Sure, the room was boring, there was nothing much to do but Stephanie could handle that if it meant she would be left alone. Mister Tom had a telly in her bedroom though and here there was nothing. But in Mister Tom's there were parties and Stephanie hated the parties. The only person she had seen the whole time she had been here was the man who had been in Nan's waiting for her in the hallway. The only time she saw him was every once in a while when he passed in food and refilled her water bottle. Stephanie didn't need much food so she had fun dividing it up and eating only little bits at a time. She tried to make it last all the way until the door opened again and the man dropped more food from a big plate onto her little one on the floor. At first she couldn't do it at all but now she always left one tiny bit on the plate when the door opened and more food was dropped in. The man only took one picture of her face. Mister Tom liked other pictures. This house won.

It would be far nicer if the window wasn't covered over. Stephanie imagined watching the other children playing in their garden next door. She heard their screeches and laughter sometimes and it made her sad. But that was better than the other noises in this house. She thought maybe if she could watch the other children she would enjoy the noises of them having a great old time. It's not so fun when you can't even watch. Stephanie wondered if she was jealous. No, she just wanted to join in, even in the littlest way. If the board was gone she wouldn't mind the noise. She'd even be able to wave at them and smile and maybe they would smile at her too and wave back. Maybe they would come and play right under the window so she could join in through the glass. But she had never asked the man to take down the board. He hadn't hurt her yet but better not try anything new. She had learned that bringing attention to herself was not a smart thing to do.

During the daytime the only light in the bare-walled room was the tiny lines that managed to squeeze their way in along the sides of the board. When Stephanie arrived she noticed the way the cracks faded and came back every day but after a while she just didn't care anymore. It just made time harder to manage. Little routines helped. Like Stephanie always made sure to sleep and before she slept, she always told herself a story. And after she woke she sat on the pipe for as long as it took to take a pee and maybe a number two. Stephanie heard the word shit a lot since she left with the man but she didn't like it. She still said number two like Nan used to. Stephanie thought about Nan's flat a lot. She hoped the old woman was alright and warm and wasn't lonely now that her right-hand woman was gone. Nan would have to walk to the shops by herself now; how would she be able to carry all the shopping by herself? Was she worried about Stephanie? It had been a long time since they had been together in the flat that was up too many flights of stairs for old bones to nip in and out with comfort. The last thing they had done was buy a school uniform for the settled school Stephanie was supposed to start in but never made it to. The man took her before she had a chance. Stephanie had never been to school. When she was little, a woman used to come to the site and teach all the kids together. Then when she went to live with her nan she just didn't go back to the site to see the woman again. This year Nan had taken her to the school where they said she could go in September. Stephanie had been looking forward to it a lot.

 She thought about her ma and the babies in their warm caravan somewhere. Eating beans on toast and watching telly together on the big bed in the back. Those memories were fading these days. It was getting harder and harder to recall the smell of bodies, damp, cooking and fags that made up the scent of her first ever home. Sometimes in Mister Tom's a grown up would light a fag and as soon as the fingers of smoke reached her nose Stephanie was transported back in time to the humming caravan and her scatty mam. She could remember the songs, and the fighting, and the fun. But when the smell of cooking and damp didn't follow, Stephanie was planted right back in her socks. It was her nan she missed the most. Her nice lovely nan, who made her sweet milky cups of delicious tea when she came in from playing with other kids from the flats. Hot chocolate before bed and clean pyjamas every night. A hot water sink to wash her face and hands in, and baths. Hugs were nice and didn't hurt at all. Her nan even taught Stephanie how to do Irish dancing. Sometimes Stephanie stood up in the dark room and danced around like she was in her nan's flat. It didn't matter if she made noise here. No one came. Anyway Stephanie was always careful not to make any dramatically loud noises but singing and dancing she seemed to have gotten away with so far. Talking to herself wasn't a problem either. The man had never said a word to her. Not since she came home that day and he told her that Nan was in the hospital where he worked and he had been sent to get Stephanie to take her there. One big talk then nothing. At first she had been scared for her nan but now she thought the man was telling lies. He lied about going to the hospital and he lied about her nan being sick. After that there were no more lies, or talks. No surprises, no shocks, just Stephanie in a room. Left to do as she liked with her time.

Today was no different except she was more bored then usual. The man hadn't been in in a long while but he would be soon. Any time now really. Stephanie was squatting over the pipe that stuck out of the floor in the corner, minding her own business and doing it at the same time. Sometimes she heard noises around the house when she was sure she was the only one there. The man would open and close other doors upstairs sometimes too but Stephanie was sick of trying to call out as loud as she dared. There was no one there. She was picking at a loose thread in her t-shirt with her sticky thumb and fingers, humming a made-up tune when she heard the front door slam. Heavy feet were coming up the stairs.

Stephanie quickly stood and pulled up her tracksuit bottoms. They made her hands feel even more sticky. The heavy feet were getting closer now. They were at the top of the stairs when Stephanie heard something else. Whimpering. Like sobbing someone was trying to hold in. Stephanie's jaw dropped.

Not again! she thought. They were going to do this to another little girl. Stephanie didn't think she could watch anything like that again, or hear it for that matter.

Not another little girl, she thought with dread. Her heartbeat seemed to flutter then bang and she could feel its movements in her ribcage. Her face got prickly and she couldn't move her feet.

No, she must be wrong. But now the noises were right outside her door and there was no mistaking it. It was another girl. How long would this one be here for? Stephanie was frozen to the spot, but they passed by to another room next door. Suddenly she regained the use of her limbs and found herself flying to the dividing wall and pressing her ear against the cold bare plaster. She could hear the door swing open and a weight being dropped on the floor, then the most bloodcurdling screech that Stephanie had ever heard.

"I want to go home...I want...to go...home! Why did you take that picture?! I'm supposed to go back!"

"Shut the fuck up. We don't make noise here." *SLAP.*

Then the boots moved to the door and the door slammed shut. Stephanie could make out the familiar clunk of a key in a tight old lock before the thumping boots passed her door again and noisily made their way back down the wooden stairs. When the louder noises faded into the distance and shut themselves behind a door somewhere, Stephanie put her ear back up to the wall. Eventually her eardrum tuned in to a low sobbing from the next room. Another little girl had been taken away from her home and brought to this place. Stephanie could not help but think,

At least she is here and not in a place like Mister Tom's.

She had to think of a way to make it better. Stephanie dragged her heavy mattress over to the wall between the rooms and plonked herself down cross-legged as close to the wall as possible.

Do you dream of brighter things, better place to spread your wings?

Do you care for one another, fellow brothers, sisters, dreamers and mothers?

It's a revo- revo- revolution.

Stephanie sang high and sweet, the first song that came into her head. She didn't know all the words so she just sang the same part over and over until she could put her ear to the wall and the sobbing had stopped. Then Stephanie lay down on the filthy mattress and pressed her little body into the wall as tightly as she could and wished some of her calm to squeeze out through her body, through the wall and into her new neighbour. Stephanie longed to hug her and explain that things weren't that bad here and if she just didn't scream and shout she would be left alone in peace.

2

"Take the next right." The English man who lived in her sat nav guided Orla down a dodgy-looking residential area just minutes away from the school. Broken cars, taped-up windows, grass growing through the tarmac of the footpaths and through the gummy cobbles of the street.

That morning Orla had been shocked to discover that Tina Madden was an adopted child. She had been adopted by Patricia and Kevin Madden four years previously when she was only two and a half. Tina had been the daughter of Patricia's disabled sister, Breda Flood Byrne, who there was very little record of. The woman had either signed over her child to Social Services after two-and-a-half years of looking after her or they had taken her. There was hardly anything legible in the thin file so it was hard to tell how Patricia Madden, the maternal aunt, had ended up adopting the child.

Patricia and her husband Kevin had been receiving social welfare for the girl and more for their two other children who were in a Catholic school at the opposite side of Swords. They were both older then Tina, a boy aged eleven called Simon and a girl aged ten called Hannah. Both had been interviewed during the adoption process and the files showed there were no red flags. She was surprised the report, as meagre as it was, was in the file at all.

Orla slowed her car down to see the wooden numbers nailed to the front doors that were almost on the footpath. She worked out that 1225 would be on her left side, and continued down the street. It wasn't there. Orla turned her car around and made her way back up the street. She noticed a little gap in between two houses and turned the car into it. It was narrow but it led to another small ring of houses. Orla would hate to live here. The ring was even worse than the houses along the street. She could see five discarded mattresses in various places amongst the six houses. Washing machines in gardens. It was bloody awful looking. One house was completely boarded up and another had plyboard over the living room window. No one was anywhere to be seen. The place was ghostly. She pressed on and started to crawl around the ring slowly, checking the numbers on the houses. And there it was, number 1225 High Park. Orla felt a lump rise in her throat.

No way is the inside of that house going to be habitable, she thought. The mouldy pebbledashed face of the house had cracked off and lay in clumps along the bottom of the wall. The roof had collapsed and instead of rebuilding it someone had covered it in transparent blue plastic that looked like it was held on with duct tape. The window frames were rotting and there was no glass at all in the window under the concave roof. Net curtains looked like they couldn't be bothered to cover the windows fully and hung pathetically on all of the windows except the empty panes of the room under the collapsed roof; there a green fuzzy thing grew undisturbed in the humus of the rotting wooden frame. There weren't any official lined parking spaces so Orla just pulled her car as close to the house as possible so that she didn't block off any other cars that might find their way down the hidden path to the ring. Gathering up her bag and files Orla noticed she was bubbling with anxiety, fear almost, at what she would find behind the front door of number 1225. If the family flipped the lid she would have to get an emergency order from the Gardaí and come in with force on another day but it would mean Tina's time in the house would be dragged out for even longer.

How could three children and two adults possibly live in that house? she thought. It had only been four years since the adoption process and the house looked like it had been in the gutter for far longer than four years. The roof caving in looked pretty recent but the rest looked like the house had been falling down and rotting for decades. *How did it pass the social worker's inspection?* She took out her camera and took two photographs of the house as discreetly as possible.

Noelle was well into her retirement but if Orla had to hunt her down and ask some questions, she bloody would. She took a deep breath, courageous after the last thought, and got out of the car. After the cringingly gaudy 'beep beep' and four-way flashers expressed the security of her car to any eyes leering amongst the filth of the cul de sac, she tucked her keys safely in her jacket pocket, within reach as always. Just in case she needed a quick get away. Just in case.

The door was the original wooden front door. It had a knocker at one stage in time. Orla could see the four holes where the screws had been and the odd shape that had missed out on years of green gloss paint jobs. But the knocker was gone, and the now dirty peeling gloss told a story; the door hadn't been painted since someone who gave a shit lived there. After three short raps, causing a shed of green flecks on her boots, the door jerked open defensively.

"What?" a short, fat woman demanded. Her face was cut from ear to ear by the silver chain between the old door and the weak-looking frame.

Orla was slightly taken aback.

"Mrs Madden is it?" she asked after forcing confidence back into her bones.

"Depends on who's askin'." Orla could not help but inhale at the smells emanating from the small gap to the house. She could not let her mind wander to its many possible sources for fear she would puke her ring up all over the little greasy ape in the doorway.

"Well I am asking Mrs Madden." She beamed her not-far-off-pearly whites and tried to look as non-threatening and non-judgemental as possible. "I am Miss Flynn from the Department of Children and Family. I just want to have a quick word with you about something small." Seeing the accusing look she was being cut by Patricia Madden's beady blue eyes, Orla kept going, trying desperately to say anything that would make the woman let her into the house.

"Don't worry, it's nothing major. It's so common you wouldn't believe. I'll only take five minutes of your time." Orla tried to keep her composure and not look like she was pleading but she knew Patricia had detected the note of inferiority and by the pleased look that smeared across her fat little face she was loving it. For a second the gap got smaller while Patricia smugly unhooked the chain, then the door opened up.

"Better not talk about things in the street. The neighbours will think I'm telling tales or something."

Orla felt her back stiffen. *What the hell is going on around here that everyone would be so worried?* She wasn't led any further into the house. Only into the damp, narrow hallway just inside the door. The place reeked. Dampness clung to the peeling wallpaper and the carpetless staircase looked sleek with moisture. Patricia noticed Orla's face.

"We're doin' up the place this summer. Don't be looking at my home like that or I'll send you on your arse, young one! Tell me what you want then fuck off." Patricia was animated to say the least, Orla was suddenly grateful for every inch that separated this piece of shit from her face. She wanted to see where the children slept so badly that she nearly just came out with it. Only her experience stopped her. She knew she had to tread carefully or the meeting would be cut off. This would be the wrong time to fuck up. This was when she needed to use her head.

She faced Patricia and gave her another beaming smile.

"Oh no, I was just thinking these old houses have so much potential. They are so much bigger on the inside than they look on the outside. I swear to God it is almost identical to my sister's house in Dundalk. And you don't even have that much to do with it now you've gotten started. Stripping is the hardest part." Orla was gushing horrible-lady-pleasing bullshit. She didn't have a sister who lived in Dundalk. She didn't have a sister at all but Patricia's face told her that she was buying it. Some people were willing to believe any old shit once it was complimentary. Patricia was lapping it up and wriggling around with a bellyful.

"Yeah, well. It will do. Now what was it you wanted?" Her teeth were as nasty as the house. Nowhere near pearly whites.

"Oh it's just that our department has noticed that your Tina has been missing quite a bit of school and they sent me to ask if she is unwell or if there is anything we can do to help you make sure she is there more often; that's if she is able of course." Orla knew that if Tina was sick, it was because of that house and God knows what else was going on under its shitty, dilapidated roof.

"She has been sick in her stomach a lot. We brought her to the doctor in the children's hospital and he said she would grow out of it. Now is that it?" Patricia was less angry looking but still managed to be just as aggressive.

Orla pushed further anyway. "Oh yes, can I get the name of the school where Tina went for Junior Infants? It's just for the records."

Patricia's response was not surprising if Grainne's suspicions were true.

"Fuck right off!"

Orla knew her time in the house was nearly at an end and for some mad, unknown reason she found her mouth open and the following words making their way across the small space between her and the brute:

"Erm…I was wondering if I might take a peep at Tina's bedroom? It's just a way of making sure we are speaking to the right parents. I should have really done it when I came in but I chanced my arm when I met you."

Patricia snuffed and crossed her arms.

"If you shoulda done it when you got here, then you shoulda done it when you got here. Too late now. Okay so, bye now. Don't let the door hit you on the arse."

Before she knew where she was Orla was being pushed by the elbow out the cracked green door. She wasn't particularly shocked at being manhandled. Being manhandled out of people's houses was another thing that wasn't particularly uncommon in her line of business but something else didn't sit right at all. She took out her keys and let herself into the car.

Wow, there is no way on God's green earth that Noelle inspected that house and that woman and found that this was a good environment for a placement. No fucking way. Orla felt her face prickle. This is exactly what Mark had explained to her when Noelle left.

"You might find that some of her dealings are less then a hundred per cent. I used to do my best to keep on top of her cases but you know how it is. She has had her favourites throughout her career; it's even in her employment file. She was made aware of it on a number of occasions and asked to be more proactive but as the years went on it got worse and worse so if you come across anything, anything at all, please, please bring it to my attention." He had been flushed in his usually pale face and was even more fidgety than during an average briefing. Orla had always been disgusted at Noelle but she was an elderly woman by the time she left and was set in her ways. No amount of quiet words or hints at irritation could penetrate her armour. She could be so sweet she'd knock the teeth right out of your head. One of those ladies who will agree with you to the last then go on and do what she likes. This adoption was a really big cock-up. Orla needed to talk to Mark. Now.

She pulled out onto the main road and indicated into a parking space outside a small, rough-looking shop while she dug her phone out of her bag. The shop door opened and four women walked out, laughing and pushing each other. They were all in or around their late twenties or early thirties and they were all in pyjamas. Orla felt her jaw clench. God people pissed her off.

Mark answered the phone on the sixth ring.

"We have a problem. Any chance you can clear off a half hour for me? We have a Noelle issue. A big one. It's about Tina Madden's adoption."

Orla could hear him suck air between his teeth.

"Trust me you need to have a look at this," she insisted.

Mark responded straight away, not wanting Orla to think she was annoying him by asking for some of his time.

"Oh I know. If you say it's serious, I know that it's serious. Sorry, I'm just driven half demented by that woman and she hasn't worked here for years! I'm stuck doing more paperwork in my office so just call into me whenever you have a chance and we'll see what the craic is. That suit you? If we need to do something more official we can sort it out after you fill me in. Okay?"

Orla was relieved.

"Perfect. I'll be back in a short while."

Tina's birth mother, Breda Flood Byrne, was born in Cork University Hospital on January 6th 1974 to Kathleen and David Byrne while they were on a family holiday. Breda had been a very sickly baby and suffered from restricted movement in all of her muscles. As an adult she was wheelchair bound and despite years of working with a speech and language therapist, provided by the Health Service Executive for most of her life, the only soul on the planet who could make sense of her strained mutterings was her matronly, devout mother Kathleen. Kathleen was Breda's full-time carer and managed well until she got into her late sixties. At that stage Breda was thirty-two years old and was having regular operations to try to release some of the tension in her tendons that had been causing the majority of her pain. Of course the physical pain was no comparison to the agony of not being able to make people understand her without her mother playing interpreter, but Orla didn't know that. To Orla, Breda was just a name with a few details on some pieces of paper.

During a check-up two months after one of her operations, Doctor Ombino, who had been Breda's doctor since she was a tot, had taken a urine sample and blood test, just to make sure there was no trace of any infection after surgery. The following day the phone rang in Kathleen's small inner-city bungalow and Doctor Ombino requested that Kathleen take Breda back to the hospital the following morning. Kathleen, like any parent after a phone call like that, was frightfully worried, but no matter how much she begged and pleaded, Doctor Ombino would only assure her that there was nothing wrong, per se, and Kathleen should not worry. This of course made her even more anxious and worried.

For the rest of the afternoon Kathleen had kept her body as busy as her brain. She hung washing on the line to be dried by the summer's weak sun then swept the floor and fussed over Breda so much that the young woman was cutting her odd looks from her perch in front of the telly. Kathleen made some vegetable soup from scratch and baked soda bread for the side, then, realising the bread wouldn't be cool enough to eat in time, she grabbed her handbag and asked Breda if she wanted to go as far as the shop at the end of the road with her. It was only a two-minute walk each way so Kathleen didn't mind leaving Breda if she heard something that resembled a "No thanks."

Breda was fed up watching the depressing English soap operas that her mother thought she was so interested in. Still, she'd rather not make her mother fuss over her all the way to the end of the road and back. The electric wheelchair meant that Kathleen didn't have to push Breda any more but still Breda felt a bit slow, and getting up and down off the footpath wasn't easy. She took a beep breath and used all her strength to make the tight muscles of her mouth make the sound "No thanks."

Breda listened as her mother took the soup off the hob and flicked the dead switch on the cooker. Then the front door closed much louder than it had any other day. Today was different somehow; the bang of the door only confirmed it. Her ma was more frenzied than usual. Breda only saw her mother like this when they had gotten bad news that hadn't made it through the channels of communication to Breda yet. This happened pretty often. The weight of the secret would put her mother into a sort of tailspin so all Breda could do was wait until Kathleen had mulled it over enough and chose the tone in which to tell her daughter whatever the 'news' was.

Walking down the street Kathleen tried to convince herself that the doctor wouldn't have told her to wait until the following day to bring Breda in if it was something dire that he was going to reveal. Or maybe it was so dire that a day and a night and a morning of waiting wouldn't affect the outcome. Or maybe he was allowing the women to have their last ignorantly peaceful few hours together before rocking the world to the core with the most dreadful news of all. Kathleen liked to worry.

She went into the shop and picked up a half-cut slab of soda bread and went to the till. She picked up two Chomp bars and paid before heading back towards the house. Of course she couldn't let Breda know that the news was most likely to be the most awful, horrible, life-ending news. Oh no, now that wouldn't be fair on the poor child. Kathleen knew that her youngest daughter was lucky to have the quality of life she had for so long. The doctor had expected the stiffness to take over her organs far earlier in her teens but her symptoms progressed slowly from her face, hands and feet to her arms, legs, shoulders, hips, pelvis, spine and everywhere else a young woman would be needing to move and shake. At the age of ten she had to leave the walking frame she had scooted around in since she started standing at the age of two and a half, and give up the last of her use of two wasting legs for the less dignified constraints of a chair with wheels.

Kathleen's sister had scoffed at Breda when she was a pretty toddler and still did to that very day.

"You have dug yourself an early grave Kathleen. It would have been best for the poor eejit if you had put her in the home. And I'd have you longer into our old age." But Kathleen would always hold up her chin and say she quite enjoyed life with her daughter and it wasn't nearly as hard on her as the outsiders gawking in loved to think it was. But the truth was, as Breda got stronger, Kathleen was getting weaker. Her heavy limbs strained when she had to lever Breda into bed or the chair but nothing was as strenuous as dressing a thirty-two-year-old woman in the same fashion she had thirty years ago when she was a two-year-old. Breda sat heavily and it was becoming almost impossible for Kathleen to twist her this way and that to pull down modern t-shirts and pull up almost-tight jeans like other women of the same age would wear. Slowly, Kathleen, much to Breda's despair, began to buy clothes for Breda without her input. Shirts, skirts, button-up dresses; not terribly out of fashion but not to Breda's taste. Still, she knew why her mother had done these random and more regular shopping sprees. She had bought clothes that would be easier to get on and off. Breda never complained and Kathleen made up for it by always making sure Breda's hair was washed and straightened with the little gas straightener she had gotten Breda for her twenty-seventh birthday. Kathleen kept up-to-date on the fashionable accessories for her daughter's sake and splashed out on little things here and there to finish off Breda's look. She didn't want her daughter to feel she was ugly and out of the loop. Breda was very beautiful. Her hair was naturally the darkest possible shade of chocolate brown. Her hazel eyes were framed by thick lashes that Kathleen often highlighted with a touch of mascara and her skin was not the sickly yellow shade that Kathleen had read people in wheelchairs had in books.

Breda had her father's skin tone, sallow and glowing. It was an unfortunate fact that Breda had to live this life as she did, but at least she was beautiful. That was the general consensus, Kathleen decided. Secretly she was thrilled that it was Breda who got her father's looks and not her older sister Patricia. Patricia had been a wonderful child; not as handsome as Breda, Kathleen now felt comfortable enough to admit, but she had still been a happy, pleasant little girl.

That all changed when Patricia reached thirteen and started with that Kevin Madden dirt a few months later. She disappeared 'til all hours and laughed at her mother when Kathleen tried to pull in the reins on her life of the Bold Reilly. No, Patricia had been cursed with the looks of her mother and the colouring of her father. She had an eyebrow that went from one eye to the other without change in its thickness or shape until she plucked them to death into two little arrows filled in with heavy black pencil. She was low to the ground and built more strongly than her mother. When she was angry, she was a bull. One push and she was off out the door, leaving her poor mother in a worried heap on the lino nursing cuts or knocks.

After the age of sixteen Kathleen rarely saw a bit of her eldest daughter, not unless their paths happened to cross in the city. Dublin is a strange city; people who know each other are pulled together like magnets and this meant that Kathleen saw her older daughter every few weeks or so. All the time she would be drunk out of her head, or worse. Sometimes she would be in the horrors but when Kathleen approached her Patricia would threaten her and swear blue murder. Out of pure shock at seeing her daughter act like a completely different person from some other, darker background, Kathleen left her to be who she wanted to be. As a girl she didn't have a thing to worry about to send her off the rails. Her dad died, yes, but she was a tot, and tonnes of children lost a parent and managed to grow up to be healthy, functioning members of their communities. Kathleen had just come back to Dublin from Cork after having Breda when their dad passed. Patricia was still colouring in pictures on the tail of her apron. There was no reason for how Patricia had turned out. Kathleen knew that and let her oldest daughter slip away out of her home and out of her heart.

Kathleen saw her low house come into view and slowed her pace. She knew why she was delaying. The soup would be cold but she had bigger things on her mind. She didn't know how she was going to bring up the hospital visit out of the blue.

If the good Doctor thinks it's better that she doesn't worry 'til she goes in tomorrow then that's what I'll do, she thought. She had made a decision and she was calmer. With the ease of a chameleon, Kathleen slipped into the disguise of a calm older mother, in control of the situation. She pasted on a smile and picked back up her pace.

Orla made it back to the office earlier than she had thought but as soon as she walked through the door Emily, the over-enthusiastic admin, had her cornered and was rhyming off a list of calls she had to make and holding up various florescent Post-its with the corresponding messages. Emily was OCD-style organised, but sane she certainly was not. Orla stood wide-eyed at the serious freckled face just inches away from hers, looking up at a very unnatural angle because of the height difference. Orla had always thought she'd like to be a bit shorter and being forced to stand face to chest with this little ferocious doll made old insecurities rustle somewhere deep in her chest. Orla swallowed them quickly and thanked God she wasn't on Emily's bad side. That would be scarier than going up against any one of the aggressive parents on the job.

"...You need to call Jean McCaile. All the other names and contact details are on each Post-it with a small *re* just so you know what they were calling about. If you have any questions or have any problems with my writing just holler and I'll come a running."

Then, zip, all went quiet, she was gone, her red high ponytail was bouncing back to reception and Orla was left holding a million Post-it's. Despite trying her very best to look and act as professional as she possibly could at all times, Orla was always left feeling a bit dazed and stunned after one of these assaults. She hadn't even had the chance to say "Thanks". She started into the office and saw Mark stressed out and hunched over a file in his little glass cubicle in the middle of the room. At least her height was good for something! Emily wouldn't have been able to see Mark through all the desks and bodies.

Moah ha ha ha! The world is just sometimes.

Orla made her way over to her desk and dumped off all her extra files. Mark would probably drop dead if she came into his cubicle with them. Two years ago at Christmas, Mark had written a little extra into the ISPCC Christmas card he had given her stuck to a bottle of White. It read, *To the woman who gives me a heart attack when I see her coming with a mountain of files.* Now Orla only brought as many as she needed in the hope that Mark wouldn't think she was too dependent on him. She wasn't really. She just got through a lot of work and it meant she had to get him to sign off on a lot of things at once pretty often.

Just as Orla tapped lightly on the glass Mark flipped over the cover of the file he had been staring at and dropped it onto a stack on the floor. When he looked up and saw Orla, his face lost its worry.

"Are you ready for me?" she asked.

"Yup. I'm ready for anything that gets me away from this for a while. Will we grab tea?" he asked, rubbing his temples. Mark suffered from stress headaches too; he was always sending crazy Emily over to scab painkillers from Orla before the normal working people left the old dogs to burn the midnight oil. Only the more dedicated social workers stayed late, everyone knew that. The younger ones had a tendency to head off at around half five or six. Orla was the only one still in her thirties who stayed late most nights. The idea of going home early in the evenings to an empty apartment made for two made Orla's stomach sick. She hated being in the apartment for long stretches, it was just so fucking lonely. So instead she kept her war paint on and worked until she was tired enough to be able to sleep after a bit of telly and a shower; if she could be bothered.

Orla smiled.

"Sure. Will I get them and bring them here or will we head into the kitchen?"

Mark got to his feet.

"Kitchen to make tea while you fill me in on the bones of this thing that has you in knots, then back in here so you can finish the story and show me what you've got in there." He gestured to the brown, surprisingly skinny, file in her hands.

The pair headed off across the office to the small kitchen whose sole purpose was to make teas and coffees. Ever since the interview rooms and playrooms were added to the premises the little kitchen seemed less friendly. No more toys and books, just a small table, sink, a kettle, and a small fridge with magnets all over it from the various resorts and destinations visited by their colleagues over the years. Mark stuck on the kettle and Orla chose two cups from the top of the press. It was a serious task. Eventually she settled on 'Don't worry be happy' with a smiley face and 'Serious shit is what we do' with a goldfish pooping. She threw a teabag and one sugar into each and sat at the table across from Mark who had plonked himself down heavily with an over-dramatic groan followed by a dragged out "Welllll?"

Orla inhaled deeply.

"Well, it's about Tina Madden's case. You know the one with the teacher calling from Divine Trinity where Dinny went?"

Mark nodded encouragingly.

"Well the teacher was right to be worried. The girl is in a jock I swear to God and I went to the house and, honestly, you wouldn't believe how bad it is. The roof is falling in, one window is missing and the mother seems worse. Went in and she had no interest in talking to me. She just wanted me out of there and the only reason she even spoke to me was because I told her it was just a common call out and kissed her arse about the rotten house. The place is a disgrace. I took a few photos just so I could show you how bad it is. I mean there aren't any words."

"Okay, so bad house, bad mother? Why not just start an investigation and monitor the girl's progress? It doesn't sound anything outside a usual case."

The kettle began to rumble loudly and with its click Mark stood and got to making the tea. Orla had more.

"Wait for it... Tina was adopted. Noelle was the social worker on the case."

Mark paused for a second and Orla heard him groan again.

"But I looked up Tina's file and there is feck all in it," Orla continued. "Only the family court ruling and an inspection and interview sheet with the adoptive parents and their two existing children. That's it. I mean there was nothing else in there. If it wasn't for the court document we would have no idea where Tina even came from. It was just pure luck that it happened to be Patricia Madden's unmarried sister Breda Flood Byrne, Flood was their mother's maiden name. Turns out she is a disabled woman who Noelle met once, going by the records. There is no way Noelle saw that house where the child has been living and if she did, then our problems are bigger then we think. You wouldn't let people adopt a dog and bring it back there. The adoption shouldn't have happened. The child is in a terrible state altogether. She came into school in High Infants and there is no record of her being in school anywhere else, but the adoptive mother said she had been in a small Catholic school in the city centre. I haven't looked into it yet, but I will. Other than that she's missing school, skinny as a rake and she was already too thin to start with. Falling asleep in the classroom up to a few times a day. She even fell asleep in the playground once. The school have only met the mother once. They have never seen the father."

Mark had stopped fussing over the cups and had turned to face Orla. He looked paler and weirder then ever.

Pity, he's such a nice guy, thought Orla.

"She can't focus in class and the list goes on. I am really worried about this one Mark. If you could see the house. I'm telling you, it's a disgrace."

Mark thought for a few second.

"And you took some pictures?" he asked.

"Yup they're in my camera in my bag."

"I'll bring the tea to the cubicle. You get whatever else you have and meet me back there ASAP. Okay?"

Orla stood and was already heading to the door "No problem. Thanks Mark."

Mark stood in the calm of the kitchen for a few minutes. He had a million things running through his head. So much was resting on his shoulders right now, more than ever before, and now another case that looked like it was going to be a massive problem. He brought his chin down to his chest and rested it there. Noelle was turning out to be a very big problem. How did he miss it for so long? How had she flown so far under the radar? His radar! Mark had only been Noelle's superior for a year or so and she had been so old by then. Old and experienced, that had been the common diagnosis. No one had any reason to suspect that she was anything other than an old lady who would be kind to you if you were kind to her. They thought her inability to be questioned or asked to explain anything, her quickness to let her sharp tongue put any young thing, fresh into the field, in their place, was down to the fact that she knew the job so well. They had all thought she just knew when to let things slide and when to press on with effort. Now Mark was left trawling through Noelle's old cases, hunting for any inconsistencies that were waiting to jump up and bite him in the ass. He had already ironed out a million different minor problems but he knew he had only scratched the surface. He hadn't even managed to catalogue the old bag's stack of notes and records that were shoved into boxes and a cupboard in the back of the record room with no order and missing information. Mark was most anxious because there were children still out there suffering because Noelle Flood had not bothered to do her job properly.

Mark froze.

Noelle Flood... It couldn't be. They couldn't be. Orla's words echoed in his brain like a radio. *Flood is their mother's maiden name.* Mark felt his blood boil and in a flash of rage he turned around and kicked the small fridge as hard as he could, sending magnets like missiles around the room and shouted out at the top of his lungs.

"Ahhhh!!!" *Who the fuck does she think she is! If I am right I am reporting her! I don't give a flying fuck what happens to me when they realise the cock-up I made. That stupid old bitch!*

Mark had to suck it up. He didn't want to tell anyone yet. Not 'til he made sure there weren't any big disasters on the horizon. Tina Madden's case would have to be straightened out before Mark could inform the department heads of Noelle's fuck-ups. He grabbed the cups of tea and, using his foot, he shoved the door open and went to wait on Orla, leaving magnets littered all over the small kitchen. He was just thankful it was her, and not one of the other social workers who he would have to tell.

Everyone in the office fell quiet. What the hell was that? They all stared at the kitchen door. Suddenly it swung open and everyone flinched. Then their usually quiet, restrained boss marched out, two cups in hand, one that read 'Don't worry be happy' and the other with a picture of a cartoon goldfish relieving itself, sloshing onto the worn blue carpet of their office. There was something interesting happening, and they all wished they had enough time to wonder about it. But they went back to work, only taking a half a second to make eye contact with a few other spectators, raising their eyebrows and making what-was-that-about eyes.

Kathleen had James pull the taxi up on the kerb outside. Now the pair were escorting Breda out of the house. James drove a wheelchair accessible taxi; it had been a regular taxi until Breda got her first chair. This chair was the biggest yet. It was electric and pretty chunky. Breda was relieved that James was there to help her mother so she wouldn't be lifting and hauling the piece of machinery. Breda also liked that, most of the time, Uncle James understood what she was trying to say. He said it was because she was always chewing the ear off him. That had made her laugh. Uncle James brought them to hospital appointments and speech and language therapy and physio, which she had five days a week in the local medical centre, as well as having it at home twice a day, even at weekends. James was her uncle, her da's brother, and if Da had been anything like James Breda would have been delighted. Ma said they were peas in a pod and when he died James naturally became the one who got called when the kitchen press fell off the wall, and who insisted on cleaning their chimney every autumn. The only difference? James didn't touch drink. Da had lived on the stuff.

"Oh we forgot the bag!" Kathleen turned on her heel and rushed back inside.

Breda tried to turn her head to face her Uncle. "James? Are you coming in with us?"

James hesitated for only a moment. "Only if you want me to. I'll stay outside either. I know the jazz."

Breda knew he didn't want to step on her mother's toes. Still she wanted him there. "Yeah will ya come in?"

"No problem sprogg," he replied softly.

Breda was as content as she could possibly have been in that situation and busied herself doing her best to help the ageing man move her into the car. This visit was very unexpected and even though Breda knew she would deal with whatever her stiff, painful body threw at her, she was deathly worried for her mother and how she would react to any bad news. Things had been too good for too long and Breda had a feeling bad news was flittering on the horizon. Kathleen treated her like a child still; Breda wouldn't be adequate support if the news turned out to be bad. Uncle James on the other hand was Da's brother. He would be able to run after her and soothe her with words that would roll freely out of his mouth, unlike the choked, stressed, broken sentences that, accompanied with the wheelchair issue, made Breda a terrible candidate for dealing with her mother's run-away emotional outbursts.

Uncle James was putting the wheelchair in the boot when Kathleen re-emerged from the house with Breda's emergency overnight bag. "Just in case," Kathleen put it merrily. If Breda could have raised an eyebrow in time to look suspicious she would have. She would not fall for her mother's positive veneer. Kathleen helped Breda put on her neck support for the journey and they headed off to meet Doctor Ombino.

"Welcome! Welcome! Good to see you guys. It is good to see you." Doctor Ombino had his ways of doing things, and this was how he said hello to the long-term patients he had come to know so well. He had only seen Breda and Kathleen the day before, but still he was thrilled to see them. His greetings could be very deceptive though. Breda had to stop herself from taking this joy as anything more than a greeting. Her mother always returned the happy gesture before turning to Breda and nodding in an excited way saying something like, "Oh this could be good." Or worse, like, "Oh it might not be as bad as we were expecting!" The last one pissed Breda off. After all her mother's efforts to act normal and totally in control she would let it all slip away just before they were going to be told what was up. *Not as bad as we were expecting?* It made Breda want to shout, "But we weren't expecting anything!" It happened a lot. Breda had tried to explain it to her once but it didn't work. Her mother had pretended not to understand and that annoyed Breda even more. She had been in her early twenties at the time, less mature. Now it was water off a duck's back. Breda would just roll her eyes and head into Doctor Ombino's immaculate office and examination room after her. This time Breda didn't wait for her mother's looks of excitement, she just headed straight for the door and Doctor Ombino stepped aside to let her in before him.

"Em, I'll just wait here Kathleen." They had completely forgotten James had been walking behind them all the way through the hospital. Kathleen looked embarrassed when she saw the sheepish man standing uncomfortably in the small waiting area outside the office.
She smiled at him warmly.
"That'll be grand James. We're delighted you're here. It's a real comfort."
James watched her go through the door with the doctor following after her.

"Okay, so I know you did not expect to see me again so soon but there are a few things I want to go over with the two of you together first, then I'll need to speak to Breda alone for a moment, then, Mom, I will call you from the waiting room and we will all talk again, okay? That would be very great."
Curious, thought Breda. This was not the way she had thought today would go but alright. This was better than "You'll be dead in a week" as soon as she came through the door. Procrastination was an amazing thing.
Kathleen looked anxiously at Breda for a moment then turned back to the doctor. "I'm sure Breda wouldn't mind if I stayed..."
"Ma!"
"I am sorry Mrs Flood but I will have to insist. Breda is a grown woman. I will have to speak to her alone."
"But you might need me to translate!" Kathleen pleaded.
Doctor Ombino smiled.
"Well I don't think I will have a problem with that. With thanks to the speech therapist and the physiotherapy Breda is

much clearer now and I am sure we can deal with it if there is a little something I cannot figure out. What do you think Breda?"

"I agree." Breda was thrilled when moments like this happened. They were rare but they reminded her that she was a fully-grown woman with a right to privacy and her own opinions and best of all she was getting more independent by the month! She loved her mother and appreciated everything she had done, but Breda dreamed of a freer life.

Breda and the doctor looked pleased and Kathleen felt a bit left out. She hated when people thought she saw her daughter as anything less than an important young woman. Kathleen longed for her daughter to have a much more independent life too. She wanted her to do as she pleased without her old mam trailing around after her. Despite truly wanting all of these things, Kathleen also knew she was guilty of clinging on too much.

Doctor Ombino got straight down to it.

"Okay, we'll begin. I didn't call you because there is anything massively wrong but there are a few little things I want to get to the bottom of. So, Breda, how have you been feeling generally since the last operation?"

Breda nodded.

"Fine."

Kathleen leaned forward.

"She has been a bit more tired after this surgery compared to the other ones. The cut is healed but it's still a bit tender, I don't think it's infected though."

Doctor Ombino smiled at Kathleen. Happy with her input, she sat back again. He turned back to Breda and said,

"Okay, okay. Good. And you are eating well and sleeping well every day?"

Breda nodded.

"Yes. I was sick for a few weeks after the operation. Vomiting a bit but fine after that. Eating a lot."

Kathleen leaned forward again.

"She said she was sick for a few weeks....."

Doctor Ombino cut her off politely.

"I understood. Breda you have to give credit to yourself. Your speaking has come on so far. Well done."

Breda smiled. "Thank you, it makes life easier."

"I bet it does. And Kathleen do you find people understand Breda more?"

Kathleen thought for a moment.

"Well now that you mention it! Gosh you're right! People must think I'm an awful gobshite for repeating everything the girl says like a parrot!"

Breda and the doctor laughed so loud that Uncle James had heard and had chuckled to himself in the waiting room. Breda knew what Doctor Ombino had done. He was changing Kathleen, making her realise what she was too close to see, and her ma had taken it like a trooper. Breda had been a bit worried she would think they were saying she was too pushy. Instead she had seemed delighted to realise her daughter's progress. Breda wanted to jump out of the chair and hug them both hard.

"You are an excellent mother Kathleen. Anyway, we will call you back in in a few minutes if Breda wants you. Okay? I hope you don't mind too much. I just have to, hospital policy, and we can't break all the rules now can we?"

Kathleen was delighted at being called an excellent mother so she expressed her non-concern and went out to Uncle James in the waiting room.

Doctor Ombino looked at Breda.

"You haven't had a period since the last operation?"

"No."

"And are you sexually active?"

"I wish. Why?"

"Well after I took the urine sample and we talked about your period going, I did a test on it." He paused for a long time as if he expected her to join dots that she just wasn't seeing.

"And?"

"Well Breda I don't know how you are going to take this. There is no way for me to gauge the best way to tell you…"

Breda chuckled. "Try spitting it out."

A flash of concern crossed the kind doctor's face, but it was quickly replaced with his standard smile. His eyes weren't in it though. Breda could read faces like books.

"Of course, of course... Breda, it would appear that you are very pregnant."

Breda laughed until her face was wet with tears and other unmentionable liquids.

"Look, you may think that I am joking but I can assure you I am not. Now we need to make sure and we do that with a very simple ultrasound. You have had that before so it should not be too ... invasive or unusual. It is just on your tummy. Right here."

Breda stopped laughing. He was serious. The doctor was gesturing to his stomach. Breda was going for an ultrasound to see if she was pregnant!

"Okay. Let's figure this out." But the most Breda expected it to be was another kidney infection.

3

At half nine the office was empty, except for the small glass cubicle. Just enough for two bodies, a desk, two chairs and three filing cabinets along one side. Orla hated that everyone in the office called it 'the cubicle'. She preferred to call it 'Mark's office', but over the years hearing it called the cubicle again and again, her brain got washed. Mark still hadn't told Orla that there was a possibility that Noelle and this family were related. He was surprised Orla hadn't twigged it yet, it wasn't exactly hard to figure out, but she still hadn't and for this Mark was very, very grateful. He felt his face blush hard at his conspiracy. Orla looked up at him suddenly with squinted eyes. He needed to distract her before she started asking questions. Keeping secrets purposefully was not his forte. All of Mark's thoughts were written on his face and in his body language. He knew he was obvious but he still had a job to do.

"It just doesn't really add up. We called every small Catholic primary school in the city and no one had Tina in Junior Infants. That's worrying. Here is the list of other schools in the county to check out." Mark handed Orla a long list with names and numbers on it. "Will you call the school where the other two Madden kids go in the morning, along with the schools on the list and we'll have to come up with something."

They had been ringing schools all evening until the phones rang out and everyone else in the world had gone home. Orla had another list of schools in the city centre that hadn't picked up and she would be calling them again first thing in the morning. Mark had been on to the solicitor Jean McCaile who would be in at 10 a.m. to see where the social workers stood on interviewing the child without her parents' permission. Jean was a godsend; she always had been in these kinds of situations. Mark only had to tell her what he needed to do and she made it legal by getting signed court orders, liaising with Gardaí and getting warrants. The woman was a weasel of the very best kind and every one of the social workers loved her for it. She would have been in the office that night if Mark hadn't told her she would need her beauty sleep for this one. She had laughed and said that she always needed beauty sleep and to expect her at ten a.m. She had to be in Naas at 8 a.m. and that's the earliest she could make it if they wouldn't have her that night.

Reluctantly the pair wrapped up their work. There was nothing more they could do until the morning, they had decided. Orla packed up and let herself out of the office with a shout of "Good night!" to Mark over her shoulder.

Mark watched her leave. Then waited until he heard the iron gates on the front of the office door open and shut. Orla was an amazing social worker. She would have stayed all night if they could have made more headway. When the gate banged Mark left the cubicle and walked down to the file room. The file room was almost as big as the main body of the office. He flicked on the light switch and in the flashing florescent lights he walked down the long passageway between the high shelving units. He walked all the way to the back wall and turned right. On the back wall shoved into corner was a large locker. A white sticker on the front had read *Noelle's stuff* but someone had scratched off *stuff* and scribbled *shit* in its place. Mark wondered if it had been Orla. That was the kind of harmless thing Orla got her kicks from. That and her brutal honesty, were never-ending sources of amusement to him. Mark wished she wasn't so bloody tall though. She made him feel tiny and he really wasn't that small.

Mark pulled the locker open and took a step back to survey the task at hand. This was the fourth time he had gone through this locker looking at every single piece of paper shoved in there. Her boxes were back in their place on top. *Orla must have put them back before she went home,* he thought. Then he sat on the ground and pulled out a bag at a time, going through everything, looking for more information about what the hell Noelle had been thinking when she set up the adoption of Tina Madden by this family. He sat there for three hours until he came across paper that had at one stage been a report on Breda Flood Byrne. Breda, Tina Madden's mother, was trying to give Noelle the child. Mark could just about read the small paragraph with the tea stains and tears. It had only been three years! There was no excuse for the file to be in this state. Noelle had been sent to the address after an anonymous tip-off to the office saying that the child needed attention. The mother was severely disabled. Vegetable state. Sent to a nursing home.

He looked at the other things in the cardboard folder. There was the court document where Patricia had officially been given custody of Tina Madden. It was very badly stained. Almost as if someone had ruined it on purpose. There was a name under *Witness* and something else. *Simon Prendergast.* Mark squinted to read the rest, *Court Clerk* and *Witness* and at the bottom a very sloppy signature. Simon Prendergast would be easy to find if he was a court clerk three years ago. Probably still was one.

Orla pulled into her parking space in the car park beneath her apartment block. She turned off the engine and put her head back on the headrest. It felt like she left here a week ago. It did not feel like she was only gone one day. She closed her eyes for just a second. She felt the lure of sleep gently tugging her consciousness. She could have fallen asleep so easily; in fact, she would have if she hadn't stopped herself. She opened her eyes quickly and severed the tie between her brain and the land of nod. Then she put her head back upright and began the nighttime ritual of gathering all the shite she was legally obliged to bring into her apartment rather than leave in the car for the world or his wife to rob. She wouldn't have left them in the car anyway. It was the obligation of it that pissed her off, and that was only because she was tired and cranky. Finally, she picked up her handbag and got out of the car.

She punched in the key code to the big steel door and struggled her way through it. It made her frustrated. On her way up the stairs to her modern, canal-front apartment with mahogany solid wood floors and wardrobe space that would make Kimora Lee Simmons jealous, an old familiar thought managed to seep its way through her defences. It would be better if there were someone waiting up these stairs for her to come home. She missed David. *He's probably off with some young one right now. He could be anywhere in the world.* David loved to travel and would go anywhere at the drop of the hat. Not just to America, Canada, or Continental Europe but to Thailand, Prague, Morocco and other places exotic sounding Orla had once longed to see. They had travelled together twice on weekend trips but nothing adventurous enough to satisfy her hunger to explore with him. His mother was Italian and he had lived near her family in Florence for two years while he went to college there. He lived in Kenya for three months on a whim. He was a journalist and could do as he liked, write about whatever took his fancy and the cultural media in Ireland and the UK gobbled it up and were still hungry for more. Orla had to live in Dublin for her career. She thought that was the heart of the problem. David of course had a different take on it but they never had the chance to iron it out. He was just gone. No talking, no chances, no acknowledgment of the seven years they had known and loved each other.

Now Orla found herself stuck in an apartment meant to be a love nest but with only one bird. Her chest always felt heavy in that apartment. She could be standing on the little iron balcony on a sunny Sunday morning and still she would feel that she could stop breathing at any second. It was as if she was missing a part of herself; or more like she lost the person she would become with David. The future Orla, who cooked amazing meals with ease and flew off to Japan on a whim but fantasy Orla would never exist now. She knew she should have moved but unlike her former flame she had a sense of responsibility and wanted to see her two-year lease through. Only three more months. She took out her keys and let herself in. Orla knew that she should have started looking for somewhere else by now but no matter how sad the apartment felt, it was the last place they had been together. It was hard to let that go.

No way. There is no fucking way! I cannot be pregnant. They must have made a mistake. However, the doctor had done two more tests on her urine. Having Dr Ombino help her get the sample was a bit uncomfortable but Breda knew Kathleen would smell a rat if she had gotten her mother to do it so she insisted the doctor did it with her. He obliged and was ever the professional during the process. Then they did the second and third pregnancy tests. Both were positive. They agreed that they would first make sure that no mistake had been made by doing the ultrasound before telling Kathleen and Uncle James. Ma probably wouldn't like that James would hear the news at the same time she would but Breda wasn't planning to be there and she didn't want her to go through it by herself so James and the doctor would have to step in and take one for the team. Doctor Ombino said James wouldn't mind and Breda had enough to be worrying about without her mother's spur-of-the-moment reaction to news she never thought she would hear. Doctor Ombino had a way with words and in the end Breda made the decision without any guilt but with just a pinch, a tiny teeny pinch, of concern. The doctor would take James and Ma off somewhere and reassure them that "Breda was just having a little test" and that there was nothing to be concerned about, the nurse would call him on his mobile right after the two minute exam to confirm or deny the pregnancy then he would tell James and Kathleen.

He had called down to the radiographer who sent two men in blue scrubs to bring her down for an abdominal ultrasound. It was all very quick. When they got to the X-ray department, the two porters helped Breda up onto a trolley. She did her best to make their job easier, shifting her weight this way and that so they could manoeuvre her better. Physio had made her legs stronger and she had more control over the movement in her arms. Breda pushed her weight into her feet and the men took it from there. Before she knew it, Breda was under yet another bright light waiting for a specialist as she had done so many times before. It didn't feel much different to the other times. It was hard to think of the news as anything other than another medical hurdle;

another blip on her journey to independence; a mistake that needed to be cleared up. Breda really did not believe she was pregnant.

"But I don't understand love!" Kathleen was distraught. "I have been with you almost every second of every day since you were born and I knew nothing about any … relations you were having."

Breda wanted to be left alone with her thoughts. She didn't know what her position was on the new revelation. There was only one thing she was sure of. She must have been raped. There was no other answer to the biological question. Breda had never had sex. She had never even been kissed! Surely she would remember something like going the full way. In addition, she didn't even know any men. Not real men, only relatives and her doctors. Breda could not remember a thing. One thing she was relieved about was that her mother hadn't brought up the idea of Immaculate Conception. Breda had half expected her too. Kathleen knew Breda hadn't been seeing anyone. Why was she still asking these stupid questions? Breda thought it was obvious what had happened. Clear as day. She had been raped in the hospital while under anaesthetic from the operation. It was the only answer. The only possible way it could have happened.

Kathleen, still begging for an explanation, was on the chair across from Breda's perch. There was a small tap on the sitting room door and Uncle James popped his head around the corner.

"Kathleen? I think you should go for a rest. You need a lie down." He went over to Kathleen, took her hand and helped her to her feet carefully. "Now this thing won't go away in the time it takes you to have a little lie down for yourself."

"Ah James no…" Kathleen began, but Breda broke her silence for long enough to back up her uncle.

"Listen to Uncle James Ma. Go have a lie down." Breda took a liar's breath. "I'll tell you everything tomorrow, I promise."

Breda knew there was nothing to tell. She didn't remember a thing. She didn't feel degraded or used. She just felt pregnant and worried for her mother.

James led Kathleen out of the room and into the hall. Breda listened as he settled her onto the bed.

"There now. Are you comfortable? Now no more worry until the morning. Have a nice rest and I'll see to Breda tonight. If you don't mind I might kip on the couch."

Breda's heart was breaking for the two of them. James was a single man. He had a wife but, just like Da, she had gone to her creator. Six-and-a-half months between them. How could James and Kathleen handle this? How could they face up to the reality that was slowly sinking into Breda?

Uncle James came back through the sitting room.

"Now, a cuppa for us two is in order I do believe!" He got the high stool and put it beside Breda's head then disappeared back into the kitchen. When he appeared again, he had two cups of tea and a bright-pink silly straw between his fingers. He was careful not to spill tea as he made his way over.

"Don't worry Uncle James, I spill stuff on the carpet all the time."

"Oh the magical non-stain carpet. Your ma is always singing its praises." James laughed at the thought of his brother's wife getting all excited about a carpet as he put one cup down on the coffee table and the other up on the high stool. Then he took the silly straw and wedged the silly part onto the rim of the cup so it would stay in the tea. Breda loved when Uncle James did things like this. They had discovered the miracle of the silly straw one night when Ma had been at a Novena and James had seen Breda's frustration at having someone lift the cup to her face and put the straw in her mouth for her. That hadn't encouraged Breda to move and try to loosen her muscles with day-to-day things. She was well able to turn her head so Uncle James had come up with the high stool and the silly straw. It might sound like a small thing to someone else but to Breda it was another thing she could do on her own and it made her eyes well up with tears. Uncle James was safe, he was kind and he encouraged her to do as much as she could for herself.

"We don't even wipe it when I spill, the carpet is so good!" Breda didn't know how they managed to talk about carpet at a time like this but she was happy for the distraction. *God, she thought, I only found out I'm pregnant and I want a distraction already! I need to focus!*

Uncle James sat where her mother was only minutes before but Breda didn't feel the scrutiny any more. She felt calm. She was with her uncle and he would make everything all right. He would not be shocked by anything she said. He was too old and wise. He was the kind of man who had lived the exciting years of his life fully with a wife who had loved him, and now was settled down by himself enjoying the peaceful years. Breda couldn't imagine him retiring. At over sixty, he still seemed so strong and healthy.

"So do you want to talk about it or will we turn on the auld box?"

Breda thought for a second. Uncle James could handle it. She could depend on him. He was the only person in the world she could have had this conversation with so informally and know he wouldn't report back to Ma.

"Let's talk," she said.

James took his cup off the table with big steady hands and sat back.

"I don't have a boyfriend Uncle James."

"I know."

"I don't remember how it happened."

"You know if there was a fling of some sorts no one would judge you. You are an adult and you are of sound mind." He quickly added, "Once it was your choice, mind."

"No. I never did. Do I really seem the sort to have steamy sessions with men on the sly?" Maybe she had made a mistake talking to Uncle James. Maybe he wouldn't understand like she had thought.

"Well then. I think we are onto the other possibility. Are you sure you're okay to talk to me about this? I don't want to interfere." Uncle James looked so concerned that Breda moved her chair towards him and reached awkwardly for his hand. James, following her lead, leaned forward and gave it to her. He gave her the time she needed to express herself.

"You are my uncle and you are never interfering! I need you and your opinions now more than ever."

"Don't you worry love. We'll get through this."

Breda moved back.

"I think it happened in the hospital at some stage after the operation when I was still under. I don't remember a thing thank God."

"You're a smart girl. If you don't remember, keep it that way and don't go giving yourself any more anxieties than you already have. But I can tell you now if you choose to go to the Gardaí, which I don't think is a bad idea at all at all, I will be with you every step of the way and so will your mother."

Breda's eyes widened.

"No. I will not be telling Ma. Never. Never ever. She has seen me deal with enough. Maybe later, when she is at peace, I will report it but not a day before."

"Understood. A mother suffers twice what she sees her child going through. I understand." James didn't know what to think after that. The child has had something awful done to her by another, fitter human man and she won't report the crime. He decided not to push the issue yet.

"And the baby?" he asked tentatively.

"I have no idea."

"Hello?"

Stephanie was asleep on her mattress.

"Hello?"

What was that noise? she thought, before falling straight back to sleep.

"Is there another girl here?"

Stephanie's eyes shot open.

"Hello?"

There it was again! The voice was real! It was a girl's voice!

Suddenly the events of the night before flooded Stephanie's mind. She scrambled to her feet. She had tried to stay awake as long as she could in case her next-door neighbour should wake up and want to try to make contact. Nevertheless, the weight of sleep was too much for the young girl and she retreated to her mattress at four in the morning. Only she didn't know it was four in the morning, she just knew the light coming in at the edge of the plyboard on the window looked like early morning. The street light yellow and the blue hue twinge gave it away. Two years ago, Stephanie wouldn't have been able to tell you the colour of early morning light. Now she knew it was blue.

"Hello?" She was on her knees against the wall.

"Hello? Talk into the pipe." The voice whispered.

Stephanie left the wall and went to the corner where the poop pipe came out of the floorboards.

"I can hear you!" Stephanie bounced up and down on her toes, nearly bursting out of her skin with excitement.

"Oh! Where are we?" the voice asked.

"We're in a house," Stephanie replied.

"I know that but where is it? Where is this house?" The voice sounded wobbly.

Stephanie thought for a while. It was close to home. Stephanie knew that because they were not in the car for long the first time she was brought here. "In Dublin I think."

There was a long pause.

"Is he going to let us go home?"

Stephanie thought. She never thought she would be here forever. God would not let a little girl stay away from her parents forever! Surely not! After all the bad things, Stephanie had to believe she would be going home. That was the only thing that kept her going. Of course she would be going home! Adults did not keep children away from their mams and dads and nans.

"Yes we will get to go home. It might not be for a while but we will be going home. I'm positive." Stephanie's voice sounded sure. Definite. It put the situation at ease. This situation wasn't going to be forever. This was a temporary thing they would have to put up with before they got to go home to kind words and hugs and minding forever, but it was hard for Stephanie to let herself think about life at her nan's. Her dad would be home and on the telephone ringing her friends' houses and checking that she hadn't gone home with someone else. The phone bill in nan's would be huge and her legs would be tired. Stephanie had been gone two months.

The long pauses annoyed her. Stephanie wanted to hear all about this girl in the next room but still she waited for the other girl to ask the questions.

"What's your name?"

"I'm Stephanie. I'm nine. What about you?"

"Nicole. I'm seven but I'm nearly eight."

Orla hung up the phone and crossed off another primary school on her list. The Department of Education hadn't gotten back to her but she was very thankful for the lists of schools they had sent over. She picked up the phone again and punched in the next number. Saint John's National School. The phone rang until a man answered. He would check the files if Miss Flynn wouldn't mind waiting for a moment. Then he came back with the same let down as the forty-two other schools Orla had called in the last sixteen hours. He had not recognised the name and he was right, there was no Tina Madden in Junior Infants the previous year. He was sorry he couldn't be of more help and he hoped everything was all right. Orla said her thank yous and hung up. Only four more schools and they were all in bordering counties.

Tina Madden had not been in school last year. Orla knew it, and two hours later the Department of Education called her and confirmed that Tina had not been in primary school or home schooled in the State of Ireland the previous year. She asked them if they could put it in writing and fax it down as soon as possible and they agreed. After giving them the fax number Orla went into her documents on her old computer and printed the legal regulations in relation to primary and secondary school attendance by citizens of Ireland. It only took two minutes for her to locate the relevant areas that had been flouted by Patricia and Kevin Madden so after they were highlighted Orla put them in the new file with *Investigation into Madden Family* printed on the front. She reopened the file that contained the photographs of the family home. The pictures flew up on the screen in an instant and Orla had a chance to see the house again. It was mesmerising. How were four or five people living in that house? Orla didn't take it for granted that Kevin Madden was still in the picture; experience had taught her that presuming leads to error. Orla had to force herself to take her eyes off the pictures for long enough to do her job. She printed them and into the file they went, along with photocopies of her notes on the conversation with Grainne Hopkins, the quiet, concerned, self-conscious High Infants teacher. When the fax arrived, she put that in the brown file too.

Ring, ring.

"Divine Trinity National School. Principal Gray speaking. How may I help you?"

The end of every sentence was so high-pitched that Orla lost control of herself for a few seconds. She laughed loudly and had to shove her fist into her mouth to hold in the outburst.

"Helllloooo?"

Scoff scoff scoff.

"Can you hear me?"

Scoff scoff scoff.

"If you are on a mobile may I suggest you hang up and call back on a land line. Good day!" Principal Gray hung up sternly.

Orla composed herself. What the hell was she playing at! This was a very serious thing! But in her head, she had "Principal Gray Speaking" repeating in the shrill voice around her brain. *Lady of the house speaking!*

Scoff scoff scoff.

Mark walked by her desk and looked at her, slightly worriedly. Now tears were running down her face. *Poor Mark!* He had no idea what was going on. Three minutes later Orla called the school again.

"Divine Trinity National School. Principal Gray speaking. How may I help you?" She said it in the exact same way she said it before! Orla squeezed her eyes shut and spoke before it was too late.

"Good morning Mrs Gray. This is Orla Flynn here from the Department of Children and Families. I was wondering if I may leave a message for Mizzz Hopkins?" She was being bold but she just couldn't help herself.

"Mizzz Flynn I hope you have been well. That is no problem once you are aware that if I am the one you ask to take the note, I will not be able to help but know its contents. That isn't something you have a problem with on this occasion is it?"

Orla smiled widely. "Oh no, not at all. I would never leave a message if I cared about who read its contents. I think I can trust you Mrs Gray, can't I? I mean it is a very important message." Now she was being obvious, but she just didn't give a shite.

"Oh! Ooh yes indeed Miss Flynn. You can trust me with any message you need to give."

"You may need to write it down..."

"I have a pen and paper right here..."

"Great. Now can you write the following:

Miss Hopkins please contact Miss Flynn in her office as soon as possible."

"Fine! Fine! I will give it to her immediately! Good day Mizzz Flynn."

Slam. Beep beep beep.

By the time Jean McCaile was due in Orla had a copy of the file on her own desk and the original was sitting on Mark's. His also had notes of all correspondence that had been requested by Orla, including a signed statement from Grainne Hopkins as well as a Community Welfare Officer who had Patricia Madden on his books for years and knew the family well. Then Orla reluctantly made her way over to Emily and asked her to take messages while she caught up on paperwork. Emily had pouted. The task wasn't challenging enough for the organisation-junkie.

"Em... any calls you want me to keep an eye out for?"

"Erm..." Orla thought for a second. Well yes there was. "Yes please. Grainne Hopkins. If she rings you can put her straight through. And if any of the people I am expecting today change their appointment times can you let me know?"

Emily was beaming! Thrilled with the additional complications she was scribbling her little heart out onto a small yellow jotter with a pink glittery pen.

"And the rest, if you could take messages and drop them into me every once in a while when no one is with me that would be great."

Emily was a freak Orla decided for the hundredth time since the young girl started, and she walked back to her desk.

Orla settled down and caught up on the work she had to put off while she had been investigating Tina Madden's case. There were a tonne of phone calls to make and she had to check progress reports from teachers and doctors and visitation supervisors. An hour later, before she had even properly bitten into the workload, she looked up and saw that Jean and Mark were in the cubicle. Two cups of tea and faces serious with discussion.

Jean McCaile was in her early forties and had been working for Social Services for ten years. She was a Dublin socialite for at least twice as long. In her college days in Trinity she had dated a very well-known Irish football player. At the time she had been what people considered 'chic' but she was something else too. She was intelligent and educated. Not just a pretty face, which was miles away from the sports star's usual 'type'. He began to act like a gentleman and people noticed. The couple began to appear in social columns in newspapers and their pictures were in magazines. Eventually holes began to appear in the unblemished picture. He began to notice the photographers and reporters were calling out Jean's name more and more. Then they were calling her name more than his. He noticed that when they were together, the photographers had begun to take pictures of them both, and then of Jean alone. He started to go back to his natural ways of using and abusing sluts as soon as

Jean's back was turned, and when the media got wind that he had cheated on her three years into the relationship, Jean had come out of it smelling of roses. He, Orla had suspected, had always been a piece of shit. Orla knew all of this because Jean loved to talk about it. She was careful about where and when she told the story but when she did, she adored it! How a pretty young college student had become the femme fatale and showed a pig for what he was, only for her to come out the other side being the sweetheart of the Dublin set.

Orla and Jean always had lunch together when they were both working out of the North Dublin office; it wasn't very often but Orla enjoyed it. They often played a little social work game where Orla would throw out a scenario where she had to do something against the rules for a case and Jean would have to describe how she would try to defend her when she got caught for it. It was totally unrealistic but Orla thought it was excellent seeing the way the invincible Jean McCaile's mind worked. She was smarter than she ever had to be; that Orla was positive of after all their games.

Orla was back at her desk on the phone again. Eileen Kelly wanted to organise her first full-day visit with Nicole. Orla was exasperated with the woman.

"So you said you wouldn't be able to make it on Saturday. Now you're saying that you can make it but only if you can take Nicole out for the day without supervision?"

"Yeah."

"That doesn't make sense."

"Well it's as much as you'll be getting out of me Miss high-and-mighty."

"Okay, okay. I'll fill out the request form but I won't pass it by my boss until you promise to do your best to show up whether it gets approved or not." Orla knew that a promise could easily be broken but she felt she needed something from Eileen.

"Fine, fine, I promise. Whatever."

Orla could picture Eileen, hand on her hip and rolling her eyes at everything she heard.

"I just need to know what time you would like to collect Nicole and what time you would be dropping her back. Other than that we just need to know what you plan on doing with her for the day."

"The bus will get there around half ten so I'd be there at eleven and I'd have her back by seven or eight. She'd be going shopping and the park with me and then to my ma's house for dinner. That alright enough for you?"

Orla let her eyes flick back over her notes.

"Yeah that's grand Eileen. If I need anything else I'll give you a call. Otherwise I'll call you with your answer in two days."

"Grand. Talk to ya." And Eileen hung up.

Orla felt eyes on her back and turned to see Jean heading over towards her.

"Okay, we have a plan of action," Jean declared when she was still fifteen feet or so away from her.

Orla smiled.

"Shall we retire to the kitchen and discuss tactics?"

Jean shook her head.

"We'll have to go to the cubicle. We can't have little ears a-listening."

Orla raised her eyebrows at Jean.

"Sounds mysterious."

Jean laughed confidently.

"Mysterious, yes. Irritating, yes. Too much for us to deal with? Absolutely not!"

Orla stood up and the women headed over to the cubicle.

Mark had been anxious before Jean McCaile arrived to meet him. He was going to have to tell her about his suspicions about Noelle. He needed to know their legal standing and if it was Noelle herself or the department would suffer the consequences of her incomprehensible actions. Why would she have taken so many big risks? What made her place children in inadequate homes and fake the paperwork? It just didn't make any sense. Possibly even her own sister's granddaughter as well! Her grandniece. Mark was worried. There were too many questions to be answered before they would contact Noelle. That would be a long way off. Jean might even recommend that they go to the authorities and report their findings so far. That would be terrible. They would come in and take over the office for God knows how long while they thumbed though all the confidential files and staff records. Mark wouldn't have minded if they would allow the office to stay open and functional but there was no way that would happen. All of the active cases the office had been dealing with would be put on hold. That would cause unimaginable suffering and disruption to any number of children and their relatives.

He had been in two minds whether to tell Jean at all yet. He had settled on just telling her about the Madden case. For the over all Noelle issue, he needed more time. He hadn't gotten a third of Noelle's career cases and already he had found fourteen cases that screamed out to him and that he would have to investigate further. They were all permanent adoptions and all of the files had the same kind of inconsistencies that caught his eye. None of them had a current address for the adoptive parents. Reports only half written up, hardly anything had been cleared by their old supervisors. There were giant gaping holes in all of them. Still they were all stamped with the same *SETTLED AND FINALISED* in bold red capitals right on the front. Mark hated a job half-done and a case not finished to the utmost standard. He hated that he didn't know for certain what situations the children had been put into. He didn't know if Noelle even knew where the kids ended up. In the file of one four year old there wasn't even a name of the adopted parents. Most of the files had no details at all about the birth mother or her situation. They all seemed to either have the details of the adoptive parents or the birth mother, but not one had both. That was probably what was most unsettling. That usually implied that someone had been kept out of the loop.

He realised she had been a master manipulator. She had been sweet as pie, played the role of the almost too sweet and kind older lady to get away with something, and only let her wicked side out when she was questioned. She could do it at the drop of a hat. No one questioned her again after they had been the focus of one of her outbursts. She would squint her eyes and lean into your face and crush you. She made people feel like bold children. Mark kicked himself for falling for it for the whole fifteen years he had worked with her. Luckily, he had only been her superior for a year before she left. When she left she had blamed Mark because she hated that this "green horn", as she put it, was allowed to ask her questions. She had never tried to go any further in the department and it bit her like a dog when Mark, a *boy* she considered too quiet and thick for the job, was over her rank-wise. Mark had been trying to get her to improve her files when she left. And when, six years after she left, he looked back at her records he made a shocking discovery. The only year she had kept even remotely adequate records was the final year of her career. Mark had hounded her out of the job without realising it. That was also when he started going back over her cases. He was so disturbed by what he found that he had spent the majority of his time in the office delegating and keeping his own time free to try to see what the hell happened before he got the promotion.

Jean suggested that Orla go ahead and make arrangements in the school to meet Tina Madden without the mother's consent or knowledge. They were well within the boundaries of their rights and by the look of the case they needed to press ahead without any unnecessary delay. Jean would head down to the family court and update a judge on the situation. Orla would make a record of her conversation with Tina and if things looked really bad she can take Tina there and then. Jean would be able to take care of the legal side of it from the court, get an order for removal. Mark agreed. Secretly he was, delighted that Jean had dismissed the whole Noelle connection as nothing more then a lazy social worker and a family. He couldn't help but bask in the relief he felt for a few more moments.

"Great! Perfect. That's what we'll do. Orla are you okay with that?" He looked at the tall brunette eagerly.

Orla nodded.

"Not a problem. I can't imagine the…" Orla chose her words carefully "…odd little principal will object. She'll just be thrilled there is something going on for her to distract herself with."

On her way out the door Mark handed Orla the week's lists for her 'meeting' with Jean. Orla took them, smiling, and headed back to her desk. Jean and Mark looked at each other and shook their heads at one another in amusement. Then Jean went off to her own corner of the buzzing, ringing, shouting room.

Mark saw Emily coming towards him, being followed by an older gentleman in a very expensive-looking suit. *Just in the nick of time*, thought Mark as Emily began her introductions.

"Mark this is Simon Prendergast, he has an appointment with you. Mr Prendergast this is Mark Tynan. I'll leave you to it. Let me know if you want teas or coffees."

Mark extended a hand to the man who took it and shook it warmly.

"Thank you so much for coming in Mr Prendergast. I appreciate it more than you know."

Simon Prendergast looked at Mark and thought, *This is a man under pressure.* "Call me Simon please. I could tell by your call it was urgent and I am a man of my word."

Mark laughed flakily.

"And I can tell you I am most thankful that you can Simon. Please come on in." The men went into the cubicle and Mark made sure the door was shut tight and there was no sign of Orla or Jean before he sat down.

It had all been off record but Simon Prendergast remembered the regular meetings between Noelle Flood the social worker and Justice Thomas White throughout the years. He had been asked to sign things after those meetings but never during. It was more like he was signing them as a favour to Justice Thomas White, just because his signature was a formality. He signed things for Justice White many, many times. So many he couldn't even pick out any individual one.

4

Breda lay awake all night. Pregnancy meant a baby. It meant giving birth. Labour. Not only that but feeding a baby, picking the baby up. Breda couldn't even pick up a cup, how could she handle a baby? Her eyes welled up for the first time since the news. She couldn't look after herself, there was no way that she could care for a child. Or give birth.

Then again, she never thought she would have an interaction with a man in order to be pregnant, and in her mind Breda still hadn't been with a man. Her body 'down there' didn't feel any different. She vaguely remembered noticing some slight soreness just before it was time to take her pain meds in the days after the operation. She had only noticed two or three times and then wrote it off as some side effect of one or more of the post-op meds. It had definitely happened in the hospital though. It would have been the only opportunity. But who had done it? Breda didn't remember any men acting strangely or leering at her the way she expected they would if they found her sexually attractive. She needed to get on with things! Not being able to remember the event was a blessing and she couldn't force herself to relive things that there is no possible way she could re-account. Breda refused to let her brain put her into the padded box marked 'victim'. How could she possibly let herself think of all of her injustices when other women went through more violent, vicious, lengthy experiences without the godsend that was morphine. No! That would not happen!

There had been a man. Not older than Breda, she didn't want anyone to be able to say he took advantage of her. He would be younger… and on crutches. They met in the hospital common room two days before she was discharged. He had understood what she was saying better than anyone she had ever met and Breda couldn't help but be madly attracted to him. She managed to lure him down and they kissed and before she knew it, they were heading to his private room. Afterwards Breda had told him that she didn't want a boyfriend but she loved him for opening her eyes to womanhood. He begged to get to know her better but Breda had said no, their meeting was brief and perfect. That was all she wanted. He was discharged that day. She was discharged the day after and Breda didn't want to see him again.

She would tell Uncle James as soon as they were alone together again. Maybe he would back her up and say he had called in to visit her only to find her room was empty. He had waited and eventually Breda came onto the ward followed by a young man who was very depressed looking. Maybe he would even say he witnessed the final goodbye. Breda hoped her story wasn't totally unrealistic. She hated to seem naive but when you learn all you know about these things from magazines and soap operas, you roll with whatever you have.

With that mess cleared up, Breda would just have to focus on the present and on what the you-know-what she was going to do with the pregnancy. But Breda didn't focus on what the you-know-what to do with the pregnancy. She fell fast asleep and didn't wake up for ten hours straight.

For the second time in a week Orla pulled into the staff car park of The Divine Trinity National School, and for the second time the only spaces left were at the furthest possible point from the door. This time it wasn't raining but Orla still didn't like walking more than she had to. She hadn't even had a coffee yet. It wasn't any earlier than a usual morning but Orla hadn't slept until four a.m. and was feeling the worse for it. It was the apartment. She knew it and at some stage between midnight and three thirty Orla had made the decision to go apartment hunting online. She would be a gobshite if she signed the lease again and put up with another two years of living like that.

This morning would be difficult. She had Annabelle on standby just in case. Jean had called to say she had spoken to the judge and he approved Tina's possible removal from the school. The judge was on stand by to give two more removal orders for the other two children all she had to do was call him if they needed them. She had already had two calls from Grainne, one confirming that Tina had shown up for school and the other to make sure Orla was definitely coming. Orla wouldn't have missed this appointment for anything. On her way through Swords she pulled in at a shop and bought four bags of penny sweets, just to ease any tension that might arise. She already had a small bucket of crayons and a colouring book in her handbag.

Grainne was waiting just inside the main door when Orla went in. Orla tried to push encouragement through her smile.
"Are we all set?"
Grainne returned the gesture and answered,
"All set. I brought her down to the library. She has been drinking tea and flicking through books since she came in. The change of routine didn't seem to faze her at all. She knows there is a nice lady coming to talk to her and she doesn't mind. Just nodded her head and let me set her up in there." Grainne pointed to the red door that read 'Staff Room'. "She loves tea so if you want to make yourselves some feel free. Just in the staff room on the right. The teachers know you are here so don't worry about seeing any of them."
"Better not keep the young lady waiting then. Will you bring me down?"
"Of course. Come on."
They took lefts and rights and went up some small steps. Orla was amazed that the building had so many nooks and crannies. For a small school, the building was deceptively large. They turned a corner and bumped straight into the Honourable Principal Gray.
"Oh hello there. Is it this morning you are coming? I thought Miss Hopkins said it was tomorrow." She didn't exactly look like a rabbit caught in headlights; she knew the meeting was today and she had been waiting.

"No it was this morning Mrs Gray. I thought I was very clear," Grainne said with concern, more to save face than for Mrs Gray's benefit.

"Oh well don't bother with me. You two just go about your secretive business and I'll go about mine." Mrs Gray pushed past them and hurried off.

Orla looked at Grainne.

"Everything I have seen that woman do and say makes no sense."

A cynical sneer crept onto Grainne's face. "That woman is a walking curve ball. See the way she pretended she hadn't been listening when I told her you were coming? It's all poppycock. I think she doesn't want to admit that she listens to what I say."

"I think she is gagging for a bit of drama and will cling on around the edges until she has had her fill. Honestly I don't know how you deal with her. I'd have strung her up by now. Fair play to you." Orla was mocking but Grainne didn't mind. She liked the tall, funny social worker.

"How long do you think you'll be?"

"I'll be out by eleven I'd say, but you know kids are unpredictable little monsters."

Grainne paused for a moment outside a door. "Well this is my classroom right here so just come back here when you're finished and we'll sneak off for a coffee if you'd like. Marianne, our special needs assistant, said that she will supervise art today." She explained further as they continued down the art-filled hallways. "It's Friday. Compulsory three hours of art. Bless the lord!"

"Marianne sounds excellent. That would be lovely. I'd say we might need it."

They had ended up outside a wooden-panelled door with a little brass plate that read 'Leabharlann'.

"Is this me?"

"Yep. I'll come in and introduce you then I'll slip out and if you need anything just run down to me. Tina is very patient. She won't mind at all." Grainne knocked lightly and pushed the door open.

Orla's heart nearly fell out of her chest. There, directly opposite the door, curled up into a tiny ball in the corner of a big red armchair was Tina Madden. Fast asleep.

Grainne looked at Orla but she didn't notice. She was staring and she could not help it. The girl was tiny. She was six-and-a-half years old and she looked like a four year old. Her jumper was so big that even though she had her legs tucked up to her chin under it, it wasn't stretched. Her whole body, including her arms, fit into the chest of her jumper and a long empty sleeve reached limply towards the floor, which for some reason made the scene all the more sad. The chair's large size made the girl a miniature. A very tired, skinny miniature.

All of a sudden Orla realised there was a lump in her throat. She swallowed hard and returned Grainne's gaze. There were tears in the young teacher's eyes.

"I am so sorry I waited so long…I…I just wanted to be sure. I didn't mean to wait until it got this bad." Her words were little more than a whisper and long silvery tears grew on her flushed cheek.

Orla's gaze hardened.

"I will need to speak to her alone. I don't expect she will be back in class today. Don't worry, her parents' will be informed of where she is." These three sentences were delivered in a low, cold monotone. Grainne still didn't make a move to leave. She just stood there crying over her mistake. Orla spoke quietly again. "If you'd excuse us please. I will knock on your door when I am leaving and let you know the definite plan."

Grainne took a shaky step backwards, and Orla closed the door.

When the sound of footsteps disappeared with the bang, Orla re-opened the library door. She stuck her head out and took a quick look up and down the hallway. The coast was clear, so she took a quick look back to make sure Tina was still asleep then she slipped out into the cool corridor. She took out her phone and called the office. Emily answered and when she heard the urgency in Orla's whispers, put her straight through to Mark in the cubicle.

"Orla?"

"Mark I have just seen Tina Madden and she is in a really bad way physically. I think I need to bring her to a hospital. The teacher totally downplayed it. Sorry, I have to whisper but I am in the hallway outside the room where Tina is."

"Bring her to Crumlin. I'll contact Jean. Is the mother's number in the file?" Mark was sweating.

"Yes on the contacts page but you might not get her."

"Has she said anything suspicious yet?"

"Mark, I haven't even spoken a word to her yet. She is fast asleep on a chair in the library but she looks like she's in such a bad way."

"Don't worry, we'll sort her out. We'll see to a placement with Annabelle when we hear what the doctors have to say."

"Okay. Thanks Mark. I have to go."

"Go! Go! Do your thing! Crumlin will be waiting!"

Orla put her phone back in her bag, taking a second to compose herself. The little girl must not guess there was anything wrong with her. She must not know Orla was upset. She put her hand on the door knob, took a deep breath, and went in. After she had settled on the couch she took out the colouring book and the crayons quietly and put them on the low coffee table. She took off her jacket and hung it over the arm rest of the couch. Tina stirred on the armchair and Orla smiled softly. "Hi there Tina. Are you sleepy?"

The girl's thick eyelashes fluttered open with difficulty.

"I'm Orla."

She still wasn't awake, only on the brink of it. Stirring she was still enveloped in dreams that Orla couldn't let herself imagine. Finally the small child put her head up straight and opened her eyes. Orla smiled at the sleepy, hollow little face.

"Hi," she repeated.

Tina's voice matched her appearance. "Hi." It was grainy and worn out.

"I'm Orla."

Slowly the girl put her arms back in her sleeves, pulled up the front of her jumper to free her twig-like legs and twisted so she was sitting properly in the big red chair. Her words came out small and weak. "I'm Tina."

Orla nearly cried. Tina was facing her now and for the first time Orla really saw her. The small brown eyes that were set in dark hollows. Her cheekbones were too prominent for a child. Her dark hair was cut in a home-made bob that was too blunt and extreme for her features, and was slick with grease and moisture.

"I know, Tina. I am very happy to meet you. I came to see you today and to ask how you are."

There was a delay in Tina responding to everything Orla said.

"I'm okay."

"You look sleepy."

"I'm okay."

"That's nice Tina but is there anything bothering you?" Orla didn't want to praise the child for lying. She was obviously not okay and Orla needed her to know that she could handle the truth. She had a feeling the "I'm okay" response was used to move the focus of attention off herself. Orla wasn't going to let her think she had to hold back like she did for everyone else.

"Not really."

"Do you know what my job is?"

Tina's face pinched itself in thought. "Are you a teacher?"

"Very good! I'm not a teacher but you're very close." Orla watched as Tina tried to figure it out. "My job is to make sure little boys and girls are having a nice life." She took it slowly. She didn't want to loose Tina in explanations. "I make sure that everyone is being kind to them and that they have nice dinners to eat and homes to live in. And most importantly, I make sure no one is being mean to them. Loads of children tell me their problems and I do my best to make it better."

Tina's eyes were wide now. She looked terrified all of a sudden. Orla kept going.

"None of the children I talk to get in trouble for telling me. Not from anyone. Not even their mammies and daddies."

Tina looked down at the beige carpet. "My back hurts."

Orla was thrilled with the progress. "Oh no! Does it pet?" she gushed encouragingly.

"Yeah."

"Have you been to a doctor?"

"No."

"Should we go and get someone to look at it for you?"

"But Ma…"

"Don't worry about your mam pet. I've already called her."

There was another long pause.

"It's not just my back."

Orla felt dread seep into her neck and claw its way down her spine. "Is it not? Where else are you hurting?"

Tina's small face crumpled and she started to cry, "Everywhere."

Orla got off the couch and went over to the chair. She picked up the tiny, weightless girl and sat, holding her on her lap. Tina wrapped her little body around Orla's torso and let Orla hold her.

"You'll be okay pet. We'll sort this out. You're such a brave girl. We'll make everything better…" Orla's face was close to Tina's neck. She saw a big purple bruise at its nape. She knew that smell. Anger bubbled up in her throat. Expertly she held it out of her voice and her body. She loosened her hug just in case she hurt the tiny precious frame. "…You're safe now honey. Just let it all out."

Kathleen didn't buy Breda's story at first, but due to the lack of any other rational explanation, she accepted it. When Uncle James had backed Breda up, she had no choice other than to decide that that must have been what happened. Sure how else would a grown woman get pregnant? So that was it. The baby was the result of a brief affair with a longing stranger on crutches in a hospital. Breda was sorry she had said anything about the crutches, it was stupid. But she had said it now, so she would have to stick with it.

Kathleen and Breda had an appointment in the maternity hospital the following day. They were meeting a family planning counsellor to discuss Breda's 'options'. Both Kathleen and Breda thought they knew what the hospital were going to suggest but the 'A' word had not crossed their lips one second before they absolutely had to approach the subject. Breda couldn't help but feel it was only a matter of time before she would face the firing squad. She would be told that there is no physical way she could continue with the pregnancy, that for her sake and for her own safety, she would have to terminate.

She felt different. Weird in the abdominal area. Her boobs were throbbing all the time, but she only noticed the symptoms after she had had the ultrasound. Now she wasn't sure that she had felt like this before she found out. So could it all just be in her head? Well the doctor said he was one hundred per cent positive she was expecting a baby. The radiographer had pointed out what she said was a ten-week-old foetus on the grainy black and white screen. It had been exactly ten weeks since Breda had been in the hospital. Ten weeks since this little thing arrived inside her. There was a little thing inside her.

The counsellor annoyed her so Kathleen agreed to take Breda home. She needed to think. She needed to talk to her own doctors. Eventually Breda settled on think now, talk to doctors later. She still hadn't really made the connection between her pregnancy and the inevitability of giving birth to a baby, and then raising that baby. How could she make a decision when she hadn't even made the connection between the baby in her belly and raising a baby?! She had done pregnancy for ten weeks. So Breda knew she could 'do' pregnancy. But labour? And taking care of a baby? That would be another thing. That would be the hard part. Money wasn't a problem. Breda got disability allowance every week and would for as long as she was unable to work, which realistically would be the rest of her life. No matter how free the operations and the physio made her muscles, she would never have full use of her limbs. It was still hard to make her arms and hands move the way she wanted them too. It was hard to pick anything up and every movement was sharp and jerky. She was not very precise but she had improved hugely. The doctor had mentioned new medication that had just come onto the American pharmaceutical market. It was designed for people with serious muscle damage but he thought it might heal the scar tissue in her muscles and tendons that was causing the pain and insufferable stiffness. He was contacting the manufacturers in the States to check it out. That was pretty exciting. The muscles around her organs seemed fine but Doctor Ombino said that could change at any time. They had been saying that since she was diagnosed. Nothing new or scary there. So there were only a few factors that really had any weight in the decision to continue on with her pregnancy. Only a few things really. Would she be alive to get her child to eighteen and independence? Would she be able to take care of a child in six-and-a-half-months time? Could she really do it to Ma? She would be the one looking after the baby if Breda didn't improve any more. Would Ma be up for it? Was she even able for it? *Not really*, Breda thought sadly. *Ma wouldn't be able for it.*

Breda couldn't believe she was considering having a baby! A baby! No way! Not possible! No freaking way! Breda could not have a baby!

"Well there is no physical reason why you shouldn't continue on in your pregnancy and have a happy healthy baby Miss Flood Byrne. You will have to deliver by caesarean section but other than that everything necessary for the task at hand is in good working order. Your uterus is in the perfect position and it's of normal shape and size. The pregnancy is in the uterus and not obstructing a fallopian tube. The amniotic fluid looks normal and we'll have the results of the tests in ten days."

Kathleen was gobsmacked. She had never thought this was possible.

"Not only is everything biologically sound at the moment but there is no sign that your amazing speech and muscle improvements are going to slow down." He lowered his tone and looked Breda directly in the eyes. "But of course, what ever you choose to do we understand. There are grounds for every option." Doctor Ombino had been waiting when they arrived.

He didn't even work at this hospital but for a well-rounded consultation to be possible they would need his input. No one knew the ins and outs of Breda's 'issues' better than Doctor Ombino.

Kathleen and Breda were in shock. They would need to go home and make a decision. Doctor Ombino had brought copies of the ultrasound pictures to the meeting in the hospital. Kathleen, ever the Irish mammy, had put all the prenatal prescriptions and medical brochures in a binder and unknowingly she had slipped them in amongst the rest. They were only in the door when Doctor Ombino called to say the pharmaceutical company had just finished their last set of studies on the drug and they were willing to include Breda in their first field trial.

"They said there would be no harm done to the baby. It might be born slightly more muscular than other children but other than that we're good to go. So now you have another thing to think about." Breda could hear his smile down the phone. *Wow this is pressure,* she thought to herself, hanging up.

5

Orla took Tina's tiny hand and they walked together to Grainne Hopkins' classroom door. Orla was so tall and Tina was so tiny that she had to bend over to hold her hand. Orla knocked, opened the door and gestured for Grainne to come out to the hall. She made sure none of the children inside saw that she was with Tina. That's the last thing the girl needed, another reason for the other little people in her class to exclude her.

Grainne came out.

"Hello there, you two."

Orla was still stiff with the younger woman but she knew that if it wasn't for Grainne's phone call, Tina would have been stuck in this horrible situation for longer. So she smiled as genuinely as she could muster.

"We're okay but we'll be heading off now. Sorry I can't hang around but I'll call you this evening if you want," she offered.

Grainne saw the apology for what it was. She was overwhelmed and before either woman knew where she was Grainne had flung her arms around Orla and hugged her. Orla just stood there, arms by her sides, in shock. Grainne, sensing that she had crossed a line there, pulled away and bent down to Tina.

"Hi Tina. You go and have a nice time with Orla. We'll see you very soon."

"Okay." She held her hand up to Orla who bent down and took it again. Then off they went through the rabbit hole corridor out into the fresh air.

"Annabelle?"

"Hi Orla. How've you been?"

"Oh I'm alright. Same old same old. I made a new friend though." Orla glanced in the rear view mirror and saw Tina sitting in the booster seat happily sussing out the car's interior. The booster seat was from a small stockpile in the boot of the blue BMW. She also had a car seat and a carrycot. Her job was unpredictable and Orla thrived on being prepared for anything. They were still in the school car park.

"Oh really? And will your new friend be coming to visit me?" Annabelle asked, not missing a beat. The phone was on speaker so Tina didn't feel like Orla was being sneaky. They had decided on this method years before and they were very good at it.

"I think so. But first we are going to see a doctor about my friend Tina's sore back. She is a very big girl. She is six and a half."

"Oh I'd love to meet her and the little girls here would love to have a new friend to play with for a while."

"Well," Orla said encouragingly when she saw that Tina was listening in keenly, "I will organise a visit soon, okay? It might not be today though but you will be excited to see her any day. Won't you?"

"Oh yes! We'll all be very excited. We'll have to organise a little party. Everyone is very friendly and kind here and they love to throw parties for their new friends."

"Brilliant. We'll see you soon and I will talk to you before then alright?"

"Sounds perfect to me. Tell our new friend Tina we all say hi and we can't wait to meet her."

"I will. Bye!"

"Bye!"

Tina was facing the window but Orla could see the small smile on her face. She started the engine and cheerily began their short road trip with a "And now we're off! That was my friend Annabelle. She would love to meet you some day Tina."

There was a long pause but Orla could see the excitement behind the tiredness when she looked in the mirror as they went off down the road to the children's hospital.

"That would be okay."

Mark had called the hospital before they had even left the school. The staff in A&E were ready for them so when Orla walked in, Tina clutching her hand, a nurse came straight up too them.

"Hello there honey," the large cheery woman called to Tina as she made her way towards them. She looked up at Orla, smiled and said, "I'm guessing you are Miss Flynn and Tina?"

Orla was delighted to be welcomed so warmly, even though she had a feeling Mark was using her unusual height as a means to get other people to recognise her. She knew this kind lady would definitely keep Tina at ease. That was what was important, of course.

"That would be us. Hi there." The women shook hands and the nurse introduced herself.

"My name is Nina and I'm going to be with you when you meet the doctor. Is that okay?"

Tina looked dubious. She looked up to Orla who nodded and smiled back at her.

"These are all good, kind people Tina. They all look after children and make them better. I will be right over there," Orla pointed to a waiting room with a TV and very stressed-out parents and guardians looking in its general direction. "See. I will be right here when you get back and maybe Nina will let me come see you in a little bit. Okay?"

"Okay." Tina let go of Orla's hand and took Nina's.

Orla straightened up and watched them go through a set of double doors to the doctor Mark had organised. She stomped to the waiting room and took out her mobile. She noticed a woman looking at her crossly and shaking her head in disapproval, so she stepped outside and dialled Jean's number.

"Jean McCaile. How can I help you?"

"Jean, my name comes up when I ring you. Why do you still answer the phone like that?"

"I didn't look. Anyway I love how I answer the phone. Do you have Tina? Are you in the hospital yet?"

"God you remind me of a certain principal I have come to know and despise."

"Nice," Jean quipped back.

"Yeah we just got here. Tina is gone down to get checked out. I wouldn't be surprised if they keep her in. She doesn't look well at all." Orla threw a dirty look at a man who was smoking far too close to the hospital doors. "Are we good with the parents?"

"Parent, at the moment. Kevin Madden does a runner every few weeks supposedly. I was on to the adoptive mother. She's a wagon and a half I was at nothing so Mark is going to try again in a while."

Orla didn't notice Nina the cheery nurse calling her name in the waiting room. She didn't see her going into the ladies and checking for her there. She didn't even notice when, slightly impatiently, Nina came up behind her.

Orla felt a tap on her shoulder mid conversation.

"Wow, sorry Jean I have to go. I'll call back if there's news. Bye." She hung up before waiting to hear a goodbye.

"Miss Flynn." Nina had started leading Orla back into the hospital.

"Please, call me Orla."

"Orla the doctor would like to speak to you immediately."

"Is Tina alright? She was only down there for…" she looked at the time on her phone "…three minutes! What could have happened in three minutes?"

Nina stopped walking for a moment.

"It's not what happened in three minutes Orla; unfortunately it looks like what's important is what happened in the last few years." Nina gave Orla an apologetic look and turned back around. Orla followed her and with every step Nina's words sunk deeper and with every step Orla's fear and worry grew. *Oh God, why do I do this job?* she thought. And in a small voice her mind answered, *Because some one fucking has to.*

"Nicole?"

"Yeah?"

"Where were you when they took you?"

"I was out with my ma."

"Yeah but where?"

"We were outside the chipper and Ma went in to use the loo. A man walked up to me and just brought me to a car. Then I was here."

"Was that ages ago?"
"No."
"Is this the first place you went to?"
"What do you mean?"
"I mean…did they take you anywhere else before you came here?"
"No. Just here. Why? Were you somewhere else before you were here?"
"Yeah."
"Was it better or worse?"
"Eh…better."
"Really?"
"Yeah."
"What was it like? Was there a nice bed?"
"Yeah."
"Stephanie tell me. What was it like?"
"I had a proper bathroom with a shower and all. There were sweets and movies and I had a lock on the inside of the door, not on the outside, and I could go wherever I wanted in the house." Stephanie briefly wondered why she had lied about the lock when there was something even better to boast about. "And I had a telly."
"You had to have a telly if you watched movies!"
"Well there was one in the sitting room and one in my bedroom. I could pick which one I wanted to watch. My room was pink and white and flowery and I had loads of toys there. No one bothered me but they left me nice food all the time. And clothes."
"That sounds deadly Stephanie. Do you think we can go there?"
"No."
"Why not?" Nicole asked.
"Just because," replied Stephanie meekly.
"Why did you leave?"
"They made me."
"What happened?"
"I must have done something really bad."

For the first time since Nicole arrived, Stephanie was glad the wall was between them. Nicole wouldn't see her face burning.

Kathleen had tried to take a few days to calm her nerves, but there had been very minimal amounts of calm around the place. There had been the awful, long, forcibly patient conversation about the conception. They had endured two days of frustrated conversation and Breda was so tired from the effort of talking alone that Kathleen couldn't help but think to herself secretly *If a child comes into this house, I'll be the only one fit to rear it.* Kathleen hated herself for it but she had wished Breda would hurry up in her explanations, even when she saw her daughter struggle to make her mouth and jaw move in time to shape the rhythm of words and sentences. The process was laborious. Sure, Breda had made progress, but it wasn't enough. Not to raise a child. Not yet anyway.

Well maybe if she gave up trying to get her legs up to scratch. Other wheelchair-bound women raise children. Kathleen had seen a good few of them over the last few years. Not so much before in the old days, but now things were different. Maybe if Breda focused on her arms and chest more? Physio worked for her. Together, and with a little help from James they had proven that. When Breda was a child Kathleen found it hard to make her daughter go though the pain of having her limbs moved this way and that. She only had it twice a week back then in a small little modern place on Harcourt Street in the heart of the city. Breda would scream until she was blue and Kathleen would be forced to go over and stop the session. It had been terrible. Kathleen still used the buses a lot back then because Breda was still in the frame. The two buses over weren't so bad; a lot of sulking but nothing Kathleen couldn't handle. The journey back? That was a different kettle of fish altogether. Breda would still be crying that she wanted to go home when they got to the bus and Kathleen would have tears in her eyes. Eventually they started calling James and he would come and pick them up. After ten or twelve bus journeys with your screaming child in honest to goodness pain, any mother would avoid it. James never charged them more than a fiver anyway. It was worth it. Kathleen had money. Well enough money to be comfortable for the rest of her days and a little bit more, only if she kept an eye on her shillings though. She was excellent with money and the carers allowance had really made a difference. Eventually Breda went to physio less and less until she was down to once a week and Kathleen didn't press her to do more than she absolutely had to. Luckily Patricia had been off in school so she didn't have to see what her younger sister had to go through. When Breda was given the wheelchair she became more dedicated to her exercises and once she noticed the progress she was making, nothing could stop her.

James and Kathleen agreed that he would be their regular driver and would continue doing his taxi work when they didn't need him to drive them. James was a widower, getting older; he wanted their company and Kathleen trusted him. When her husband had died from the belly that grew from the beer, James had made sure it was not made public knowledge, even though Kathleen was sure he didn't care what people's opinions were. He had done it so Kathleen could save face, and save face she did. She had to bite her tongue when she saw the smelly liquor flowing at her own husband's wake but she forced herself to remember that these people didn't know what had got him in the end. The general assumption was a heart attack, which was right, and she with a babby on the hip and a babby on the floor. Terrible sad. Terrible sad. And they shook their heads and looked at the ground and did strange things with their cheeks.

Men were unusual creatures in the eyes of Kathleen Flood. They were so formal, like they all knew their roles so well. They all knew exactly how to act in so many different situations. Kathleen had been running about like a headless chicken passing sandwiches and desperately offering those with pints a nice cup of tea. And there they were, standing around in little circles and semi-circles, not looking at each other but all doing the exact same things. Even down to the same movements. Men were all so formal, then one day you meet one who isn't and you have a thing with him. Kathleen had married that one. That had been her husband and the father of her children. But times were changing she supposed and people didn't marry all the time anymore. Single mothers were part of the scenery now. Maybe Kathleen needed to get with the programme. She had a few good years in her yet. Her blood pressure was a bit high but other than that she was in perfect health.

Eventually Kathleen decided that more conversations needed to be had. She stood up from the kitchen table and went into the sitting room where Breda was sitting in front of the window. Kathleen had intended on walking over and switching the television off, telling her daughter they would need to have a discussion in the kitchen and getting the binder with all the medical information in it from the mantle. Then she would have the discussion of a lifetime. But she couldn't. She walked into the room and saw her thirty-two-year-old daughter in the morning sunlight. Her hair shone and her skin glowed. She was laughing at something on the television. Kathleen wondered how she was able to laugh. But Breda had always been able to laugh. After the bad news was delivered, after the operations, after the pain from the physio, Breda had always been able to laugh. In that moment Kathleen was overwhelmed with love and awe for the vivacious young woman in front of her. She couldn't stop herself from laughing along. Breda looked at her, a bit confused, but then they just laughed together. They laughed at the new mad situation they were in together. They laughed at the mad situations they had already been through together. It was wordless but it was all the communication they needed right then and it was perfect.

Nina guided Orla into a small examination room. Her eyes darted around the room. Tina wasn't in there.

"What's happening?" Orla asked as the nurse closed the door behind them.

Nina walked to the other side of the small room and leaned against the hospital bed. She spoke softly, like she was breaking the news to a relative and not the social worker who had only met the girl a little while before.

"Well there is proof of long-term trauma and the doctor strongly suggests we photograph it before we take any further steps. We didn't want to scare Tina so we thought you could talk to her before we take any more of her clothes off; she seems to have taken a shine to you already. That's if you give your consent of course." Nina looked Orla square in the eye for a long time. "You know what I am telling you about her mental state don't you?"

"Of course I do. Jesus. What are we talking about here? How bad it is?"

Nina saw the pain in Orla's face. Most social workers she dealt with had lost that a long time ago. Nina decided she like Orla Flynn.

"We think the signs are there alright. We could be looking at sexual abuse. As well as that she is severely malnourished and dehydrated. Then there is a bad rash on her wrists and ankles. Some definite trauma to the chest and back. That's as far as we've gotten and that's really at a first glance. It is obvious she has suffered neglect as well as other things. The doctor wants to put her straight on fluids after we take the pictures. Then he will take bloods and send her to X-ray to make sure we can find what's causing the pain."

"Okay. Okay. She'll be kept in then?"

Nina was a very honest woman. "We'll have to see what shows up on the X-rays and in the bloods but by the looks of things her general health is plenty to cause enough concern to warrant a stay."

Again, Orla pushed her burning anger deeper down inside her chest.

"Okay let's get to it then. Will I use my camera?"

"We have to use the hospital one and we will have copies made for both the hospital records and for your own. We can get them on film or a disk for you too so you have them more permanently." Nina had her hand on the handle of the door now. "We have a few consent forms for you to fill out first. All we are photographing is her back, chest, ankles and wrists. Just what we saw in the preliminary checks."

"No problem."

Nina opened the door. The hustle and bustle of busy doctors and assistants and little patients and concerned parents just didn't exist to Orla. She felt like the only people in the hospital were Nina, the doctor, Tina and her big awkward self.

Two hours later Orla was sitting in an old-woman armchair in a room with smiling suns and pots of gold at the ends of giant brightly – and pretty inaccurately –coloured rainbows. There were six beds in the room and all of them had occupants, although some had come and gone during the hours Orla had been sitting there. Others had been fast asleep the whole time and one poor little girl who had her daddy with her had been collected by porters with a wheelchair, to be brought off for God knows what kind of cruel procedure. Her dad went with her, saying reassuring things in a low tone that Orla couldn't make out. When they got to the door of the ward he gave the porter the eye and the porter stood aside kindly and let the man push his daughter out of Orla's vision.

Her mind wandered to Tina's adoptive dad. Was he leaving because he didn't agree with his wife's behaviour? Was it him? Most likely it was both of them. Orla knew that. They were certainly both to blame. Even if only one of them was putting their hands on Tina, the other would have a responsibility to get the child out of there or report it. No matter what. This meant both were responsible.

Mark had his eyes closed. He was leaning back in his chair, lolling for just a second before he had to get back to work on this fucking joke of a case. He sighed and opened his eyes reluctantly. Then he leaned forward and flipped Tina Madden's file open to the contacts page. Jean had called five minutes ago and they were all clear for removing Tina as well as her older brother and sister who were the biological children of Patricia and Kevin Madden if they needed. Mark had to call Patricia and let her know Tina had been removed. Jean had tried a short while before but she couldn't handle Patricia Madden's abuse.

Simon, the eleven year old, and Hannah, the ten year old, were still in school but not for too much longer. After one of their children was found in such a bad way, all three would be removed temporarily. They wouldn't mention them to Patricia until he had been to the school and removed them but because Tina was now officially in the care of the state, they were obliged to inform her mother and father of the situation.

Mark ran his finger down the list until it settled on Patricia and Kevin Madden. He had added an updated number to the contacts sheet after he had called the community welfare officer and gotten a mobile number. He wasn't at all surprised that Tina's school didn't have a way to reach them but the community welfare officer certainly did. It was a little trick that Mark had figured out years ago. These people didn't want to be bothered by schools or anyone other than the man who handed them a cheque each week.

Mark punched in the number, taking out his anger on the tiny plastic buttons, which clicked loudly on impact.

"Yeah?" Patricia had answered the phone on the second ring, Mark hadn't been ready for that. He didn't really know if he had expected her to answer at all. He blubbered and bumbled his way through his introduction.

"Eh... Hi there...eh....Is that Mrs Patricia Madden?"

"Yeah, what of it?"

"Eh.... My name is Mark Tynan. I'm a social worker here in the Dublin North office. I'm just calling you to see if I can pop out for a chat? It's about Tina." Mark heard as Patricia moved the phone away from her ear and grumbled, "For fuck sake."

"What now then?" she growled.

"Well are you free today? I would really like to have this conversation face to face," Mark continued.

"Fuck that. You lot have taken enough of my precious time in the last while so just tell me whatever it is you have up your hole then piss off."

"I am calling to inform you that we have had to remove her from the school. She won't be coming home tonight."

"Fine. Grand. Whatever."

"Or until we carry out a full investigation." Mark knew this final piece would bite hard.

"Not in my fucking house you're not!" Patricia was pissed off.

"I will need to call out Mrs Madden. I'm sure we can clear this mess up pretty simply. It's just with her health and after my colleague Miss Flynn called out to your house she expressed some serious concerns."

"Fuck off! Tina is grand. Not a bother on her. You can have her if you want her though. I don't give a shite what you do."

Mark was taken aback. She really and truly didn't seem to give a crap. Maybe he could tell her about Simon and Hannah now too since she didn't seem so bothered. It could save him a bit of time later.

"I am meeting with Simon and Hannah in a short while too. We really do have to meet Mrs Madden. I have documents for you."

"Don't you fucking go near my two! They are mine and you can't go near them! Do you fucking hear me you little prick?! Those are my fucking kids and that fucking school isn't just givin' them out to any strangers with a story about being from the social. I won't let it fucking happen! I fucking won't! Do ya hear me?!" Patricia slammed the phone down. Mark just sat still, eyes wide and the receiver still up to his ear humming away. *Oh shit!* he thought. He had taken a chance and it had blown up in his face. A switch turned on in his brain. Patricia would try to get to Simon and Hannah's school before him. Mark jumped up and threw down the receiver. He opened the door of the cubicle and shouted "Emily!" out into the masses. "Emily!"

He grabbed his file and other necessary papers and almost tripping over himself he ran out the door and towards Emily, who looked slightly confused at seeing her boss in such a hurried state.

"Call Jean and tell her I need the other two orders for removal. Take messages. If Orla shows get her to ring me ASAP. Call Annabelle and tell her to hold two more beds just in case. Even if she has to get a travel cot out. Not a baby cot, the bed cot, Okay?" He hadn't stopped walking. They were going towards the door, Mark with Emily running behind him. Mark was going through his pockets of coins and far too many sets of keys to find the ones that would let him into his Mondeo. Emily was glowing with the excitement and she was scribbling in her little pad, nipping at his heels.

"Okay, no problem, consider it sorted."

Then he was gone out the door and Emily stood watching it close after him.

He put his phone in the hands-free kit, and called the school while he was driving. He had the number stored after he had called them only a few minutes earlier that morning to explain that he would have to speak to the children. Mark had spoken to the principal a few times before. He was younger than Mark had expected a principal in Ireland to be, and was really, really into his job. Mark liked him a lot. The first time they had met was at a conference in a hotel in Citywest on the latest from the ever-changing child protection laws in Ireland. They had ended up sitting together and missed most of the lecture because of their talking.

Robert had liked Mark ever since, so when Mark had called the school in a professional capacity Robert had been on the ball right away.

"That's no problem Mark. We'll have them ready and waiting for you and if there is anything at all I can do, please just call."

Mark had thanked him profusely. The second call was a bit different to the first.

"Good morning, principal's office."

"Hi I need to speak to Robert ASAP."

"One minute. I'll get him right away." Mark could hear the phone being put down and footsteps running off on a hard floor. He took a right turn and stopped at a set of traffic lights. More footsteps and the phone being picked up.

"Hello? This is Robert."

"Robert it's Mark from Social Services here again. We may have a bit of a problem. Patricia knows I'm coming. I think she will show up there. She might cause a bit of a scene."

"We can handle that Mark if that's what you want us to do. Do we give her the children?"

"Absolutely not. If you can avoid it at all please keep her away from the children. I understand if you really can't stop her but I would suggest calling the Guards if things seem a bit hairy."

"Are you on your way?"

"Yeah. I'll be less than fifteen minutes; she is closer though but she doesn't have a car."

"Well the way I see it is whether you get here before her or not, she'll still be throwing a fit if she wants the kids that bad and can't have them. Maybe I should ring ahead to the Guards. Just so they are prepared?" Robert had no idea what was going to happen but he was sure he didn't want a scene outside his school.

"You're a smart man Robert. Go for it. I'll see you in a few minutes."

"Okay. Go team!"

And both men hung up. Mark chuckled.

"We can afford it you know," Kathleen pressed. "And I will help you."

"And me. You're not by yourself you know," added Uncle James.

"Yeah, you're not by yourself. You have help. We can even get a nurse if we're under pressure," suggested Kathleen.

Breda was looking at them both; at one, then the other, then the first one again. She felt like she was a spectator at a tennis match.

"And there's the box room. That's big enough for a little one. It did the job grand for you when you were in there."

"What do you think?" asked James. He and Kathleen were dying to hear what Breda would say. *And*, he thought, *she could do with the adventure. They could all do with the adventure.*

Kathleen on the other hand thought it would be motivation. A reason to push the limits of her body until the movement that caused pain became part of her day-to-day abilities. Already she was able to move her hands and arms to lift non-delicate things. She just wasn't exactly accurate, but with enough practice that would come too. Breda stopped them both from talking by looking at the floor until they fell silent. After what seemed like an eternity, she faced them again.

"Let's do it."

Kathleen and Uncle James jumped up from their seats and bounced up and down with joy!

"A baby!" cried James.

"You're having a baby!" cried Kathleen, cupping her daughter's face before spinning around and doing a jig of glee with Uncle James.

Wow! thought Breda. *What am I letting myself in for?*

The doctor told Orla that they would be keeping Tina Madden on the ward for at least three nights. She needed serious medical attention and he had written her a report to that effect. He handed the stapled A4 pages to her and continued explaining the many problems Tina was up against in the next few months to recovery, but Orla had zoned out. She looked down at the long list of ailments. It was incredible. She looked back at the tiny body, hardly making an impression on the fresh clean duvet that was tucked around her. Tina had fallen straight asleep when she had been brought to Orla and what would come to be her bed. Orla had watched the small girl give in and loose her fight to keep her mind in the present and drift away. The only tube coming out from under the bed didn't make any difference in the process at all. Orla felt a sort of pride that Tina hadn't complained about the needle being put into her tiny wrist; that was until Orla realised that this little girl had suffered much, much worse than having an IV put in her arm by a registered professional. Then that made Orla very sad again.

The list was two pages long. The photographs were awful. Orla had only looked at one. It was a small back bent over.

Orla had seen the little bones of her spine and ribs and three big red lines right across the middle of her back. Under her right shoulder there was a fresh blue bruise. Orla turned back to the doctor.

"So as you see we are currently saying three nights but that will just be to re-hydrate her and to feed her up a bit, but really that's when the hard work starts. There are various procedures and minor surgeries she will need over the next few weeks, possibly months. With time in between for healing of course."

Orla closed the file and put one hand to her mouth. "I understand. I just can't believe that it's this bad."

"I agree, it's definitely hard to look at. Well, that's all yours." The doctor gestured to the report now under Orla's arm. "At the back there you can find a time line showing you what we suggest doing in what order and when. Please take it with you. We don't need to know your decision on the next two surgeries until the day Tina is either leaving or staying for the first of the procedures to correct the ribs and the right wrist."

Orla thanked the doctor, he walked to the door and got whisked away by the traffic in the hallway outside. It was only one o'clock and already they had a full plan of action for Tina's recovery. That was something. Tina would sleep until late afternoon so Orla thought she would head back to the office for a few hours and come back after six. She gathered her things and wrote a small note for Nina to read to Tina should she wake up before Orla made it back.

Dear Tina,
The doctor says you are brilliant, and I think so too. I will be back this evening to visit you.
Your good friend,
Orla

Then she drew a little picture of a tall, wide stick woman bending down and holding the hand of a very small stick girl. Then she put speech bubbles from their mouths. In the big stick woman's bubble she wrote, *Hi I'm Orla. Let's be friends.* In the small stick girl's bubble she wrote, *Hi I'm Tina. We are friends silly pants!*

Before she left the ward Orla went to the top of the bed and made sure Tina was definitely asleep. She had done it a million times when she realised the doctor was going to talk to her right there with Tina fast asleep only feet away from them. She was still deeply asleep. Totally out for the count. Orla put her note on the bedside locker and took out the two bags of penny sweets from the depths of her handbag. A bit squished but they were still pretty good. She arranged the sweets, the colouring book and the small box of crayons on the top of the locker and moved the note in front of them. Then she walked away. When she passed the nurses' station Orla stuck her head in to Nina who looked up at her from a file.

"God! Our jobs aren't so different at all. You look like me in there with your files," Orla joked.

"Ha ha ha! Now all you need to be able to do is change a bed." Nina chuckled at her own joke. "Are you heading off?"

"Yeah just for a few hours."

"I'll keep an eye on her don't worry."

"I know you will," said Orla appreciatively. "Oh, I left a few little things with a note on her locker. Could you read it to her if she wakes up before I'm back?"

"I'd be only delighted." Orla wished everyone she dealt was as nice as Nina.

6

You have a message from: Emily!

You missed a call from: Eileen Kelly
At: 12:30 p.m. today
Could you: Please return the call.
Re: Day visit with daughter Nicole

Mark was only two minutes away from the Swords Catholic School when a squad car flew past him with the flashing lights on. *Fuck! Patricia made it to the school before me,* and he pressed a little more on the accelerator. Pulling onto the street he could see two Gardaí disappear in the front door. Mark pulled up the car and walked as quickly as he could into the building. He could hear the shouting when he got to the small white gate in front of the school's happy little garden.

"Get! Your!…. They're mine!.. Get the fuck off me! I'll sue ya!"

Mark walked in the gate and almost ran up the garden. There was no way the children hadn't heard that and whatever else she had shouted before Mark got there. Just when he was about to walk through the door Mark saw Robert running towards him.

"Oh thank God you're here! She freaked. We had to call the Gardaí to come down. She was going mad." Robert was pretty composed even though he was jogging and talking quickly. "Careful now. She's coming. The Guards have her. You better hide. You won't need her seeing you." Robert grabbed Mark by the arm and dragged him into the school. Patricia's protests were getting louder. Right inside there were two doors. One with a little boy on it and another with a little girl. Now Patricia sounded dangerously close. Robert shoved Mark into the little boys' room. "Sorry," he hissed though the shut door.

Mark couldn't help but be a bit weirded out by the tiny urinals. *No grown man should be in here unless they are cleaning it,* he thought uncomfortably. *Someone might still be in here!* He fixed his eyes on a point on the tiled wall and listened to Patricia Madden scream insults at Robert, who was thanking the Gardaí right outside. Eventually Robert opened the door and Mark almost ran out.

Robert laughed.

"Yeah it's just a bit weird in there the first time. Come on, I have Simon and Hannah waiting in my office."

As they headed off Mark realised there was music playing somewhere. And it was loud too! The closer they got to the office the louder the music was. It was The Beatles 'Love Me Do'. *So pleeeeeeeaaaase! Love me do! Wa wa wa wa wa wa. Wa wa wa wa wa wa.*

"What the heck is that?" Mark asked.

Robert didn't look at all embarrassed.

"I thought it might be better if the kids didn't hear their mother freaking out. I know her and she is what I call a C.C.M."

"What's a C.C.M.?" Mark asked sheepishly.

"A Case of a Crazy Mother," Robert replied.

The music was blaring by the time they got to the gleaming glass door. Inside Mark could see one slightly chubby, very pissed off looking boy and a terrified looking little girl. Robert opened the door and walked straight over to the CD player on his desk. "Well what did you think?" Robert asked the boy as he switched off the racket.

"That was not good," the boy sulked.

"And you little miss? I bet you loved it! I bet you two were grooving around the room while I was gone!" he exclaimed. They replied with looks of disgust.

"Well, I can't win 'em all. Simon, Hannah this is my good friend Mark. He is going to talk to you two for a while. Is that okay?"

Both children nodded.

"I can stay or go. Your call guys." Robert was excellent with children. Mark felt a bit like an old potato standing beside him in the moody boy's glare. He hoped the children would ask

Robert to stay, and luckily Hannah asked him to. Simon rolled his eyes and called her a looser.

"Don't be rude now Simon," Robert warned as he took a small stool from between the chairs Simon and Hannah were sitting on and put it in the corner beside the door. "Mark, please. Sit down there. You can have my seat. I'll just sit right here Hannah."

Mark dragged the chair around the table so there was nothing but air and knees between them and himself.

"Well guys I have a bit of news for you. You know your sister Tina?"

Hannah nodded.

"She's not our sister," spat Simon.

"What is she then?" Mark asked.

"She's our cousin," Hannah was adorable. Neither of the children looked malnourished, definitely not Simon anyway. Both could do with a bit of a wash but as far as Mark could tell they looked alright.

"She's a retard," added Simon slyly.

Mark straightened up instantly.

"Why do you say that Simon?" he asked.

Simon's face went from smirking to utter shock at being asked to explain his smartarse comment.

"She just is. Ma says she is," the boy tried.

"And her real ma is. She's in a wheelchair."

"Shut the fuck up Hannah!"

"Simon! That language is not allowed in my school! You know that. Now correct your behaviour or I will have you doing tables 'til you get into first year do you hear me?!" Robert spoke from the corner. "Mark, maybe it's best if I take Hannah into the next room to do some drawing so you can talk to Simon. Then we can bring Simon next door to do his last night's homework so you can speak to Hannah."

"Maybe that's best," Mark agreed. "Why don't you bring Simon out first?"

"No problem. Simon come on, grab your bag and we'll set you up next door." The boy was staring at his sister with a warning so obvious that it sent chills down Mark's spine. "On you go Simon," he said to break the boy's stare and free his little sister from the pressure that made her rigid in her chair.

When Simon and Robert left Mark tried to make things easy between Hannah and himself.

"Do you want to wait until your principal comes back in Hannah?"

She shook her head slowly.

"I only wanted him here 'cos a Simon."

Mark was getting a glimpse into this little girl's life and he was scared for her. She was terrified of her brother and it was written all over her face.

"He is a bit bold alright isn't he?"

"He's really bold," Hannah agreed.

"What else does he do that makes him bold Hannah? Can you tell me?"

Hannah looked at him curiously.

"Are you bad?"

"No I'm not bad at all. Well I forget to brush my teeth sometimes but other than that I am a goodie. I help children get away from things that upset them." Mark's face was honest and open and Hannah trusted him. He was like the principal, just plain good.

"Do you really help children get away from bad stuff?" she asked with a spark of hope in her voice.

"Yes I do."

"Can I see them?"

"See what Hannah?"

"Your teeth. Can I see your teeth?"

Mark pulled back his gums and let the girl see as much of his teeth as he could show.

Hannah inspected them.

"They don't look like you forget to brush them."

"Why thank you." Mark smiled. "Would you mind if I asked you some questions about your house?"

"I knew that's what you needed to talk about. I hoped it anyway. I wanted to tell someone like we are taught in school but it's harder than the teachers say it is."

"I know, but did you know most people don't tell until someone who can help asks them?"

"Really?"

"Yip. I have been doing this for a very long time and most children I talk to aren't able to tell until someone asks them. It's not something easy to bring up is it?" Mark spoke to Hannah as if they were equals. She was smart and he wanted her to know he knew that; he wasn't going to lie.

"Da is horrible to Tina. Ma is too. They bring her off all the time and when she comes back she is crying and they put her in a room until she stops." Mark didn't take notes or anything. He just listened. Hannah spoke for an hour about food being kept under lock and key, missed birthdays and washing themselves in a basin in the kitchen before she said the words Mark had been looking for.

"Her name is Noelle. She comes around and her and Da go off together. Then Ma takes it out on Tina. She says if it wasn't for her the auld cunt wouldn't be around taking Da off all over the place." Once again Mark thought of the Noelle connection. *Time to come clean,* he thought. *As soon as I get back.*

"How do you know Tina's mammy Hannah?"

"I sawed her."

"Where was she?"

"My house. She's loud."

"Was she there long?"

"Not really. She's gone now."

"And did Noelle ever talk to her?"

"No just called her a retard and shouted at her and stuff."

"Then what happened?"

"She went away."

"Oh." But in his head, it sounded more like *Oh Fuck!*

"And do people ever shout at you or Simon?"

"Yeah at me but not really at Simon 'cos he's a boy."

"What do they say to you?" Mark was careful. He already had what he needed to get them out of there, and soon he would reach the limits of what he could ask her. *Better not take it as far as physical abuse yet,* he thought.

"Lots of stuff. Can you get me and Tina away?" Mark felt the prickle of tears behind his eyes. This little girl was lovely. Truly lovely. How anyone could shout at her and call her names Mark would never know. It just wasn't in him. Time to nail Patricia and Kevin.

Patricia Madden would have only gotten a warning from the Guards if they hadn't walked in on her hurling abuse and small plastic chairs at staff in the school. Instead they had to hold her and give her the warning down in the station. A written warning but there was no fine issued. They had kept her in the station until Robert rang to say they had left. Mark had thought that was quite impressive. It had been their Plan A when Robert had called them the first time about the possibility of trouble and it worked like a charm.

Mark removed Hannah and Simon and brought them straight to Annabelle who had made appointments for both the children to see a GP and a child psychologist the following day.

On the drive back to the office Mark got a call from Orla. She had been back two hours already and was playing catch up.

"Okay, a few things to run by you," she said before he had a chance to protest.

"But I'll be back…" he began.

"No! It will take a sec I promise," she begged. Orla had a strange control over Mark that, like a lot of things, made him slightly uncomfortable. *She'd like Robert,* he thought suddenly out of the blue. *What the hell am I thinking about!*

"Okay, okay what is it?" he asked, taking his brain off the matchmaker idea.

"Well first off Jean needs you to sign some stuff before I can put it in Tina's file. She's in hospital and they have to do surgery. They want to know when they can start."

"As soon as they can I suppose. The sooner she's better, the better." *God I am a tool,* he thought, rolling his eyes.

"And I have written up the reports for the warrant request, it's on your desk with the pictures of the house ready for the Gardaí. All you need to do is throw an eye over it and sign it. We have to hand it in soon because they will need it before going in to the house."

"Okay. I can do that as soon as I get back. That's a two-second job."

"Oh and there is a request from Eileen Kelly to take her daughter Nicole out for the day from Annabelle's. She has been doing better but she tried to get out of the last visit."

"Tell her if she shows up for four visits in a row and actually involves herself in those visits we'll give her five hours in a month's time. That alright?"

"Yep. That's it. I might be gone by the time you're back. I'm going back to the hospital to Tina. I need to organise a psychological evaluation so we know what we have to do and so we can put that in to give to the Gardaí as well."

"Great job Orla."

"How are the other two?"

"Fine now. You were right though. This is a very extreme case. There's going to be a lot to it."

"I know, but we will prevail Marky Mark. We will prevail."

They both hung up.

Orla's body was at her desk in the office but her mind kept floating back to Tina, bruised and broken in that big hospital by herself. It was hard to sit still and harder again to stop herself from getting up from the chair, walking out the door and driving to the hospital. She sighed loudly and picked up the phone to call Eileen Kelly, Nicole's mother.

"Hello?"

"Mrs Kelly? It's Orla Flynn. I have the answer for your day request with Nicole."

Eileen was uncharacteristically excited, Orla noticed. Weird. Maybe she was really missing her little girl.

"Oh deadly Orla! I hope it's good news!"

"Well it is. Basically they have granted the request on the condition that you do a few things."

"Okay, what?" Eileen's usual impatience was nowhere to be seen. So far she was playing ball.

"Well if you make it to your next four visits with Nicole, and you interact with her properly during those three visits, then we will grant you a five-hour unchaperoned day visit."

"Oh that's perfect! Fecking prefect! Not a problem at all!"

Orla was thrilled with Eileen's reaction. She really and truly wanted to take her daughter out for the day.

"Okay so make sure you show up and on time, and make sure the visit reports are glowing and I'll call you in three weeks to organise it."

"Great Orla. Look thanks a million. I can't wait. I really can't," Eileen gushed.

"No problem Eileen. I'll talk to you soon. Say hi to Nicole for me."

"I will! Bye."

Only six more calls and a handful of small errands and Orla could go back to the hospital. *Better buckle down*, she thought as she crossed *Call Eileen* off her list and tapped her pencil under the next item to tackle.

Mark came into the office half an hour later. He thought about Noelle's original personal file on the case. *Definitely time to come clean*, he thought. He walked straight over to Orla at her desk.

"Orla I need you. Can you bring everything you have on the Madden file. Even the few things from the original file you dug up. Meet me in Jean's office in five." Then he strode off.

Orla was totally knocked for six. Never in her six years of working here had Mark spoken to her like that. There was no *Oh your still here*, nothing.... and she kinda liked it! She gathered her things as quickly as she could – her copies of the doctor's lengthy two-page report and suggestions, the photographs, the file marked 'Investigation into Madden Family' and her own notes from talking to Tina, Patricia and Grainne – then she picked up the thin cardboard file that she had dug out of the record room and went over to Jean McCaile's office.

Mark stood up and asked Orla to take a seat beside Jean. Orla felt like he was going to give them a presentation. He stretched over and closed the door. The atmosphere thickened as he took a seat, looking at the two confused women without saying anything for a long time. Finally he spoke.

"I think Noelle is related to Tina." (*Relief!*)

"But she was over her case," said Orla on autopilot, without seeing that her words defined the problem they were facing.

"Oh shit!" Jean blurted without her usual restraint.

"What's the connection then?" asked Orla after doing a double take.

"Well Noelle has a sister I'm guessing. A woman called Kathleen Byrne, maiden name Flood. Her daughter is Breda Flood Byrne, the disabled woman who had Tina." The room fell silent as Orla and Jean allowed the information sink in.

"That explains the lack of paperwork," Orla realised out loud. "The file I found had a bit saying something about interviewing Simon and Hannah three years ago and all was well. The same thing about the house inspection. They must have been bull."

"So where is the birth mother?" asked Jean.

Mark thought about his conversation with Simon Prendergast.

"I think I might have to do a bit of leg work on that one but she has been in the Madden family home for a period over the last few years. Not anymore though."

"Okay. Now, we need all original documents on the table first," said Jean, dying to put some order on the proceedings.

"Good plan," Mark agreed, taking out the tattered pages and placing them carefully on Jean's desk. Orla stood and pulled all of her original documents out and started lining them out on the table too. Jean went to the corner and dragged over a whiteboard on wheels.

"We need the information in bullet points. You two go through what you have there and call up the facts so we can figure this thing out."

Breda's pregnancy had not been as easy as the doctors had hoped. She had low blood pressure and found it hard to keep down the prenatal vitamins as well as her own regular medication. She had to take eight tablets in the morning, four after lunch and eight before bed. It was a trial and a half every time and Kathleen was worn out going up and back to the doctor's to get prescription after prescription when Breda threw them back up into the basin Kathleen and James kept beside her all the time. Her stomach was causing her massive problems and as the pregnancy went on the doctors worried that the baby wasn't getting enough nourishment with Breda vomiting as much as she did.

Uncle James had been a saving grace during the four months after she found out she was pregnant. He kept Breda sane and Kathleen calm. He was doing a lot of the heavy work for Kathleen like helping Breda in and out of bed after Kathleen helped her to change. Kathleen had noticed how much harder it was for Breda to move under the new weight of the ever-growing baby. She thought to herself a million times that this had been a bad idea, but every time she disregarded it as being something they couldn't change now.

One cold afternoon when Breda was six-and-a-half months gone, she and Kathleen were watching the News at One like any other day when their appointment book was free. Kathleen was sorting a small mountain of socks and Breda was focusing hard on keeping her lunch down. They didn't expect the day to be any different to any other until the phone rang. Kathleen expected it to be sales people. Sometimes she put them on the phone to Breda so she could practice making people understand her. It was fun and practical and the women usually had a giggle at Breda pretending to be the bill payer and at the general bold nature of their entertainment. But it wasn't a sales person. It was a doctor from a hospital in County Kildare. James Byrne had named Kathleen Byrne as his next of kin on his medical card. Breda heard the cracking in her mother's voice as she confirmed that she was indeed Kathleen Byrne.

Kathleen felt her heart stop as she listened to the words spilling from the receiver.

"James was bringing a couple to Naas from the airport. The wife was wheelchair bound. Unfortunately James had suffered a massive stroke while helping them get into their home. I am very sorry to inform you but James Byrne passed away before the ambulance could get to him. The gentleman who he was dropping home at the time did CPR on the scene but he just wasn't able to keep him alive. I am so very sorry. We are sending a van to collect you and your daughter now. They should be there in an hour."

7

Orla went back to the hospital after their meeting to give the doctors the go-ahead for Tina's surgeries and to meet her psychologist. Jean and Mark worked on their information for reporting Patricia and Kevin Madden's abuse and neglect of their children. Then they made a start on the tangled web left for them by Noelle.

Orla had her task for the following morning: hunt down Breda Flood Byrne. She looked at her phone. Only half four. Still time to make a start. She turned to her computer and went online. In Google Search she typed in the words *Special needs live-in care facilities County Dublin*. Orla was delighted that she was excused from the mess in Jean's office. What she learned from going through the options thrown up by Google was that loads of nursing homes catered for younger people with disabilities too. Orla found a page with a full list of all the facilities in Dublin and printed it off. Only fifteen looked like possibilities. The rest were either too expensive or only dealt with older clientele. So yet again Orla started to work her way through another list of phone numbers armed only with a date of birth and a name.

Jean was in her office pacing like a mad woman.

"So how many adoptions are there here?" she asked, exasperated at the administrative mess Noelle had left in her wake.

"Four in the 'alright but check up on them' pile. Nine in the definitely dodgy pile. And one in the 'no idea if it even happened' pile," Mark told her, again.

"And there are still loads more you haven't gotten around to yet?" Jean asked for the third time.

"Yes Jean. There are tonnes more."

"Oh God." She threw her arms up in the air. "We're fucked. This is going to take hours and hours of hands-on work. Then we have to report it all to the complaints department so they don't think we're involved. That's more paperwork. And we have to go to the Guards at some stage with the details Tina Madden case, and on top of it all we have to decide if we will tell them everything about Noelle at the same time or just her involvement in this particular case."

Mark shook his head.

"We don't know what we are reporting when it comes to Noelle yet. All of these files look like things have been left out on purpose. Names blotted out with ink and coffee, half-finished reports leaving out the vital details; and obviously she faked inspection and interview reports."

Jean nodded and plopped down in her chair.

"I agree fully. There are holes in all the cases we have in these piles. That could not be coincidence. And so many times too. No way could it happen. Has to be a billion to one. So we need to figure out why."

Mark looked up.

"She did it for a reason every time?"

"Exactly."

"So if we can fill in the blanks we could put together the files where half the info is missing, thus finding the dodgy cases and files she tampered with deliberately?" Mark asked, enlightened.

"Yes exactly," Jean agreed. "It's all very vague at the moment. We need to know what we are talking about when we are reporting Noelle. The Maddens we need to nail now."

"Hello Oak Hill Nursing and Care Home. How can I help you today?"

"Hi there. My name is Orla Flynn. I am a social worker in North Dublin and I am trying to track down a child's birth mother. I was wondering if you might be able to help me?" Orla tried to be as pleasant as possible. This was number five.

"Oh yes. And how can I help you with that?"

"Well I was hoping you could check for a Breda Flood Byrne...."

The woman cut her off quite rudely.

"Hang on and I'll have a look." Orla wasn't expecting much from call number five. The first number she'd called, Newport Nursing Home, said no, they had never had a Breda Flood Byrne with that date of birth but they wished Orla well. Number two had said that they couldn't give out client information on the phone. Orla had said that was no problem at all and she would send them a written request via snail mail. Number three had said no, plain and simple. Their quick response made Orla question if she should cross them off her list or not. She hadn't, and instead moved on to number four, who said they had a Brenda Byrne Flynn. Orla crossed them off half way. If none of the others worked out she'd call them back, just to make sure.

The line cracked back to life.

"Mizz Flynn?" The lady asked.

"Sorry, yes?" Orla had begun to hate when people called her Mizz Flynn.

"We don't have anyone by that name here. I checked the computer and I need a date of birth."

"06/01/1974, I am sorry to put you out like this."

"Oh don't even think about it. We take it in turns to sit behind the desk here. There's never anything to do. Hang on I'll take a better look." Orla heard the woman hurry off again. She waited. And waited. Then she got the news that Breda Flood Byrne, date of birth 06/01/1974, had been a resident until a year and a few months ago.

Mark and Jean drove to Pearse Street Garda Station where they said they needed to report a very serious case of child neglect and physical abuse. The young Wexford man behind the desk blushed and excused himself. He quickly got the Sergeant on duty.

Sergeant Martin was a fatherly man in his fifties who listened intently to everything they said and asked for further explanations here and there. They knew he was taking them very seriously. By the time they had finished explaining, he already had a plan of action. "I'm going to need statements from both of you and from the social worker over the case, Miss Flynn. Once we have everything we'll get the search warrant and possible arrest warrants started. Well, let's see to it!" He hoisted himself out of his chair like a sea captain going to bark orders to his mates before a storm, and bark orders he did. Two Gardaí were shouted at to get ready to take statements. "O'Connell you're in Interview Room One! Fisher! You're in Two. Now get to it. These people might need teas or coffees. McCarthy you see to that!" Then he re-entered the room briskly. "I'll be taking charge of this one. Mr Tynan you're in One there. Miss? Mrs?" he fished, looking at Jean with raised eyebrows.

She smiled.

"Jean. Just call me Jean."

"Jean you are in Two. Hopefully I'll have some answers by the time you're out."

Stephanie was bored with Nicole. She didn't want to tell stories or talk to Stephanie often or anything. Stephanie decided that Nicole was the worst companion that the stupid food man could have brought. She was utterly useless. Useless! She didn't help pass the time at all like Stephanie had thought she would.

"Stephanie?" The loo pipe whispered.

Stephanie sat on her mattress trying to flick three peas through two stripes on the patterned mattress material. After already loosing half of her six peas to squishing and layer-peelage, she had learned to flick them lightly. She was ignoring the pipe stubbornly.

"Oh yeah. Talk when you want to talk, not when I want to talk," she muttered to herself, careful not to be loud enough for the pipe to hear.

"Stephanie? Do you hear the noise outside?" Oh, she was trying to get her all curious! Stephanie wasn't born yesterday. That wasn't going to make her talk. Slowly and quietly she got to her feet, careful so next door wouldn't hear her movements. She put her ear up against the boarded-up window. Nope. Nothing. She sat back down and played peas for another while until her tired and heavy hands squished one of the three surviving peas.

Stephanie made herself put the last two peas down carefully in case she had another dreadful accident that would leave her with only one pea to play with. She lay down on her mattress and tried to think of warm things as she succumbed to sleep.

Bang bang bang. Stephanie's eyes shot open. Heavy footsteps on the stairs and she had only just gotten food that day. *This isn't right*, she thought as she scrambled to the pipe. It could be another girl; it could be one of the girls from Mister Tom's. They had come and gone before. But no. This sounded different... and familiar...bad familiar. Stephanie hung around the pipe like a baby monkey to its mother. Then the door. A key was going into the lock of her door!

"Nicole! I'm sorry I didn't talk to you last night!" but the man had come up behind her and all Nicole could hear was the screaming as her friend was dragged down the stairs. Then, even more terrifyingly, she fell silent. The man's heavy boots went out the door. Nicole was more scared than she had ever been before. Stephanie's apology was ringing in her ears. She was more scared than when the man had taken her. More scared than she had been in the boot of his car. More scared than when she heard Stephanie tell her lies to make life seem better in the house. The end was clear to Nicole now. The end was getting dragged down the stairs only being able to scream.

For a few hours Nicole just cried. She thought of where Stephanie might be now. Did he kill her? Did he drag her back to the other house? Nicole froze when she heard the front door open again. Then in a frenzy she scraped up her thin body and scuttled her way across the floorboards until she was hiding under the heavy bulk of her mattress, shaking like a leaf. The boots came up the stairs and a door opened and closed again. Nicole stayed very still. She could make out some faint far-off noises but she couldn't make out what was happening. She missed Annabelle. She wanted to go home.

Breda and Kathleen weren't doing so well after uncle James died. They waked him in their house, which was more than uncomfortable. Neither Kathleen nor Breda had any idea of how well known he was. At the funeral Breda saw the long line of mourners and how they stopped and shook Ma's hand like she was the Queen and shared in her misery like they were family. They weren't of course. In amongst the sea of tear-soaked tissues and cap less taxi drivers one pair of eyes were burning into Breda's back. When James's friends, in-laws and co-workers waddled their way up to the front of the church like penguins lining up to jump into the sea, Kathleen could sense her coming. It had been a long while since she had spoken to her sister.

Noelle's sorry smile and disingenuous empathetic face turned her stomach. Out of the corner of her eye she watched the vision hobble towards her with the aid of a walking stick. Even here she was putting on a show. Noelle got closer and Kathleen's anger grew, and by the time she was the next in line, Kathleen knew what she had to say. She let go of the last hand and immediately reached for Noelle's. The sudden movement didn't give Noelle a chance to do anything, other than offer her sister her hand in condolence. Kathleen looked Noelle square in the eye and then in one quick and less than discrete move, Kathleen tugged on it hard. Noelle fell towards her sister's chest and her head was caught there by sharp fingers pressing hard into her scalp.

"I am done with you. My daughter is done with you. Keep the fuck away from us." The words were said in no more than a whisper, right into Noelle's old-woman ear. Kathleen meant her words. She made sure Noelle knew and afterwards she shoved the old woman back up where she landed on her feet without any need for the cane. Breda knew there was more to the meeting. Noelle pushed Kathleen's buttons but Kathleen was not a woman to strike out, Noelle must have done something really bad this time.

Noelle stood there, disgusted by the assault.

"A nurse told me about a pregnant retard. See you when it's born," the old woman hissed down at them. Then off she went, the walking stick dragging along behind her. No one mentioned a thing and the line continued. Then the penny dropped. Noelle must have threatened Kathleen before they met in the church.

The words rang through Kathleen and Breda's heads for days, but neither of them brought it up. It wasn't until they flipped the calendar one day and were stuck staring at a big looming X that Noelle's words ignited a conversation between the anxious pair. Kathleen was straightening Breda's hair after they had washed it. Breda eyeballed Kathleen in the mirror and eventually caught her mother's attention.

"Can she really do it?"

Kathleen knew what her daughter was talking about right away.

"I don't know love."

"How can we stop her?"

"By giving them no reason to come knocking. The money James left you has set the baby up."

"Fair play to Uncle James. He always put us first."

"That he did."

And that was it. No more conversation.

It was eight a.m. and Orla was driving to work but she couldn't concentrate on the road. Things had slowed down in the Madden case. It had been a full two weeks since Tina had been admitted to the hospital and Orla had spent a lot of that time at her bedside reading stories, playing games and, most importantly, talking. She wasn't talking to the psychologists at first. She wasn't even talking to the doctors, despite their coaxing. She hated men, Orla had come to realise. It took the psychologist one whole week to get Tina to even acknowledge him. During their conversations Orla began to realise why, and it was keeping her awake at night.

Every night after she had left the hospital Orla had driven back to her horrible empty apartment, curled up on the couch with her laptop and written detailed accounts of their conversations. Then she would eat something, anything that happened to be at the back of her kitchen presses, and go to lie in bed for a few hours. Then she would get up, drive to work and give the reports to Mark. Mark was getting regular reports from Hannah and Simon's therapist too and he spent much of his time comparing the reports for corroborating details, of which there were many. He wrote up those details and had Emily fax them all to Sergeant Martin.

Something else was bothering Orla too. It was bothering all of them. Breda Flood Byrne. She had been taken out of the nursing home by her sister Patricia and her Aunt Noelle Flood. Mark told Jean to call the Sergeant and see what he made of the Breda Flood Byrne mystery. Sergeant Martin had asked Orla to come in. She did and she too had given a statement. Hers had taken seven hours. Orla handled it like a champion but when she walked out the door of the Garda station she was hit by a wave of exhaustion like she had never felt before. The days seemed to drag after that.

Orla pulled into her usual parking space outside the office and prepared to start another day. She had gotten in before Emily thank God, which saved her the few minutes that would have been spent taking a barrage of orders. Mark was in the cubicle already. On her way past she waved to him and gestured with her hand that she was making tea for them before she joined him. She left her bag and coat at her desk and switched on the screen of her computer. Expertly she slipped her USB stick from her key ring, stuck it in the little port on the computer hard drive and ordered it to print. Then she headed to the kitchen to stick on the kettle and spent a bit too much time picking her morning cup. 'Be Fabulous' and a pig in a hat was up against 'Don't worry be happy' and a smiley face. She took 'Don't worry be happy' and gave Mark 'Be Fabulous'. *One thing to smile about*, she thought as she poured in the milk and stirred the tea. She dropped them into the cubicle and said a quick "Hi", before going over to the printer and collecting her three-page report. When she turned back around from her desk she saw Emily in reception. If she moved quickly she could slip by without having to say hello. Emily loved to get through the messages on the machine as early as possible. Orla and Jean were convinced it was so she could hand them out like late slips to the social workers when they came in in the morning.

Orla made it to the cubicle just in time to see Mark taking a sip from his 'Be Fabulous' mug. It made Orla smile and she took her seat. The moment was broken though when she saw Mark focus on something at the other side of the office. As he began to get out of his seat he said,

"Gardaí are here." Orla twisted in her seat. Emily was bobbing across the office being followed closely by a young Guard that Mark recognised to be O'Connell, the young man who had taken his statement.

"I believe it's D-Day!" Mark exclaimed excitedly.

Garda O'Connell was brief. They were going to search 1225 and arrest Patricia and Kevin Madden for the neglect and abuse of a minor in their care.

Breda wasn't asleep when the doctors lifted the tiny baby from her belly. On the table she was treated like any other mother having a C-section, or so she thought. She would have been mortified if she had known about the hours of discussions and debates that had gone on behind closed doors about her delivery in the maternity hospital. Doctor Ombino was there so much they had given him a room to work from when he needed a quiet place.

To Breda it was heaven on earth having her baby placed on her chest. Just like she had seen a million times in films and on television, only this was better. It was real and it was happening to her. This was Breda's baby!

"Congratulations, Breda. You have a healthy baby girl." Then the little pink beauty was whisked away out of Breda's sight.

Breda had been sewn up and cleaned and she was back in her bed when a nurse wheeled in the squeaking bundle in a little clear plastic box that had been lowered on its trolley so Breda could watch her little girl sleep. Mother and baby slept for hours. Granny Kathleen sat beside them, proud as punch, looking at this one then that. Rubbing their cheeks and brushing back Breda's hair as she slept.

Doctor Ombino had been in the delivery room and when he came to see Breda on the ward he wasn't at all surprised to find her fast asleep. He smiled at Kathleen's exaggerated motherly posture before he crept up to her, making sure he didn't wake the worn-out mother and newborn.

"They are both doing excellently Kathleen. You should be very proud." He fed her assurances in hushed tones.

"Thank you so much Doctor. For everything."

His dark skin crinkled and a small chuckle escaped from between his lips.

"You are talking like our journey has ended Mrs Byrne. We have just gotten started. I can assure you of that." He cooed over the sleeping baby for a moment before patting Kathleen softly on the shoulder. "I will come back to when they return from their travels."

It was only when he left that Kathleen realised that he was right. She wouldn't be around for ever and her blood pressure was though the roof in her last check up, yet here she was getting ready to raise another child. Was she a fool? They would have to get Breda ready to do as much as she possibly could for her baby girl so when, God forbid, the day came, Breda could go on caring for her daughter. Not alone of course, but maybe with a kind older live-in carer? Or a nurse maybe? They had the money for one. God there was so much to sort out! There was no point putting any hope on Patricia stepping up to the plate. Kathleen made a decision to go to see a solicitor and make up a will sooner rather than later. At least then Breda could prove the baby was provided for after Kathleen's death.

8

Orla was driving and Mark was in the passenger seat. They were on the tail of three squad cars heading to the Madden house. The silence in the car was not because they were worried about what they might find; it was because Orla was finding it hard to keep up with the speed of the high-visibility Fords. Mark didn't dare break her concentration after she had taken the first bad bend at 110. Mark had been very close to peeing his pants.

"Jesus Orla! Will you slow down!"

Her eyes were wide with concentration, "It's like a video game! Why are we even driving this fast? It's not like they know we're coming."

"It's just how the Guards do things I suppose but not social workers." He urged, "Social workers are safe people, who keep under the speed limit."

Orla had ignored him.

They had been waiting for this day for what seemed like an eternity and they were excited to have some progress. Orla didn't want to miss anything to do with the Madden case. She wanted to look Patricia Madden in the eye and inform her that her children would be safe now.

They don't like me very much. Either do their friends. Well some of them do and then they don't and then they do and then they don't. Orla could hear the six-year-old's voice in her head. *I don't like cars. They only bring people to bad places.* Oh this would make up for it. This was step one to justice for Simon, Hannah, and poor little Tina.

When they got into the estate Orla and Mark saw Jean pulled up in front of the overgrown lane down to the ring where 1225 High Park stood. They slowed down to let her pull out in front of them then they followed the procession down to the house. They had been warned to stay well back from the action. One group of Gardaí were banging on the front door and a second lot had jumped the locked gate that had divided the back garden of number 1225 from the already hidden street. Eventually, after a lot of knocking and shouting, they broke down the front door. A Garda with a German Shepherd ran in first. He was in there for a good five minutes before he re-emerged shouting, "Clear!" Then five officers accompanied by Sergeant Martin marched in and were in there for another twenty-five.

Jean, Mark and Orla wished they hadn't bothered coming so early. They had been with Gardaí when they had gone into houses before. They should have known things wouldn't have moved that quickly. Jean was getting impatient. Mark watched her jump from one high-heeled foot to the other. Still, he was impressed that her complaints never went further then a loud tut or a sigh. This would take as long as it would take. When Sergeant Martin came out he said the Maddens were gone. They would keep looking but now that it was just the two of them and they didn't have the kids in tow, it would be easier for Kevin and Patricia to slip away.

"You can go in and have a look, just to get an idea of the house, but we will be sending you full reports after the scene investigators have given the place the once over."

Deflated, they listened to their instructions. They could go in after the Gardaí had photographed the whole place. Under no circumstances were they to move anything or step anywhere they were told not to. They would be walked through the building by Garda O'Connell.

Outside the front door and out of earshot from his boss, O'Connell had seemed to have found some authority.

"Okay we have put peg markers in the floor. Please keep between them and try to remember not to touch or put your hands on anything." Orla thought that he wasn't bossy per se, but he was definitely getting close. As soon as he pushed open the front door, the same rotten smell rolled out to greet them. It had gotten stronger. Much stronger.

"Oh my God! What is that smell?" asked Jean, scrunching up her powdered nose. O'Connell kept walking while he answered.

"Cigarettes, dampness and grease from the deep fat fryer makes up the bulk of it. The sealed windows don't help. Other than that it's just rubbish and dirt and dirty clothes."

"Oh. Okay." Jean really hadn't been expecting a detailed account for the smell. She pulled the sleeve of her cashmere jumper over her hand and cupped it around her nose and mouth.

"I want to show you the kitchen and living room before I show you the bedrooms. That's what you will be interested in." Mark and Orla exchanged knowing glances. This was not a good sign.

The house was incredible. It was hard to see how anyone could live there. After the small, relatively clear entrance hallway Orla had already seen, there was a door into the main hallway of the house. A tide of what she would describe as shite, papers, junk mail and clothes had been piled all around the walls with only a thin path in the middle to walk to the kitchen. Little white pegs with red tips stuck out of the piles in two neat rows with the clear patch in the middle between them. They squeezed past five pegs to the kitchen where the smell was so overpowering that Jean gagged and turned back, leaving the other three to go on without her. She apologised later when they made it out. She just couldn't hack it. It took all of Orla's curiosity to keep her in the stinking house. It was like something she would expect to find in a squat; a squat with some pretty out of place expensive things dotted here and there though. The air hung thick and heavy with the smoke from a million fags and rotting food. The living room was adjoined to the kitchen by what had once been a set of double doors, now covered up by piles of more garbage. A filth-encrusted blue three-seater couch and two armchairs didn't look very old despite their grubby appearance. They faced towards a dusty flatscreen television in the corner, propped up on a blanket box. If that had been all that was in the living room it would have been fine but with all the piles dominating the space, no one could have relaxed in that room.

Next they were shown a downstairs bedroom. It was like the rest of the house, filled with shite and dirty as hell. Orla couldn't even make out who could have possibly slept on the broken bed. It was the clearest space in the room but there were no hints as to whose room it was. Children's clothes as well as women's and men's clothes were strewn all over the place and were covered in footprints and whatever had been dragged across them on the soles of shoes. This room didn't have any expensive things.

Upstairs was far more telling. Two rooms were not as messy as the others downstairs. Not as disgusting, but still not good. They were Patricia and Kevin's room and Simon's room; they even had duvet covers and small televisions. But the other two bedrooms were a different story altogether. The first had been set up into a sort of twisted cinema room with stacks and stacks of pornographic DVDs lined up along one wall, with the giant television on a chest of drawers in between them.

"We had a quick look through their collection. So far nothing underage but they have some other pretty sick stuff in there," O'Connell told them. The television was much bigger than the one in the living room. In one corner there was a stack of what had to be porno magazines that reached up to Orla's shoulder. In the other there were cardboard boxes stacked on top of each other. Money had gone into the collection. Most disturbingly, there was a double bed on the same wall as the door, facing the television. There were ropes screwed into the headboard and two cameras on the floor. On the headboard Orla noticed hundreds of tiny scratchings.

"Do we know what's in the chest of drawers or the boxes?" asked Mark gravely.

"Not yet. We've only taken the pictures. We haven't started moving things out or properly going through things yet. That will be after you guys go." Mark took the not-so-subtle hint on the nose. The next room was the worst. Only plastic bags were between its occupant and the stars. Mark was terrified to think that this could have been Hannah's room. He would go and visit her soon.

Orla wanted out. She had seen enough. She went down the stairs, walked out of the house and straight to her car. Mark was left going to see the bathrooms by himself. He had to see if he could see any sign of Breda Flood Byrne. A wheelchair, a bathroom with hand rails – anything! But no joy. Their trail on her was still cold. Only for a moment did he let the worst go through his mind. Then he knew that wouldn't do Tina any good and he pressed on.

Orla had almost left her boss behind in her rush to get away from the house but luckily when she started the car she saw him walk out after her. She sat there waiting like a anxious parent in a car outside a teenage disco while he and Jean spoke again to Sergeant Martin. Eventually he came to the car and Orla got to drive away from that horrible house.

Things were going really well for Breda and Kathleen. They had gotten into a routine and it was suiting them. Kathleen had even left Tina with Breda after three weeks and went all the way into the big baby store in the city centre to buy a baby sling. Tina was asleep in her pram and Breda was in her wheelchair. Kathleen planned these little trips regularly from then on. She knew she had exactly one hour and thirty minutes before Tina would spit out her soother and start to make kitten noises. Even though she liked her daughter to think that she shared the responsibility of minding baby Tina, she still wouldn't have liked to let Breda hold her sitting up without her chest strap or try to get the top of a bottle into Tina's tiny mouth.

Doctor Ombino had come to the baby shower. It had been a small affair. Hospital staff made up the majority of the twelve guests; the surgeon who had delivered Tina, the nurses who were so thrilled to see them take on the challenge of raising a newborn together. All of them had come out of kindness and they all came with beautifully wrapped gifts just for Tina and her new mum. They had all been so thoughtful, giving Breda contraptions and machines to make caring for Tina easier, more hygienic and more confusing. They were difficult to use and Kathleen was having problems trying to stay focused reading the lengthy instructions. They didn't have things like this when Kathleen had been rearing Patricia and Breda. They had to make do with the basics. One little cushion was for feeding and it meant Breda could hold Tina while she feed. They had been delighted and Breda couldn't stop crying with the joy of feeding her baby by herself. Kathleen then began to think of other things that might help. Basic but functional things. It was then that she had first thought of a baby sling. She was surprised it hadn't occurred to her sooner. Breda could use a baby sling when she had the chest strap closed around her in her chair. Kathleen was grateful for all the presents and good wishes from the guests. It was the support for Breda she had been most grateful for. And maybe for giving herself a bit of support too, she had thought happily as she strolled once more into the pastel-filled shop.

They hadn't gotten them. They hadn't really expected Kevin to be there but they had hoped to get Patricia at least. They still didn't know where Tina's poor mother was. She hadn't been registered dead but hopes of finding her safe and well were slipping away.

Mark sat in his cubicle and watched his hive of worker bees zipping over and back all around him. He had a mountain of Noelle's 'files' on his desk. He had been sorting them according to Jean's system. Three piles: one definitely dodgy, one complete but check, and one miscellaneous. The definitely dodgy turned out to be nearly all adoptions. The massive gaping holes were only in the adoption cases, which just happened to be Noelle's speciality. Mark wasn't thinking about Noelle though. He was thinking about Patricia and Kevin Madden. He hadn't been too hopeful of Kevin being there with his history of disappearing off for days on end, but Patricia? She must have been out at the time. Maybe she had gone back to find the house taken over by Gardaí and slipped away again. Probably to her husband. So where would Kevin Madden be? Mark picked up his photocopied copy of the investigation into the Madden family file and opened it on the contacts page. Again he found the number of Patricia and Kevin's community welfare officer. Odd, he thought. These people had been receiving social welfare for years. Why were they still dealing with a community welfare officer? Usually people only went to them before their payments started to get cheques to tide them over, but he was under the impression that Kevin Madden had been getting disability allowance for a really long time. Mark picked up his receiver and dialled the number.

"Hey Annabelle," Orla chirped.

"Hi Miss! You said you would call down and that was nearly three weeks ago. I had to give the fancy biscuits I had gotten for your visit to the savages before there was mutiny." Annabelle chuckled on the other end of the line.

"Awh, I'm sorry. I've been bogged down in the Madden case. How are you keeping? How are Simon and Hannah fitting in?"

"They are out with a potential foster family at the moment," Annabelle cooed.

"Oh! Good for them!" Orla was excited. If Simon and Hannah were fostered soon it meant that there was a chance that when Tina was well enough, she could still be placed with Annabelle. There had been doubts about keeping the three children together. Orla didn't like the idea of it either despite how much she wanted Tina to end up in Annabelle's care. Tina rarely spoke about Simon or Hannah and when she did it was only to say she didn't like Simon. When asked about Hannah she just clammed up. "Does it look promising at all?" nudged Orla keenly.

"Orla Flynn! Why do I have a feeling you are asking for a reason other than the brother and sister's wellbeing?" Annabelle accused jokingly.

"I have two reasons for asking actually," Orla began matter-of-factly. "One, because I want to see after their wellbeing and two, because Tina Madden will be out of hospital soon."

"We have had a bed ready for her for weeks. She won't be a problem once Simon and Hannah move in with the Nolans."

Annabelle sounded excited to have the little girl come to her big happy house. Orla really had no idea how she did it. The idea of caring for one child scared the pants off her, let alone twenty-odd at a time.

"Is it really looking that promising?" she asked.

"Yep. This is their third day trip. All is going well and the parents, John and Sharon, were in with me this morning saying how eager they are to move forward. I have to ask the kids first off. Then get a recommendation from their psychologist and if that is green then I will be putting in the application to Mark and Jean before the end of the week."

"Excellent! And what are the family like?"

"Good people."

"Great. Oh, speaking of day trips. How has Nicole been getting on with her visitation?"

Annabelle sounded confused. "I don't see the connection, but better. Eileen seems to be making a bit more of an effort."

"Has she shown up for the last three weeks?"

"Yes, on time as expected. Why what's happening? She isn't taking Nicole on the day trip is she? Nicole mentioned it." Annabelle didn't sound very pleased.

"Well that depends on her turning up this week or not." Orla winced as she broke the news. Annabelle was blind in her caring for the children. Once she knew someone had wronged them she found it difficult to help parents develop a relationship with their children again. Annabelle would have been happy to place all of the children with parents she hand-picked herself whom she knew, without a doubt, would never harm a child in any way, shape or form.

"I'm not happy about it but alright. I bet you a fiver she is late bringing her back though. Mark my words!"

"Well it's on next Saturday; only if she makes it this Saturday."

"Fine."

"Please don't be upset with me."

"I'm not upset with you. I'm upset at the system."

"I know. I am too sometimes but all we can do is our best and I must say Annabelle, you do such an amazing job. Really."

"Awh stop would you! Now I'll call you when I know what's happening with Simon and Hannah. I'll get one of the girls to call the good doctor and hurry things along."
"Perfect. I'll talk to you soon so."
"Oh and you owe me fancy grown-up biscuits."
"I'll bring some I promise, and a little extra something else to distract the masses."
"Oh I think bringing them a new person to play with will be good enough!"
Orla noticed Mark making his way across the office towards her with an armful of files.
"Okay I'll talk to you really soon."
"Bye Orla!"

"Guess what?" Mark asked her as he slammed the files down on her desk. Orla wasn't used to playing guessing games with Mark.
"You want me to make those disappear?" she asked innocently, pointing at what was obviously going to be her load.
"Community welfare officer thinks Kevin Madden has a job somewhere. He keeps missing appointments and his days to sign on. That's why they have to work through the community welfare officer so often. They keep getting cut off because Kevin is too busy to show up when they need him too. Patricia used to be down there every week until we took Tina."
"So you want to find out what Kevin's job on the side is?" Orla didn't really understand the relevance, unless they wanted to do him for social welfare fraud too but surly that wasn't their job.
"No, I want to find out where he is going when he disappears. He has to stay somewhere. I'd bet you any money that Patricia is after running off to meet him."
"She'd have to go back to the house though surely?"
"I don't think so but I need to see if I can find out where they might be. Will you do my job for a while and keep going with this? I am going through some of these old adoption files and checking them out on the system to see

where they stand. Well, to see if they ever even made it onto the system."

"No problem. Where are you going now then?"

Mark thought for a second before he answered. He didn't want to seem too eager. "To get some inspiration." And off he went across the office and out the door.

Orla rolled her eyes and opened the first file. She didn't even get to sink her teeth into it before her phone rang again. It was the young Garda O'Connell.

"We have spent the last two days going through the house with a fine tooth comb. The Sergeant asked me to call you because we have found evidence that Breda Flood Byrne had been in the house for a period some time ago. We found a neck brace and a few empty bottles of medication with her name on the labels." There was a pause. Orla could tell there was more. Garda O'Connell continued. "The state of the house alone tells a lot, but we found other things. We also found a lot of sexual material; magazines, DVDs and toys. Far too much to be normal. We are sending it off to be tested. We've gotten samples of Tina's DNA from the hospital. They say we will have the results in a week or so."

Orla rang Mark right away.

"Hello?"

"Mark the Guards rang. They found evidence that Breda was staying at 1225 a while ago."

"After the nursing home?"

"Must have been."

"Are the Guards at the house now?"

"I don't know. I don't think so."

"Okay. Well at least we're getting somewhere."

Orla got back to her files. They didn't even have file numbers on them. She had to use the names and hope to get a hit.

One

Child's name: Zoey Clarke

Birth parents' names: ?
Adoptive parents' names: Tanya and Brian Norris
Social worker: Noelle Flood
Witness: Simon Prendergast
Family court judge: Justice Thomas White
NO RECORD.

She went to the next.
Child's name: Sarah Quinn
Birth mother's name: Ann Quinn
Adoptive parents' names: James and Monica Dunne
Social worker: Noelle Flood
Family court judge: Justice Thomas White
Witness: Simon Prendergast.

Orla was noticing a pattern already. Quickly she flicked through all the adoption files. Noelle of course had been the social worker on all the cases, but only one judge's name came up time and time again in each file.

Justice Thomas White.

No freaking way!

Mark drove to 1225. Then he sat in his car looking at the empty house for a while. All of the houses looked awful but this one had a darker feeling, like the house had been corrupted by everything its walls had witnessed on the inside. Hannah had told her therapist that all night she would hear little girls shouting and crying. Mark was scared one of those girls had in fact been an adult Breda Flood Byrne. Hannah didn't know who they were because she had never been allowed out of her room, but Simon had. Simon had been brought around with Da a lot. But Simon, so far, wasn't talking. He was fiercely loyal to his father. The therapist had said that despite the trauma Hannah had suffered, she had a strong moral compass and had known it was wrong. Still there were some things she just wasn't able to talk about yet. They had asked Hannah if he had ever hurt her. She had said no, he would hit her every now and again, and call her names but he never hurt her like she was used to being hurt. They could not get either Hannah or Tina to say if anyone hurt them sexually. Both were only able to talk about the other, lesser offences. All of a sudden Mark had an urge to talk to Simon. He had to talk to Simon. Man to man. He would call Annabelle and sort it out as soon as he was back in the office.

"I never hurt anyone in me life!" Simon shouted.

"That's not what I asked Simon. I want to know if you ever saw anyone hurting Hannah or Tina?" Mark hadn't been accusing in his tone when he was talking to Simon Madden. Simon was being defensive out of guilt. Mark hadn't even mentioned the possibility of Simon hurting anyone. He had brought the idea up on his own.

"No, now piss off. I'm not talking to the other fella and I'm not fucking talking to you, dickhead."

That hadn't gone well at all. Mark quickly wrote down the details of their brief meeting so he could write up a fully accurate report later. He was wondering if he should talk to Hannah. Even though he had spoken to her before and she had been open to talking to him it was too soon to ask her the adult questions. He would come to visit her later. She might need a bit more time. She still hadn't opened up about the real details of who, when and where with their psychologist yet so Mark knew she needed to build more trust before she could go there.

Breda sat in her chair at an angle so she could push her baby girl's buggy back and forth. Tina was fast asleep, smacking her lips at something or other. She was such a good baby. Other than feeding and changing her she was really very easy to look after. If only Breda could steady her hands more and get her arms strong enough to hold the baby without worrying she might drop her. She couldn't wait until she could help out more. Breda wanted to cancel her speech and language therapy and focus instead on her arms and back day in, day out with the physio. She would say it to Kathleen when she got back from her latest trip into the city. Breda knew exactly when Kathleen would be back. She never left for more than an hour and a half when Tina was down for a nap. Breda was so grateful for the time alone with her little one. She felt like a mother.

She heard a key in the front door and manoeuvred her chair around the sleeping baby. She arrived in the kitchen just in time to hear Kathleen's warm, happy greeting and to see the big green bag of new purchases.

"Not more baby clothes! She has too many clothes!" Breda joked with difficulty.

"Nope. It's something better!" cheered Kathleen. She shoved her arm into the big bag and pulled out a box.

"More gadgets?!" guessed Breda, feeling the excitement building.

"Kinda. Here look." Kathleen turned the box so Breda could see the picture on the side.

"A baby sling?" she asked.

"Yup. For you my dear!" Kathleen took the sling out of the box. She checked Breda's chest strap was fastened and then helped her get her arm into the sling. "Now you can carry around Tina in your chair with you."

Breda was speechless.

9

Simon and Hannah moved in with their foster family only a few weeks after being placed into care. Hannah loved John and Sharon Nolan and their beautiful home. Simon, on the other hand, would take more time to adjust. Tina would be released in just a few days so the timing couldn't have been more perfect. Still, Orla couldn't just focus on Tina as much as she seemed to want to of late. It was the day before Eileen was due to take Nicole out for the day and Orla had to finalise the plan. That, along with half an A4 page of other To Do's.

Annabelle knew to expect the visitation supervisor at eleven in the morning when she would collect Nicole and bring her to meet her mother in Swords Medical Centre where usual visits were held. Then the visitation supervisor would meet Eileen back there again at eight that evening to bring Nicole back home to Annabelle. Eileen had complained to Orla that five hours wasn't long enough so she had gotten Mark to extend the visit.

Orla rang Eileen to make sure she was all set to entertain her daughter for a day. She had been so ecstatic on the phone that Orla didn't know if it was an act or not but for Nicole's sake she hoped it was genuine and so she played along.

"We'll be going to this massive park first that I found outside the leisure centre down the road. Then I'll be taking Nicole back to the flat for a bit of lunch and to hang out together. Last we're going to me ma's for dinner like I told you. I'll have her back on time I swear."

Orla felt uneasy. Everything was in place, the wheels had been set in motion and Nicole would be going with Eileen on the unsupervised visit. The following morning Annabelle dressed Nicole and gave her a big breakfast. She waved her off from the front door and promised to see her in the evening.

Annabelle rang Orla to say Nicole had been sent as promised with the supervisor.

"My stomach is in knots Orla! I feel like we have just taken a risk. We didn't do enough supervised visits to know Nicole will be safe. She could be using again."

"Don't worry. It isn't a risk. It's a routine day visit to a park and to her granny's house with her mam. In a few hours time when Nicole is back in your herd, you will be wondering what you were so scared of. Everything will be fine, I swear."

Famous last words. At half eight the visitation supervisor called Annabelle. Eileen hadn't showed up to drop Nicole back yet.

Annabelle's heart sank.

"Wait longer."

For an hour Annabelle prayed that Eileen would bring Nicole back. She prayed hard with every inch of her body and soul. She willed Eileen to feel her and take Nicole to the Medical Centre. At half nine Annabelle rang Orla's mobile again.

Orla was letting herself into her apartment when her phone rang. She was so sure that Eileen was only running late that she had just gone on about her usual day.

"Hello?"

"Nicole didn't come back."

"Fuck! I'm on my way! Don't worry we'll find her." Orla wanted to kick herself. She wanted to slam her head against the wall. She felt that something wasn't right and still she let the visit happen. "Fucking idiot!" She kicked the wall with the soft toe of her boot, winced in pain and dialled Mark's number.

Ring ring

"Hello?"

"Mark it's Orla. Eileen Kelly didn't show up to bring Nicole back. I'm going out to Annabelle."

"Okay. I'll meet you out there. I'll ring the Gardaí on my way."

"Okay see you."

"See you out there."

Sergeant Martin didn't come down in the last shower. He knew the social workers were keeping something from him and he had a feeling it was this Noelle Flood character. All of them reacted when they spoke about her. When he asked questions about her, they rolled their eyes and tightened their jaws, like they weren't saying everything they wanted. This Noelle one had seen Tina, Breda Flood Byrne's biological daughter, move in with the Maddens. She must have been soft in the head.

"O'Connell!" he bellowed out into the main reception. "O'Connell where are you?!"

"Here Sergeant," replied a weary-looking Garda O'Connell, appearing in the office doorway.

"Call Mark Tynan from Social Services. Tell him I want to talk to him as soon as he can."

"Yes Sergeant."

He had just gotten back to his work when the young Garda stuck his head back around the door.

"Mark Tynan is on the phone Sergeant. He wants to speak to you."

The Sergeant huffed loudly.

"Did you not tell him I want him to come in to see me? A phone call won't cut it."

"I didn't get around to calling him yet. He called you."

"Okay put him through."

O'Connell disappeared again.

"Mark? What can I do for you?"

"We have a missing child. Her mother had her parental rights revoked and we had been trying to get them back on track. She got a one-off unsupervised day visit and she never brought the little girl back."

Sergeant Martin clicked his tongue off his teeth.

"And has that Noelle Flood woman had anything to do with this case?"

"No. She retired, I told you before. It had been her case, but that was years ago. She isn't involved anymore."

"She had been over the case?"

"Yeah but then she retired and it went to Orla Flynn."
"But she *had* been involved in the case?"
"Well yeah."
"I want to find this mystery woman. I think she might still have her fingers in some pies."

Mark was a bit put out because Noelle wasn't the problem right now. The problem right now was a missing child taken by her ex-junkie mother.

"I'll send O'Connell out to you. Where are you now?"
"I am going out to the residential care facility at the other side of the motorway. It's run by a woman called Annabelle Hart. She is really distraught. I'm meeting Orla Flynn out there."
"Okay give me the address and I'll have him out there in fifteen."

Annabelle opened the door and she looked a mess. Her long wavy hair was in a tight frizzy bun on the top of her head. Her eyes were red-rimmed and rubbed raw.

"Oh Annabelle. You poor thing." Orla opened her arms wide and Annabelle fell into them.

"I just need to know where they all are. I can't not know where one of the kids is."

"I know. We'll know where she is soon. It's not your fault," cooed Orla.

"I knew. I knew before she even left the house. And she was excited. Not jumping up and down excited, but pleased that her mam was trying." Annabelle crumbled again. Yvette, the assistant on duty, was putting the older children to bed but Annabelle insisted on going around to all the rooms to make sure the children were safe and accounted for while they waited for Mark. Orla went with her. It broke her heart to see Annabelle so upset. She had always been very matter-of-fact when children left legitimately but someone disappearing? Orla worried she wouldn't be able to handle it. She had already voiced her failing confidence in the Irish social system. The last thing they needed was for the one woman who could handle twenty-odd kids at a time to give up on her good work. Annabelle was the last person on earth who deserved any sort of pain. She was one hundred per cent kindness and generosity incarnate. She had given up her life for this job. *Her second name is Hart for Christ's sake!* Orla thought to herself.

Mark showed up soon after. It had taken him longer to get there than he had expected but he made it. Orla went to the door to get him.

"She is so upset Mark. I hope to God we find her."

"The Sergeant is sending out his wingman, that O'Connell guy."

"Good. We need to get the ball rolling if we want to have a hope of finding her." Mark and Orla went back into the sitting room to be with Annabelle and five minutes later Garda O'Connell showed up at the door.

"I'm seeing a lot of you lately Mr Tynan. We should get you a loyalty card." Mark was not impressed and the young man could sense it and got very professional in the same instant.

"Okay, first I need to talk to the three of you to get the details of the mother and child, and I need to know what they had planned for the day as well as all contact details for the mother, her family and friends. Then I'll need to talk to the woman who was in charge of the child's care and the social worker who organised the visit. We already have people checking hospitals and the like in case there was just some sort of miscommunication."

Mark thought it was a bit full-on for a doorstep briefing but he said nothing and just led O'Connell through to the brightly-coloured living room and the two women. Orla and Annabelle were sitting on a big green sofa that had been set up with some other furniture at the far end of the room in a circle intended to be a 'hangout' for the older kids who were too cool to watch the little kids' shows on television.

As soon as Orla saw the navy-clad Garda she remembered how uncharacteristically enthusiastic Eileen Kelly had been to see her daughter. A daughter she didn't seem to give two shits about before. Why was she so keen on looking after Nicole for the day? Maybe she missed the child allowance. Orla made a note in her head to tell Garda O'Connell about the curious change of heart.

They went through all the details of Nicole and Eileen's case with Garda O'Connell before he took them one by one into the homework room for individual interviews. Annabelle went in first stony-faced and came out just as steely. Next Mark went in so Orla could stay with Annabelle and finally it was Orla's turn.

The only furniture in the room was four children's school desks, each with four tiny chairs. Surely they could have picked a more suitable room with appropriately sized tables and chairs. "There is something strange that I only thought about just when I saw you come in," she began before her butt had even made it to the chair that was far too low for her long legs. O'Connell pulled his seat closer to the small table. Orla couldn't help but think how odd they must have looked. Two very tall people sitting in tiny chairs, at a tiny table. The fact that one of them was a Guard just seemed to add to the comic value of the scene in Orla's head.

"Eileen never really showed much concern about seeing Nicole. She never called to see how she was or ask if she could talk to her. She only showed up for the visitation because it was court ordered and the only way she could stay out of the Dochcas, but she really, really wanted a day visit with her. It was just pretty out of the blue you know?"

"That would make sense if she had this all planned." O'Connell added.

"But we picked the day of the visit. Not her. So it couldn't have been for a particular event that would be held on a particular day."

"Okay this could be important. Let's go through it from the start. When did the idea of a day visit come up for the first time?" He asked keenly.

"Five weeks ago. Eileen rang and said she wanted one of her three court-allocated annual day visits."

"And was that the first time she had contacted you about any sort of visit with Nicole? Had she ever rung about the usual weekly visits?" O'Connell probed.

"Only to try to cancel her third week, but then she called about the day visit and she showed up. She was scared that if she missed the visit that week that we wouldn't even consider the day visit," she explained.

"So she wasn't going to show then she did?"

"Yes."

"And she asked for the day visit soon after?"

"Yep. She asked a few days after she had cancelled the Saturday visit but Mark made it a condition that she had to see her for four supervised visits before he would approve the day visit. I have it all in their case contact log in the office. I can photocopy it and fax it to you first thing in the morning." Orla was getting weary, it had been a long day and it was catching up on her.

"That might be a very good idea. And is Eileen still in contact with her previous social worker, Noelle Flood?" O'Connell was digging for something. Orla wished she knew what he was thinking.

"Not that I know of but they had been close while Noelle had been over her case. I wouldn't be surprised if they were."

"Hum…"

Orla explained the Noelle situation a bit further to the Garda; if he was onto something Orla wanted to give him all the information she had.

"We are planning to make a formal complaint about her very soon to you guys and to the Minister of Children. She is a sly old bitch in my opinion and I didn't even know how sly until years after she retired. There were definitely some really dodgy things going on with her adoption cases but I didn't think there was anything up with her standard cases. If your suspicions are right then that means we'll have to go back to the drawing board. We'll have to go through every single case she dealt with."

"And when were you planning on reporting this activity?" said O'Connell disapprovingly.

"When we figured out what the hell we were reporting! You can hardly investigate a case of bad bookkeeping can you? No. So we want to figure out if there is a reason or if she was just lazy and a bad judge of character."

"Okay, well I'm going to need you to come into the Sergeant very soon Miss Flynn, you and whoever else knows about the inconsistencies in the work." O'Connell had crossed the line into bossy. Orla decided she didn't like him anymore.

"Mark would be the man you want. He knows the problems better than any one. He was her supervisor for a year before she retired."

O'Connell raised an eyebrow.

"Mark it is then."

Mark left to follow Garda O'Connell to the station to talk to the Sergeant. Orla stayed with Annabelle for another hour then she went to meet the visitation supervisor. She had stayed in the car park until it was locked up and then she pulled onto the footpath right outside but they knew Nicole was not coming back. Not this late. Orla sent the tearful woman home.

Kathleen's hair had gone completely white. She didn't bother dying it any more like the other women on her street did or like she had for so many years before the arrival of little Tina. No, she didn't have the time; she would have to grow old gracefully. She picked up a tea towel and went through to the sitting room. Breda was on the floor propped up with her back to the couch. She was watching Tina colouring in a picture of a smiling circus elephant with a hula hoop.

Kathleen bent down and started wiping up the spilt tea from the well-used carpet.

There was a time when Kathleen was overjoyed that it didn't seem to stain. Those days were long gone too. Her back clicked sharply as she straightened herself up. She would have to go to the GP and see what he could do for her soon. Her back had gotten weaker as the years had passed. Now Kathleen had a major concern; she might not be able to help her daughter into and out of bed for too much longer. Maybe it was time to finally bite the bullet and get Breda a contraption to help her get into bed. Kathleen had seen them in advertisements in different medical magazines down through the years. Over the last while she found her eyes gravitating towards them more and more often. Maybe it was time to have a look into them. Surely they wouldn't be that expensive.

Tina was a great help in looking after her mammy. She would get this and that and hold her hand steady when Breda was working on her precision by picking up marbles from her tiny daughter's hand and dropping them into a plastic bowl. Breda was at it for hours every day and Tina would stand there and give praise for each one landing correctly. Kathleen wasn't sure if she was happy with the toddler helping so much. Even though she didn't seem to notice that what she was doing was really helping them out, Kathleen felt a pang in her heart when she saw the little girl doing things for her mother. She had lost her life to slavery, she wasn't going to let her granddaughter do the same! Kathleen needed to get things in order. For the second time, she thought about doing up her will, then maybe she'd look into getting some help. Maybe.

Nicole was thinking about her bed in Annabelle's house. And the big kitchen table with all the friendly faces around it. She thought of her little wardrobe and all of her lovely clean clothes hanging up. She thought of the older girls and how they loved doing Nicole's hair. She loved it too. She loved being included, especially by the older girls. Now she was being punished for it. She knew it. Nicole was supposed to be in filthy flats with smelly beds. Nicole was never supposed to go to Annabelle's. She had thrown the world off by going there. Now the world was getting her back. Someone had arrived in the room next door in the night time. She wasn't talking but Nicole could hear her crying. She must have been bad too. Stephanie had been bad and a liar; Nicole was bad; the new girl had to be bad.

Then there was a different noise. The back door? And a woman's voice! There was a grown-up woman in the house! Nicole got to her feet and ran to the door. With her little hands bent into fists she beat on the door as hard as she could.

"Help me! Help! I'm up here! Help! They took me from my ma! Up here!"

A woman would save her. Some women were mams and nurses and stuff and no matter how bad they were they wouldn't let this happen. Annabelle said Nicole didn't deserve being locked up. Not even Nicole's ma would let this happen with the strangers and all. There was pounding on the stairs and Nicole thought she would faint with fear. Then there was pounding on the upstairs landing.

"Shut the fuck up you little prick!"

Nicole was frozen. Oh oh.

There were people outside the door now and Nicole heard a key being shoved roughly into the key hole. She could hear her heart beat.

The door swung open and Nicole saw a short, fat, scary woman raise her meaty fist and then the world fell down.

O'Connell had been given a piece of paper with an address on it and was told to go. It had taken him an hour and a half to make his way up and down the Wicklow Mountains, but finally he had got there. On the way he had seriously considered putting on the siren and giving it socks on the roads to make the journey a bit quicker and a bit more exciting but he had forgotten just how badly twisted the roads were up here and it was dark. It was nearly two am in fact.

When he had started fresh out of Templemore, he had thought that there was no way on God's green earth that people actually answer their doors after they have gone to bed. No way, but he was wrong. He hadn't had a door go unanswered yet; well, except little scumbags hiding out, but that was different. They weren't exactly normal people keeping normal hours.

He pulled the heavily marked squad car onto the gravel drive and stopped the car right in front of the shiny red door. The house was very modern but still had a very traditional feel to it. It was brand new. Built maybe in the last five years. No more than that anyway. O'Connell and his new wife were looking into building a house. This was very like the design he had tried in vain to draw and describe to her. Except he definitely wanted his drive way tarmac'd. The gravel made the whole place look more old-fashioned then the building actually was.

He got out of the car and walked up to the front door. He took the address out of his pocket and turned the page over.

Noelle Flood. Like he'd forget!

Knock knock knock

"Mrs Flood?" he called loudly. There were no neighbours to interrupt so he kept it up until he saw the upstairs light flick on, then waited for a few minutes to pass before he knocked again.

There was no answer.

Orla called into Tina before she went into the office the next morning. She had gotten home after one o'clock the night before and then had spent an hour on the phone with Mark. Nonetheless she was up at half six to squeeze in a visit. Tina was like herself, a real early bird. But when Orla walked into the hospital she still felt like crap. Nicole was still out there somewhere. God knows where! When Mark had called Orla after leaving the Garda station he had said that he had been told Eileen's landlord had let them in. Eileen wasn't in her flat and some of her things were gone. That was a good sign. There was still a chance Eileen and Nicole were together. Sergeant Martin had told Mark that they still need to explore all avenues of investigation.

Orla had been instructed to get a photograph of Nicole, preferably one with Nicole and her mother, and do up a flyer and press release from the department's perspective first thing that morning. She had already called Annabelle the night before and asked her to email across a few photographs. Orla had heard the energy come back into Annabelle's voice when she had told her about Mark's plan of action. She had jumped at the chance to do anything to help, but of course, when you care for as many children as Annabelle you hardly have time to change your socks, let alone aid a search for a seven-and-a-half year old.

So with everything that was on her shoulders, Orla definitely felt worse for wear when she walked through the doors of Crumlin Children's Hospital at seven a.m. She was still grumbling to herself when she turned the corner into Tina's ward. Then she saw Tina, and it all just melted away. All the stress, and the rushing around to meetings with Gardaí, Mark and Jean, it was all worth it when she saw Tina in that hospital bed, on that ward, on that morning. It had only been twenty-four hours since Orla had been there but Tina had changed totally. She was sitting up in bed with a bear sitting in front of her. She had a small plastic tea set made up between them and there she was, proud as punch, pretending to feed Cornflakes to the bear and explaining why food was good for you.

"... so you can play all day long and if you don't eat your breakfast you'll be sleepy all day. Do you hear me Mr Bear?" she asked, putting a spoon of cornflakes up to Mr Bear's mouth then, at the last second, diverting its flight to her own.

This is why we do it. This is exactly why we put ourselves through this. Orla breathed in and smiled hugely when Tina looked so happy to see her. Whatever bad was locked inside her mind was the responsibility of the psychologist, and right now Tina looked like she was doing very well indeed. Patricia would be caught; Orla could feel it in her bones. People don't get away with the things she did. She strode over to Tina's bed merrily.

"Hello there Tina and Mr Bear. How are you two this morning?"

"Hello. We're fine thanks." Tina didn't stop feeding Mr Bear; she just smiled and continued on. Orla took off her coat and put it with her bag on the ground before sitting down on the chair beside Tina's bed. She bent down and began to unzip her boots.

Tina suddenly stopped playing. She was staring at Orla's boot with wide scared eyes.

"What are you doing?" Tina muttered.

"I am just taking my boots off for a minute so I can put on a pair of socks. Mine got wet this morning and I had to buy more." Orla had stopped what she was doing and was looking back at Tina with concern.

Hardly a normal reaction, she thought.

"What did you think I was doing Honey?"

Tina turned her head and stared hard at the crisp white duvet cover.

"Tina are you okay?" Orla reached down and zipped her boots back up.

"Look I have them back on now. I will do it in the loo later. Don't worry. I didn't mean to upset you." Tina turned back to Orla. Her little face was softening.

"I'm okay. You can change your wet socks but you can't get in okay?" Tina spoke matter-of-factly, in a calm but warning voice.

"Get in where Tina?"

"Get in here. You can change your wet socks but you can't get in here with me okay?" Tina carried out this negotiation in such an adult way that it sent chills down Orla's spine.

"Why would I want to get in with you? I have my own bed in my own house. That's where I slept last night. Did you have to share beds often in your house?"

Tina was taking in Orla's explanation of her own bed in her own house. People didn't only sleep in beds. Didn't her new friend Orla know that? Tina wasn't going to be the one to explain it to her. Already she felt her face prickle with embarrassment. She had talked herself into a corner, and over wet socks. Not all grown-ups were bad. Tina was only figuring all this out.

"I don't want to talk about this anymore. But you can change your wet socks."

Then Tina turned back to Mr Bear and wiped some cereal off his face with the sleeve of her pyjamas.

"Thank you." Orla changed her socks as quickly as she could without looking like she was panicking. She kept up a strained conversation with Tina.

"I hate wet socks. The rain got me when I was parking. Thank God the lady in the shop had socks for sale downstairs." Orla felt like this was a bit too grown up a topic to get the interest of the little girl but to her amazement she saw Tina nodding along in agreement.

"That was a lucky one alright."

Orla could have laughed if they hadn't just brushed off a topic that scared her to death. She would have to go and speak to Tina's psychologist as soon as possible.

"Have you ever had wet socks? I hate the way they make your shoes squish," Orla continued.

Tina nodded knowingly, still focusing on her bear.

"How did you get it all in your boots?" she asked.

"I stood in a giant puddle when I got out of my car. I wasn't minding the ground when I parked so when I opened the door and put my boots on the ground I was up to my ankles in water."

Tina looked up and giggled.

"You're funny."

"I suppose I am."

Tina went on playing with Mr Bear.

"I told you about my job didn't I honey?" Orla asked softly.

"Yep you help children get away from baddies and get better." Tina rhymed it off like she had been thinking about it a lot.

"That's exactly right. And you know that I don't like baddies at all at all?"

"Yep I know that." Tina was holding onto Mr Bear's paws and was bouncing him up and down on her knee.

"Well I want you to know that I will never, ever, ever hurt you. I am on your side."

Tina stopped bouncing Mr Bear.

"Okay."

10

The Sergeant had been on the phone to Mark for only a few minutes and already Mark's head was on overload with all the updates. They were still out on the streets looking for Nicole. The little girl had been missing for three days and they hadn't got one official lead other than Eileen running away with her. Sergeant Martin was trying to get Noelle to come in informally to see if she could think of anywhere Eileen might have taken her. Orla hadn't been much help other than to let them know Eileen wasn't around much. They were going to formally question Noelle but only after Mark's office gave over all of her files and any other case files that she had dealt with. Until then Sergeant Martin would be making a trip to meet "the old bag" as he called her and try to sweeten her up. Mark was freaking out. He hadn't gotten through the files. He needed to go through them all first before the Guards and before Jean and Orla.

"We'll start to dig it out but it will definitely take us a while to get them all together. We have files in storage all over the country, and locating all of Noelle's might take us a while. I'll do it as quickly as I possibly can though."

"Well you must have some already pulled if you were able to highlight the inconsistencies that you have already come across? Just get us what you have already and send us the rest as you find it. Alright?" Sargent Martin wasn't messing around. He was shocked when Mark had told him about what he had discovered already, a huge number of children that couldn't be located all of whom had been Noelle's clients at one point.

"No problem." Mark was sweating. Why hadn't he been tougher on the old woman? Why hadn't he made her run all of her cases by him? Why hadn't he had the balls to do his fucking job?!

Mark hung up the phone and started to make calls file by file. Orla had said Justice Thomas White had signed off on all of the files he had given her. He had signed off on every court order in Noelle's old cases. Every single one. Mark had hoped he would come across something, anything, else important done by another judge. He rummaged through file after file hoping to see something, but no, they were all Justice Thomas White. Some dating as far back as the 1980s.

Mark picked up the phone again and dialled.

"Margaret? I need you to dig up files. Anything signed off by Noelle Flood; any thing she touched or was involved in. If you just take a flick through you should see something with her signature." Mark gave Margaret Noelle's years of employment and jurisdiction even though Margaret had been there so long that she knew all about Noelle and her hatred for paperwork. He wouldn't be surprised if she knew all of Noelle's file names and where they were stacked by heart.

Mark hung up and got back down to typing names into the computer and calling adoptive parents.

Breda woke up to the sound of Tina screaming.

"Nana! Nana! Up Nana!"

It sounded as though the child was in agony. Breda was in her bed. How could she get to her baby? In desperation she looked around and realised she would have to try to figure out a way to get herself out of her bed and onto her chair. She stretched her right arm painfully to the plastic-coated hand rail at her bedside and urged her hand to make a fist around the bar. She watched in amazement as they naturally did as they were told. Then she pulled and tried to jump her body up and down to drag herself as close to the edge of the bed as she could. Thankfully, her chair was lined up beside it. Tina was still screaming and Breda knew something was terribly wrong. Ma would never leave little Tina scream like that. She hauled her torso up and let her weight fall roughly onto the chair. She shouted out when she landed on her hip painfully, legs folded beside her, stuck between her hip and the armrest of the wheelchair. She reached for the ON button and managed to get it clicked. Then she got two fingers on the lever and she was off zipping into the living room where her little daughter stood screaming in her play pen, chubby arm extended, pointing at the floor.

Then Breda saw her. Kathleen was on the carpet. Face down. Her hands looked blue. Her beautiful ma was blue.

Orla spoke to Tina's psychologist for an hour before she left the hospital. They were both looking out for the same thing, anything that would give them a new window into Tina's time in the Madden household. Orla had to report back to Mark right away and he would have to report their suspicions to the Gardaí and give them the reports. The paperwork was surprisingly simple and wouldn't take long. Investigating on the Tina side of things would be far more difficult but Orla truly felt that Tina was opening up to her more. It was only a matter of time.

Orla had to call out to Annabelle to make sure she was okay. She was not surprised to find out that Annabelle had hundreds of people looking for Nicole. Friends, family, school parents and many other concerned people who had seen the two-minute announcement on the six o'clock news the night before. They all could be seen in high-vis vests handing out flyers and walking in and out of establishments all over the city. Still not a dickeybird and Annabelle had taken to calling Orla regularly for support. Of course, Orla was happy to help but she was really feeling the toll of living on so few hours' sleep. Her phone could ring at any hour of the night with all the drama that had taken off in the office. Mark was stressed to the hilt. Jean had been buried under a mountain of Noelle's files and hadn't been up for air since Nicole disappeared.

All the stress made Orla miss David even more then usual. She had found a vacant apartment near work and the letting agents were so keen to get her in that they were handling everything for her except the move itself. Without David Orla was alone in the city. No brothers or Dad to come and help her move. No in-laws or sisters to call. She hadn't been close enough to her foster parents in Laois to call them for anything. Moving was a very depressing thing to do when you are all alone, and she would have to do it in one month's time. One month and she would have to suffer the agony of loosing the apartment she had shared with him. The apartment where they had last made love. Moving was depressing. Work was depressing. Life was pretty fucking depressing. Orla decided to work longer hours over the next few months. She got into her car. *First to the office then on to Annabelle's,* she thought as she pulled off.

Twenty minutes later Orla walked into the cubicle without knocking.

"I think Tina was sexually abused. I know the doctors said it but I really think it was serious. I have done up my report as to why. Here it is." She thrust the report out into the air. "Now can we please figure out what the fuck Noelle Flood has been doing sending kids to these places?"

Mark looked at the report, then back to Orla. He took a deep intake of breath before he put it all out on the table.

"I just rang six adoptive parents. All of them are gone off the radar. Landlords are all saying the same thing. They were here for a short while this many years ago then they were gone. Some of them have come up on the social welfare database. The two I managed to get hold of told me to piss off and refused to talk to me. I think Noelle was setting up adoptions to dodgy people on purpose. I don't know why yet but I know that Justice Thomas White was a part of it. Simon Prendergast was just the clerk. He always worked with Thomas White but he never once got suspicious or asked questions. We have to hunt down some of these kids and see if they are still with their adoptive families or if we are dealing with worse." Mark had aged overnight.

"Like what? Adopting the babies out to dodgy families then buying them back and selling them in higher-priced adoptions? That's what I thought but Tina was still with the Maddens. She hadn't been sold on to rich people." Orla said, trying to make sense of the mess.

"Maybe Patricia Madden felt too bad to let Noelle sell on her sister's child?" Mark shook his head. "Sorry scratch that. That's the last reason why. They didn't give a crap about Tina."

Orla clicked her tongue and nodded in agreement.

"Well, if what we think happened to Tina really did happen to Tina then we have a whole other avenue to explore."

The words were out there. They couldn't be taken back or ignored.

"We need to find the children. Then we'll know what she has done with them. The only way we can do that is to keep hunting down the adoptive parents. We have to tell the Guards everything now. This is too big," Mark exclaimed.

"But we aren't sure yet," she threw back in a fluster.

"But by the time we are sure it will be too late for Nicole." Mark dropped his head down on his desk, hard.

Orla left to go to Annabelle's to see if she had noticed anything in Nicole's behaviour that suggested that she had had similar experiences to Tina. If so then they would have to look into all of Noelle's cases, not just the adoptions and placements.

Mark was a bit thrown when he picked up his work phone to hear Sergeant Martin on the other end for the second time that day.

"I believe we have something to discuss Mr Tynan. We have found our mother of the year. Eileen Kelly is straightening up in a cell as we speak," he had boomed.

Mark bubbled over in excitement.

"Oh that is excellent news! How is Nicole? Is she there with you now? I can get Orla to go collect her now if you'd like."

"Well Mr Tynan that is what I am calling about I'm afraid. We found Eileen Kelly. No sign of any child. I had the lads search the building. No Nicole, just the mother."

"And did you ask Eileen?"

"She was under the influence of a number of substances by the time we got to her. We won't be expecting to get a clear response until late tonight. I still have the lads out looking though. We'll let you know. Bye for now."

"Bye." Mark didn't know what to feel. He was dreading telling Annabelle. He decided to call Orla and get her to tell Annabelle. He hoped she hadn't left yet.

Another Garda stuck his head around the door of the Sergeant's office.

"There is a woman here who is desperate to talk to you Sergeant."

"I'll be out in a minute."

"She's a bit…odd sir."

"Sure aren't we all," replied Sergeant Martin.

The Garda left the office and went back to the station reception.

"He'll be out to you in a minute. Do you want to take a seat over there and I'll give you a little wave when he's out? It wont be long at all."

"Thanks a million."

The woman shuffled over to the rows of orange plastic chairs and took a seat along the back. Her face was heavily lined and she looked wild in her long skirt, her curly grey-blonde hair and woollen cardigan.

"Where is she?" Sergeant Martin asked appearing in the doorway.

The Garda nodded in the delicate traveller's direction.

"Let me know if you need anything."

"Fine so." Sergeant Martin went out through the door into the waiting room.

"Hello there. I am the Sergeant on duty. I hear you want to have a quiet word?"

He sat down in the seat in front of the woman and twisted around to face her. She looked scared as a mouse but he knew how to make people feel comfortable.

"Would you like if we nipped into a room in the back, so we can chat properly?"

The woman nodded, tears were filling her eyes and Sergeant Martin noticed she was visibly shaking.

"Right so, you come on with me then and we'll have a big room for ourselves. Don't be worried now. You won't be in trouble at all but we will have a cuppa."

He called out to the Guard to stick on the kettle and come on in to get the lady's order. Leaving the door wide open the Sergeant led the woman into Interview Room One and got her to take a seat. Tears were now falling freely down her sun-beaten cheeks. After ordering two strong teas with milk and sugar in both Sergeant Martin folded his arms and rested them on the table between them.

"Now tell me. What has you in such a state? No one has hurt you have they?"

The woman shook her head slowly.

"It's my ma and my youngest Stephanie." Mrs Connors took a grubby photograph from underneath one of her layers and slid it across the table to Sergeant Martin.

"Are they alright?" he asked softly, picking up the picture of the smiling young girl and her grandmother sitting in a field of wild flowers on stools. It was a truly beautiful photograph of the pair and the Sergeant could see their closeness.

"No." Missus Connors began to bawl in long loud gasps. The sound startled him.

"Okay. Okay. Let's start at the beginning. Where does your ma live?"

"She has a flat in the towers. Me daughter went to live with her because I have a problem…with me nerves. Only sometimes, and the other kids are big and hardier then Stephanie." The woman was taking all this badly and the Sergeant was mindful of his approach.

"And what happened to make you think something is wrong?"

"I have been callin' over to the flat every week for three months. I'd bang on the door and think that I just missed them every time. But this morning I tried to have a look through the windows." The woman burst into tears again and her sobs rang through the building like an alarm.

"Okay, okay. It's alright we'll sort it out what ever it is. Can you tell me what you saw?"

"It was the smell that made me look through the window." She was blubbering and mucus was beginning to trickle onto her thin lips.

"Okay I will need to get your mother's full address. We are sending a car over right now. You were very brave to come in to us. Very brave. You can stay right here for as long as you like. The lads there will make you as much tea as you can drink and if you need a smoke, it's just out the door there." He was looking her directly in the eyes and she knew he was on her side. "And if you forgot your fags there is an emergency packet behind reception and don't worry about using them up," he added with a nod.

Then the other Garda arrived in with the two cups of tea.

"Now we'll give this lad the address 'cos I'd bet he has a little black notebook in this top pocket," joked Sergeant Martin. Of course the Garda did, and he took the address before being followed out to reception by the Sergeant.

"Could be bodies. Older woman and a child. Break down the door if you see anything from the windows."

Don't look! Tina needs you now so don't look! Don't look! Breda moved the chair as quickly as she could over to her baby girl standing screaming in her playpen in the corner of the room. Her knees banged into the wooden side panel painfully but she was blinded by the need to soothe the two year old. She twisted in the chair and managed to get herself into an almost sitting position. Leaning her torso as far forward as she could, she let her young daughter use her neck to pull herself over the side of the playpen into her lap. Tina clung on for dear life and cried and cried into her mother's neck. It took all of Breda's strength to keep her back upright with the little girl's weight. She had never carried weight without a back strap before. Still she managed and even got her chair all the way to the door. Then she struggled to lean forward and raise her arm to unlock it. She hit her head on the inside doorknob hard and felt blood trickle from her forehead down to her eyes but she reached up with every inch she could muster. Finally her fingers caught hold of the slip lock and she backed the wheelchair up to pull it open. She shot through the door up the small sloped driveway and out into the street.

Breda knew there was no point in trying to make sense so she just screamed and screamed at the top of her voice until one of the neighbours heard and called an ambulance from behind her living room curtain. Eventually, a man coming out of the shop at the bottom of the road stopped in his tracks when he heard the commotion. He looked up the street and seeing the woman in a wheelchair, distraught, with a child on her neck, he took off in her direction. The rubber soles of his runners pounded their way into Breda's conscience and she started towards him.

"Help me! Help me. It's my mother. In the house!" The young man paused for a second to hear and seeing her desperate gesturing towards the small white bungalow he sprinted in as fast as he could. Breda tried to compose herself. Tina was now a ball in her lap with big eyes peering up at her.

"It's okay baby. Everything will be fine now." Breda's unsteady hands stroked her daughter's hair.

Then the sirens came into earshot and there were flashing lights and people shaking their heads. Two men gave her an injection and everything was getting hazy. Then Auntie Noelle was there and then Tina was gone. Then someone said that Ma was dead and the young man had been doing CPR all the time until the ambulance had arrived. Then she fell asleep. Then she was moving and she was in a car of some sort.

Breda woke up in the nursing home. Tina was gone.

Power of attorney was granted to Noelle and she got to decide how all of the money Kathleen had left to her daughter was spent. By getting power of attorney, Noelle knew she had bypassed her sister's ridiculous wish list for her retard whore of a daughter. The daughter, who she had said for years, would put her sister in an early grave. Now Noelle had all the control that Kathleen had meant for Breda, even the house. All it took was going to her very good friend Judge White and telling him that her confused sister had left everything to her mentally disabled daughter and asking him for help. She didn't even have to give him any medical records.

Patricia hadn't exactly been a challenge to Noelle, especially after seeing how her mother's will favoured Breda over herself. She had been counting on that house. So Patricia agreed when Noelle told her she would get her share and put the house on the market. Noelle had removed Tina. The child should never have been born, she was made out of the closest thing to incest. Kevin had only meant to scare her into convincing her mother she wanted to be in a home. The child was an accident. Kevin, Patricia and Noelle met in the house so Noelle could convince them to take Tina in. Patricia didn't like the girl for obvious reasons; she was after all her husband's child that her sister bore. They agreed but only because she was old enough to be used. Noelle knew she would do well out of Tina. And so she did. Tina turned out to be the best business venture of their despicable career. And they had no intentions of stopping until there were no more set-up adoptions to exploit.

Annabelle took the news pretty well under the circumstances. They had all gotten hope from the thought that Eileen and Nicole were together and that when it came down to it, Eileen wouldn't let anything really bad happen to her daughter. But that hope was gone now and they wouldn't have any answers for hours until the junkie sobered up enough to tell them what had happened.

But life goes on and the women planned Tina's move from the hospital to the house. Orla gave Annabelle a cheque to get clothes and school things for Tina's scheduled arrival in two days. They had to give it enough time to make sure Simon and Hannah had settled into their new family in case they needed to come back to the house. In that case Orla would have had to put Tina with a short-term foster family. Thankfully everything seemed to be going well so far and everyone had high hopes for all three of the Madden children so they got to work on getting Tina set up in the community.

They had called the local primary school and called the kids' GP along with half a dozen other little jobs.

After all that Orla managed to get back to the office at a fairly reasonable hour. Mark was never so happy to see her in all his life. He stood up in his cubicle and beckoned her over as soon as he saw her come in.

Jesus Christ! There were boxes stacked high off the ground lined up at the back of his bubble.

"They're Noelle's cases," Mark said, defeated. "All of them. Margaret pulled them for me. I need help."

Orla raised on eyebrow.

"That you do."

Orla took off her coat and her bag and lay them on the floor before picking out her first box.

"I'm guessing we are looking for any adoptions and other dodgy-looking things?"

"That's the one. Thanks Orla."

Orla was already on her knees flipping through the first box.

"No problemo Marko."

Together they got through the first load in a few hours. Far quicker then either of them had expected. Orla talking about Tina and her progress was getting to Mark. He had guilt over the little girl's experiences. He had been over the department for years and Tina madden should have come up. How ever bad Hannah had it, Tina had it worse and Mark was finding it hard to have her status mulled over in front of him.

Eventually Mark just cut Orla off while they were on their last box. "Why don't you go any see her?"

Orla stopped what she was doing. "Are you sure?"

Mark nodded, "Yes go on. I'll finish up here."

Her smile affected him somehow. He was so happy that he had made Orla smile like that. He had to focus his attention on what she was saying because the feeling had come so out of the blue, it took over.

"Thank you, Mark. I owe you one big time for this," and then she was up and gone and her smile went with her.

Tina was absorbed in the comings and goings of a small swallow building a nest on the sill of the permanently shut ward window. Her small eyes struggled to keep up with its erratic flight path. Orla didn't know if Tina had noticed her or not. The little girl's voice caught her off guard through the bustle of the children's ward.

"Is that bird a ma?"

Orla shrugged her shoulders, giving her mind a bit of time to come up with the answer.

"I'd say she's building a nest to lay her eggs in. When she has her eggs she'll be a mammy."

"Are birds good mammies?" Her eyes not moving from the window.

"Yes. Birds are excellent parents," Orla answered honestly.

"All of them?" Tina asked.

"Maybe some of them aren't," she said, quickly changing her stance on the subject.

"There are birds that will go around and lay eggs in other mammy birds' nests and let them feed them and all. My teacher said."

"Well that's not very good is it now?"

"No it's not," Tina agreed with Orla.

"Maybe those mammies need some help and the other birds offer to take their babies until they are bigger." Orla paused. "You're very clever to remember that you know."

"I'm too smart for my own fucking good," said Tina angrily.

"What?" asked Orla. "Who told you that?"

"Pat. She always says it. I'm too smart for my own fucking good."

Patricia Madden, Orla thought instantly.

"Well this Pat doesn't sound like a very nice person then!"

"She is a smelly old bitch." Tina swore like it was nothing at all. Water off a duck's back. She was like a parrot reciting off what she had heard over and over again. Orla let the language slide.

"What does she do that makes her one of those?" asked Orla, feeling her way through the conversation.

"She sends me off and that's not fun at all. I just wanted to stay with Hannah all the time. Not Simon though. He is bad. Even Hannah knows he's bad."

"Gosh that sounds tough to deal with."

"Yes it was and I'm finished up talkin' 'bout it now." Tina was incredible. So well spoken at times. Far too mature.

"Okay then what will we talk about now?"

Tina looked up at Orla.

"When will I get to meet Annabelle?"

"Two more sleeps then you'll have your very own room in Annabelle's house."

They chatted a while longer until Orla left. As soon as she was off the ward she called Mark. He was Simon and Hannah's social worker, he had to hear what Tina had just said.

"Mark it's me. Tina says Simon is bad. She says Hannah even knows how bad he is. You might want to take a trip to the foster family. It might be something small and I'm sure someone would have picked up on it by now if the problems Hannah is having with him are serious, but I just heard it from Tina."

Mark sounded scared.

"Shit! Why didn't we look into it more?! I'll call them right away. Did she say anything else?"

"Yeah, that 'Pat' would make her go off with people and she hated it. She wanted to stay home with Hannah but not Simon. Simon is very bad, according to Tina."

"I'll sort it. Orla you're a fecking star!"

"I know."

They hung up.

It wasn't long after Mark was on the phone to Orla that he got the call he had been waiting for from Pearse Street Garda Station. Garda O'Connell explained that Eileen had come around that morning.

"She said she didn't remember a thing but Sergeant Martin says she remembers something alright, she just won't say it yet.

Guilty conscience. She has been whimpering since she woke up." He promised to call back if they got anymore out of her. Mark thanked him before grabbing his car keys and leaving the office. Time to talk to Hannah.

On the way in his car Mark slipped his phone into the hands-free and pulled up the number of the Nolan household where Hannah and Simon had been placed. He couldn't help but say a little prayer that nothing had happened to Hannah yet.
"Hello?" A refined voice asked.
"Hi is that Sharon?"
"Yes it is. How can I help you?"
Mark cleared his throat.
"This is Mark Tynan here. Simon and Hannah's social worker. How are you keeping today?"
"Very well thanks. I am delighted to hear from you again so soon. I was actually going to give you a buzz later."
Mark was curious. He had only brought the children there a few days before. "Oh?"
"Yes. It seems we might have a little something to discuss. Would you mind paying us a visit?" Sharon was a polite lady. Mark was glad Hannah had such a fantastic role model.
"I would be delighted. I was calling to ask if I could pop out now."
"Excellent! The universe works in mysterious ways Mark!"
"That it does Sharon."
They made plans for Mark to call out and hung up.

Sergeant Martin walked into Interview Room Three and saw the sorry shape of Eileen Kelly sobbing on the wooden table. She looked a right state. He had a female officer come in with him, just in case. Garda Hanlon stood at the door and listened to every word. The Sergeant was definitely someone she could learn a thing or two from.
He sat down across the table from Eileen.
"Okay, okay that's enough now. You and I both know that you are crying over more than being picked up by us love, so

let's get this thing sorted before you end up getting yourself into real trouble." He sat up straight with his hands neatly folded on the table. "Alright?"

Eileen looked up through her tears. Her face was death warmed up. This woman had been on a bender and a half and the Sergeant was well aware of it.

"I can't!" cried Eileen after her dramatic pause, and she fell right back into her hearty sobbing.

"Oh yes you can," he told her, like when a father tells his daughter to go upstairs and wash that muck of her face. She looked at him, startled. He was a no-nonsense kind of a man and he certainly had no time for Eileen's obvious self-pity.

"Now you're going to dry your eyes and take a sup of your water there, then we'll sort this mess out."

Her face screamed that she thought Sergeant Martin already knew everything she had done. His face screamed that he knew everything she had done and wanted to sort it out for her. Garda Hanlon knew the Sergeant was playing mind games, and she knew that it was going to work. Eileen wiped her eyes on the bottom of her pink t-shirt and took a long drink from the plastic cup. Then she sat up and put her hands on the table; she was ready to answer this man's questions.

"Do you remember the day you brought Nicole out?" Sergeant Martin asked calmly.

"Yeah I brought her to Phoenix Park playground."

"And do you remember what you did after that?"

"Yea we went to Leo's on Dame Street for chips."

"And Nicole was with you then?"

"Yeah but not for long. I went in to get the chips and she was out the front. When I came back she was gone." Eileen started fidgeting with her t-shirt.

"I am sorry now Eileen but I don't believe that for one second. You and I both know there is more to this and I don't think lying to me is going to do you any favours." Sergeant Martin was sitting perfectly still the whole time. It made Eileen uneasy. They knew. She had to tell them. They already knew.

"If I tell you do you think you can get her back?" asked Eileen quietly.

"I don't know. We are already working on that. We're hoping you can give us something that would help us out on that one."

"Well I had two social workers. The real one is Noelle Flood. She offered me money for Nicole."

Half an hour later the Sergeant stood up and walked over to Garda Hanlon.

"Take a statement and stick her back in a cell until we figure this out." Then he walked out of the room into the reception.

"O'Connell!" he shouted. "O'Connell! Go get that auld one. We need her for questioning now!"

The Sergeant had hoped to make the journey himself but he had bigger fish to fry and they had to be fried right now before Noelle Flood arrived at the station. He walked into his office and dialled the number for Beaumont Hospital. Stephanie Connors' mother was resting in a ward there after identifying the body of her mother earlier that day. She hadn't taken the news that Stephanie was missing well. Her family were travelling up to be with her but they wouldn't be arriving until later.

The ward matron told him that Mrs Connors was looking less stressed and that she was more than able to talk to him for a moment or so. Mrs Connors had been going on all day about his kindness. Sergeant Martin thanked her and hung up the phone.

"Lads I have a run to do. Someone come with me. We're pulling out." With that he headed towards the back door without even picking up car keys. Two Guards went to follow him but the one who got to the door first was the victor and got to play driver to the Sergeant while the other man had to fall back and give in.

11

Nicole heard more people coming and going from the house than she had ever heard before. When she got there it was only the girl next door and the man but now there was a woman. Nicole knew that they weren't the only people there. She had heard the woman shouting at other people too. She was a horrible, nasty woman and Nicole hated her already. She had hit her so hard that she fell like a doll. Then she went to sleep for a while and when she woke up she was lying in her own puke. Two days later a man came. The woman had brought him in to meet her. He seemed kind. Very quiet though. He just stood at the door and looked at Nicole, who was sitting cross-legged on the mattress. He was smiling so she knew he couldn't have been too bad. Then they walked out again. For the hours that followed Nicole had some sort of hope that the man would come back and save her, but he didn't come and she was worn out hoping.

The next day, Nicole heard a car pull up and someone else coming into the house. It was another girl. She made just as much noise as Nicole had when she arrived. Then Nicole was moved out of the big room at the front of the house and was brought to another, smaller room at the end of the hall. It stank. The smell made Nicole's already upset stomach even worse and there was no pipe to go. Only a well-used looking plastic basin in the corner furthest from the door. There were tracks worn in the carpet to and from the toilet corner. Someone else had used that nasty basin for a long time. Nicole just hoped she wouldn't be in there as long as whoever had been in there before her. With the mattress and the basin, there was very little floor room.

She heard some awful noises in the rest of the house in the next few days. Terrifying, scary noises. Two more men came to look at her with the man and woman as well that time. These meetings were looking more and more threatening each time. There was something about them that made Nicole's skin crawl. The same way that her skin crawled when she saw her mother with a man.

Mark pulled up to the house and saw Hannah waving out from a downstairs window. He caught himself thanking God that the ten year old didn't hate the sight of him. By the time he got to the front step both Hannah and Sharon were standing in the open doorway. Sharon gave him a friendly handshake and Hannah went straight in for a hug. That was a drastic improvement. One giant leap for a little girl like Hannah.

"We are delighted to see you. Simon and John are gone on a little fishing trip so us girls can talk to you properly." While Sharon was talking she looked at Hannah for approval. Hannah didn't miss a beat and nodded back reassurance.

"Well I have to say I'm delighted to visit again. I have been dying to hear how you're getting on Hannah." He smiled at the happy looking face beaming up at him.

"I'm fine thanks. Sharon and John are deadly. Come in, we made you hot chocolate and we have cookies from Marks and Spencers," Hannah told him as she took his hand to lead him into the house.

"She has a lot of important things she wants to tell you Mark. I had to explain how you are a really good man and how you stop bad things happening all the time because children will tell you things. Isn't that right?" Sharon coaxed, making faces at him in the hope he would catch on. She needn't have worried. Mark was a dab hand at this sort of situation. Social workers have to be.

"Yep that's exactly right. Children tell me about some really bad stuff and I make sure they are safe forever. That's my job and I am very, very good at it." They made sure Hannah was taking in every word.

"I know that!" Hannah piped up, sensing what they were up to.

They presented Mark with his hot chocolate and a choice of white or milk chocolate chip cookie and they all settled down around the Persian marble kitchen table. Sharon pulled her seat closer to Hannah's and for a while Mark chatted to Hannah about school and her new room and all her new clothes. Then Sharon took Hannah's hand and turned to the little girl.

"I think we better tell Mark why we wanted to talk to him today. What do you think sweetie?" Sharon ran her free hand through Hannah's long, conditioned hair in support.

"Alright. Well, you know when you asked me what it was like livin' with Ma and Da?" Hannah began without much fear at all. Mark was in awe at how open and direct she was.

"Yes. I remember," Mark said kindly.

"Well I don't think I could tell you everything then. There are bad things...like really bad things." She stopped in her tracks so Mark spoke up.

"I always knew there were bad things that happened. And whatever happened, it wasn't your fault and you have every right to tell me so don't feel one bit bad." Mark's words hit home and Hannah began to well up with tears.

"I think she needed to hear that. I have told her she can talk about it whenever it feels comfortable but it means a lot more coming from you," Sharon explained as she rubbed Hannah's back protectively. "You needed to hear that from Mark didn't you sweetie? You're alright. You're such a good, kind person. You take as much time as you need," she cooed, until Hannah wiped her eyes and looked back up at Mark.

"I'm okay. My Da has friends and they are bad. He used to take Tina off to them all the time. There is another house somewhere close to mine and there is something bad happening there. I hear Ma and Da talk about it with their friend. Tina has been there lots. Sometimes Ma and Da bring men back at night time but I don't think the men live in the house. Tina says they meet Da there to bring her off. She says it's real close. The men are all bad, except Da. They all do bad stuff except him. Even Simon does bad stuff."

Mark listened to a child's haphazard description of a horror house. It was a paedophile ring. Noelle had been involved in a fucking paedophile ring!

"Do you remember the names of any of the men you saw? Or any of the women?"

"Yeah. Noelle was always there with Da. She came in to Ma a lot too. They are great friends but she doesn't party with them.

Ma doesn't like Tina at all. That's why she is always sent away to the men and the other house and gets hit and stuff. I don't think the names the men used were real. They all seem a bit fake now when I say them back. Like loads of people have those same names." Hannah was calm and her words came together more fluidly.

"Well anything you can remember about them will help me loads and loads," Mark pitched in.

"I don't mind telling the Guards. Sharon says you won't let anything bad happen to me. She says they will even send away Simon if he keeps being weird." Hannah looked up at Sharon who was nodding at Mark as if to say, "We'll talk about it when Hannah leaves the room."

"It would be really helpful if you would talk to the Guards, but let's take it one step at a time. You did an excellent thing telling me about this. You are such a brave girl Hannah. You have no idea how much good you have done by telling me all this. You should never have had to go through any of that. That was not fair and your ma and da should have known better and minded you and Tina more."

Sharon bent down to Hannah's ear.

"Why don't you go out and have a can of Coke from the fridge, sweetie. Have a little breather outside for a minute or two?"

"Yes please. I am okay though," Hannah told Sharon.

"We know you are honey and we are so, so proud of you." Sharon kissed her on the top of her head and Hannah went to the fridge, took out a Coke and headed out of the room.

"Thank you so much for this Sharon. You have done so well with her," Mark gushed as soon as he was sure Hannah was out of earshot.

"It's my pleasure. Now the other big issue of the day is Simon. He is being totally inappropriate with Hannah. Just O.T.T. rude and crossing too many lines. I don't think we should have both of them together, but ideally we would love if Hannah could stay. I know it sounds selfish and unfair but you have to understand what I mean by inappropriate. Needless to say, if you guys and the doctors think we can make things right between Simon and Hannah we have no problem giving it another shot. We are just very concerned for Hannah." Sharon was really making the most out of their few minutes alone. Mark was trying to digest what was being flung at him as quickly as it was being thrown but it was difficult.

"Do you think Simon could have been sexual with her?"

"Yes definitely, and generally abusive. He can't even walk past her with out hitting or pinching her."

"Okay then he needs to be out of this house. Is there any way your husband could stay with him in a friend or relative's until the morning? This is serious and we need to act now." The gravity of the situation hit Mark. It looked as if Simon was affected by all the things he had witnessed, and possibly acted out himself.

"We can do that. John is not particularly keen on Simon staying here. Hannah doesn't know I have been keeping John up to date. I would really appreciate it if you didn't tell her. I really don't want to loose this trust."

"That's not a problem. You can tell John I will call him first thing in the morning to let him know the plan." Mark now understood the pressure these lovely foster parents had been dealing with... what Hannah had to deal with!.. what little Tina had to deal with! It was enough to make a grown man sick.

When Hannah came back into the room, her eyes were puffy but she was composed and purposeful.

"Hannah you have been so good. Do you mind if I ask you a few more questions? It would really help me." Hannah took her seat beside Sharon and was already nodding her answer.

"That's okay."

"Are you sure Hannah? You have already done enough for one day. Are you sure you don't want to have a break and Mark can come back another day?" Sharon asked.

"No I'm fine. I haven't even told him the bad people's names yet. You only know about Noelle and Simon," Hannah responded simply. She looked up at Mark. "You should write it down so you don't forget them."

Mark smiled.

"You are such an unbelievable person Hannah. In a really, really good way. I have a notebook in my bag. Hang on." Mark stood and went over to his bag, which was propped up on the breakfast bar. After locating his notebook and pen he went back to the table. Everyone was silent.

"Ma, Da, Noelle, Tom, Mike and Dunnie. They're the only ones I know."

Mark wrote down the names. He wanted to wrap up this conversation; Hannah had been through enough for one day.

"Hannah, you said before that you wouldn't mind telling the Guards everything you told me. Are you sure about that?"

"Only if it's a nice Garda. Maybe a woman or something? Then I wouldn't mind."

Mark sat in his car. He was parked outside the Garda station but he needed a few minutes to gather his thoughts. *There is another house…* Hannah's words rang in his head. Noelle was a friend of Pat and Kevin. Hannah didn't know she was talking about her own grandaunt … *and it's close to mine…*

Is the house in High Park?

How involved is Thomas White?

How involved are Patricia and Kevin Madden?

Are there other adopted kids mixed up in this?

Mark's head was a mess. Lots of mixed up adoptions and a group of paedophiles working out of some house somewhere? He couldn't comprehend it. It was too big. He had come across a horror and he needed help.

Sergeant Martin wasn't in the station so Mark said he would wait. He took a seat in the back row of the waiting room and took out his notebook again. Like a mad man he wrote down every detail he could remember from Hannah's interview, before the smallest little bit slipped away from his memory. For over a half an hour he scribbled like a man possessed. Then he sat staring at the ceiling with the pen hanging out of the corner of his mouth and the notebook still open in his lap. Only when he was sure he hadn't missed anything did he reach into his bag for his folder. He rooted through pages and pages of A4 and eventually found a blank incident report. He spent another forty-five minutes filling it out. He even had to attach a further two notebook pages so he could get everything down. When he was finished, Mark packed back up his bag. He didn't think he would have to wait this long but he'd wait as long as it took to see Sergeant Martin.

"Get your filthy hands off me! I am perfectly capable of walking on my own!" Mark knew that shrill voice. Straight away he turned towards the ruckus and saw Noelle on the other side of the reception desk being led towards a door by Garda O'Connell. She kept trying to stop walking and face the tall young man but he kept moving her on, and this only frustrated her more. Then her eyes fell on Mark. The sight of him watching shut her up and Garda O'Connell guided her with ease through the last few steps through a door into the belly of the station. Five minutes later Garda O'Connell reappeared without Noelle. Mark was in shock.

The first morning that Breda Flood Byrne woke up in the care home it took her nearly half an hour to piece her last memories together. Tina screaming. Trying to move. Finding Ma....Ma was dead. Breda's lovely, kind, soft Ma. Tina was taken out of her arms. By who? Noelle. Aunt Noelle was there. That's never a good thing. Her head began to swim so Breda closed her eyes again. *Where is Tina? Where is my little girl?* she thought sadly. *Where am I?*

She opened her eyes again and tried to make sense of what she could see around her. She was lying on a bed in a very white room. Too white. Too sterile. It didn't look like a room in a hospital exactly but definitely somewhere that was cleaned thoroughly. The grey carpet on the floor was the only thing that wasn't shining. The room was furnished with a bed, a small table and chair at the other side. There was a window but heavy white curtains were hiding the view that Breda could have used to get some idea as to her location. Her body was heavy and even lifting her head took too much of her energy. Her head was very foggy so before she managed to bring her thoughts back to her missing daughter and her dead mother, Breda fell back into a deep sleep.

She had no idea how long she had been out when she awoke for the second time. She was still alone. No one had come to explain what was happening or even to see if she was alright. Breda felt abandoned. She missed her mother desperately. She wanted her chair but she couldn't see it anywhere. She wanted her daughter but she knew something dreadful had happened to both of them since Noelle had Kathleen out of the picture. What had she done? How was Patricia involved? Was Tina with Patricia? Was she taken into care?

Breda let her head fall back onto the pure white pillow and cried her heart out noisely, and still no one came. Eventually her tears subsided and her sadness was melted by anger. How dare the world ignore her! How dare they take her baby away! Was Ma buried already? Had they allowed Breda to miss her own mother's funeral? Where the fuck is Tina?! Where is everybody?! Why hasn't anyone come?!

Breda pushed her weight onto her weak right elbow and pushed herself over on it until she fell heavily off the bed and onto the floor. She dragged herself as close to the wooden door as she could and banged it with her arm and head. She made as much noise as she could. She shouted and screamed and banged her head until she was positive she was minutes away from knocking herself unconscious. Then after what had to have been an hour, Breda heard the sound of someone rushing towards the room down a squeaky floor. She was expecting the door to be locked but it wasn't and someone tried to walk straight in. The door hit Breda hard on the top of her head.

"Shit!" a young voice muttered. "Are you alright? How did you get down there?"

"Where am I?! Where is my daughter?!" But Breda knew the young voice wouldn't understand her.

"You stay right there and I'll get one of the girls to give me a hand to get you back into your bed, alright Miss Byrne?" Then the door closed and Breda listened to the shoes squeak away into the distance. She just lay there on the floor. Worn out but relieved someone was coming. Maybe they would tell her where Tina was.

But they didn't. When the two women came back into the room they just hauled her back into bed and left again, paying no attention to her pleas. They ignored the desperation in her eyes and didn't even check her head where the younger one had hit her with the door.

Breda was left alone again, exasperated. She needed a plan if she was ever going to get out of there, and Breda Flood Byrne was a very smart woman.

Even though the odds of Mrs Connors having dealt with Noelle Flood before were about a hundred to one, considering he didn't even know if she had a record in social services, Sergeant Martin had a very strong feeling that he was on to something here. Noelle Flood had been involved in the Tina Madden case and the Nicole Kelly incident, why not go for three of three? All three cases were very recent as well. He hoped he was right; if he was they had a chance of finding both girls at once.

He got to the door of the ward and was met by an attractive woman in a navy blue suit.

"Sergeant Martin? I'm Roisin Mullan. I am the patient liaison on duty this afternoon. I was told you would be in and came to ask if I can be of help in any way?" Sergeant Martin hardly noticed her tightly fitted suit or the extra sparkle in her eyes. He was almost on tip-toe gawking over her head down into the ward.

"Nice to meet you. Would you be able to show me to Mrs Connors please?" He put his weight back onto his heels and looked at the over-made up liaison. "She and I are working on a little something together."

"Oh certainly Sergeant. I'd be happy to. This way please." She detected his professional tone and reacted accordingly, exaggerated to camouflage her failed attempt at dazzling him. A Sergeant. Who probably had an ugly old wife. She gotten excited at the thought. But she didn't mean to make a fool out of herself. *Another opportunity missed,* she thought as she offered the Sergeant tea or coffee.

"Two teas with milk and one sugar would be great thanks," he asked, with only half his attention on the request. Then he marched towards Mrs Connors who was now in front of him sitting up, tidied and waiting.

"Sergeant."

"Mrs Connors. How are the kiddies doing since the bad news?" he asked as he took a seat at the head of her bed.

"Grand. Sad about their gran and asking where Stephanie is, as we expected really. My sister has them near the Red Cow and my husband is on his way back from England to take them." Mrs Connors was younger than Sergeant Martin had thought. She was a bit mad-looking from the drink but she had been sober since long before she had arrived in the station. *Unlike Eileen Kelly,* he thought bitterly.

"That's great to have family isn't it?"

Mrs Connors smiled genuinely.

"Thank God for them. My sister is made of tougher stuff than me. She has been great."

"And for the other fella to come back all the way from England, you and yours must mean an awful lot," Sergeant Martin offered.

"That's kind of you to say." They both knew why he said what he did but still she was grateful.

"I want to ask you a little something if you wouldn't mind?" He made an effort to keep his face as soft as he could.

"Of course. No problem. No problem at all." Mrs Connors leaned forward and opened her eyes wide to show just how willing she was.

"Have you ever had any dealings with social workers from the North Dublin office?"

"God now I have had dealings with a few alright but there is a one who we all know far too well. We moved to get away from her after livin' in the one spot for three years. A few other travellers seen her too. Well she would come in and ask questions about this child and that one. Not a very nice one but other than that there was the woman who came to see if we were sure we didn't want to put the kids in a settled school after we had been in the site for long enough. She was nice enough. And after that we had a few dodgy council men and stuff moving us around and trying to get us to move three feet this way," she gestured off to the right with her hand.

"The first woman you mentioned, Mrs Connors. You wouldn't remember her name would you?"

"I have a funny story about that. None of us knew her name for months and months. Nearly a year I think. Then one day she came and flashed her card for long enough that one of the kids was able to read it. Noel it was and we all had a laugh that she was a Mister." Mrs Connors chucked heartily before her face hardened quickly again.

"You don't think they did something?"

"Not at all. We are on it though don't you worry." Sergeant Martin pretended to change the topic by leaving Noelle Flood out of it altogether. "So you were on one site for three years? That must have been nice for you to stay so long."

"Ah it was. We had everything we needed sure. But these things always end. That's just the way things happen."

"How long ago did you leave there?"

"Around a year tops I'd say. Ah we miss it a bit alright but there will be more Ballyashs in our lifetimes."

"And you moved because of Noelle Flood?"

"True. Right enough."

When Sergeant Martin had politely ended the conversation he felt like he had won the lottery. Exactly how long ago had Mark Tynan said Noelle Flood had been retired? On his way out of the door of the ward he saw Roisin Mullan heading towards the lift with two cups on a tray accompanied by a plate of biscuits;

nearly an hour after the offer had been made. She didn't see him and he didn't care to stop her. Mrs Connors would like the biscuits. He doubted she managed to have anything sweet at home with all those kids. It was the same when his kids were little.

As soon as Sergeant Martin got back to the station he shoo shooed away all pleas for his attention to get to his desk and write everything down. He was on to something now. They had leads to investigate. Mrs Connors' story was something they could easily prove with the number of families Noelle Flood seemed to bother. She had been impersonating a social worker after she had retired if Mrs Connors had been right. The typed interviews with both Mark Tynan and Orla Flynn had said she had retired three years ago. Mrs Connors said she had been forced to move out after Noelle Flood's harassment a year ago. The Sergeant had a lot to go through, but first Noelle Flood was in to be questioned about Nicole Kelly. He had just gotten started on Stephanie Connors and needed to put a few more pieces together before he would question Noelle about her. The murder was a second priority for as long as the children were still missing.

When the Sergeant opened his office door he couldn't help but notice Mark in the waiting room. Standing staring at the giant clock on the magnolia wall. *Shit! How long has he been waiting here?* he thought.

"Why didn't anyone tell me Mr Tynan was waiting for me?" he asked the entire reception, hoping Mark would hear and know he hadn't ignored him purposely.

"Sorry Sergeant," chorused the Gardaí together. All of them knew there was no use in pointing out that they had been shushed. The older ones knew that his scolding was for Mark Tynan's sake. The Sargent was just covering his ass. Leaving Noelle Flood to sweat for a little while was not a bad thing, so Sergeant Martin made his way straight out to Mark and shook his hand firmly.

"Mr Tynan good to see you. I am very sorry to leave you waiting."

"Don't worry about it. I have bigger things on my mind."

"We'd better go into the office," Sergeant Martin said, looking around.

When they had settled into their seats, the Sergeant behind the old oak desk and Mark on the opposite side, a silence fell over them both for a few seconds. In that brief moment both men were exasperated at the information he would impart to the other. Sergeant Martin broke the spell.

"I have more information but I have a feeling I should hear what information kept you outside for that length of time first." He gestured towards the waiting room.

"Yeah. I have a feeling you should. Well there are two things really." Mark sat forward. "Firstly, I have been getting Noelle Flood's files together for you."

"That's good. That's good." Sergeant Martin had expected a bit more than that.

Mark saw the note of confusion on his face.

"That's not why I'm here." He inhaled deeply and started into it. "While I was getting the adoption files and the removal files together I noticed something strange in the cases. One family court judge has resided over all of Noelle's cases. He granted everything she ever asked for by the looks of things. That's not normal practice. In fact it is too abnormal to be a coincidence in my opinion. You can see for yourself when you see the files. They're all missing parts and other parts have been purposely blotted out with food stains and stuff. It looks bad. Really bad."

"What is the judge's name do you remember?"

Mark raised his eyes to heaven.

"It's burnt into my brain. Justice Thomas White."

"Okay. Okay. I'll add him to the list of possible co-conspirators with Noelle Flood, and Kevin and Patricia Madden. You need to get those files to me as soon as you have them together. We need to get this ball rolling. What was the other thing?" Sergeant Martin asked as he continued scribbling into a shorthand notebook.

"I spoke to Hannah Madden at her foster family's home this morning. It was disturbing to say the least. I have a report written up for you but would you mind giving me a copy for my records? I had to write it up in the waiting room out there." Mark was hoping Sergeant Martin would just take the report rather than asking him about it. This meeting was informal. They both knew it. He would end up describing the conversation twice. He took out his folder and removed the incident report with its extra notebook pages folded onto the corner and handed it over.

"We can do that," Sergeant Martin replied while he ran his eyes far too quickly over each individual page. Then he stood up suddenly and walked to the door, report in hand. He opened it and bellowed out that he needed something photocopied. A hand appeared and took the report from him. The Sergeant closed the door and took his seat again.

"Give me the gist of it."

"She has been sexually assaulted on a few occasions by men Kevin and Patricia Madden brought home. So was Tina. Tina had it far, far worse. She says Kevin didn't touch either of them in that way but he allowed the other men to. She called Noelle Flood a friend of her parents. Said that she was in the house at 1225 High Park a lot with her mam and dad."

The Sergeant didn't even flinch when he head that Noelle Flood was in the Madden residence only recently. Under different circumstances it would have been simple for Noelle to avoid the families after she had organised one of her dodgy adoptions. But the Maddens were family. Even if the children didn't know that, it was enough for Noelle to have a legitimate reason to be around them, so close to the abuse, even after she had committed her own crimes. But the Madden case was different for a hundred other reasons.

Mark braced himself for the next part.

"She also said that there is another house. A house where Tina was repeatedly taken by Kevin Madden. Tina would come back in pieces and Hannah would have to look after her for a few days. Tina told Hannah some of the things she went through but not everything. Men met Kevin at this other house and took Tina for a while and dropped her back when they were done with her. Tina said there were other girls in the house as well as her, with the other men." The size of it all was sinking in for Mark. It was hard to keep talking.

Sergeant Martin couldn't ignore the uneasiness washing over Mark's face. This was a hard thing for a soft man to deal with. Mark was only a young man. Maybe in his mid thirties. He had a lot on his shoulders and the Sergeant didn't want him to crack before he heard what he needed to hear.

"Do we know anything about the men? Or more importantly the house? Find the house, find the vermin as they say." His attempt to ease the heavy air failed.

"I have three half-names. They are the men Kevin and Patricia would bring home. They were also three of the men that Tina said were at the house."

"And the house?"

"Hannah thinks it's close by. Kevin nips over and back regularly." Mark swallowed. "He brings food over from their house and gets back really quickly. Hannah said she would talk to a Guard. She would prefer a woman though and you might want to give her a day or two after what she had to go through this morning telling me."

"We can arrange that."

"There is one more thing. Simon Madden sexually abused Tina and Hannah too."

"You're not serious!" Now Sergeant Martin looked shocked. Mark had finally shocked him.

Mark shook his head.

"I know. I'm removing him from the foster carers until you guys get Hannah's statement and decide what to do. I haven't dealt with a possible child predator before. I have to wait to get back to the office and see what the protocol is."

"We'll deal with that in the interview. I'll have a look into it on my side and see what we can do." Again there was silence while Sergeant Martin wrote in his notebook.

"I saw O'Connell bring in Noelle," Mark mentioned sheepishly.

The Sergeant glanced up at him from his notebook.

"We want to ask her a few questions about Nicole Kelly."

"Are you going to arrest her?"

"Not yet. Just in for questioning for now. We need to figure out what we are up against first. This thing just keeps getting bigger and bigger." Sergeant Martin hinted that the story did not stop there. He wanted to remind Mark that he had something to say too. Mark got the hint and straightened up in his chair to attention.

"Has Noelle had dealings with many members of the travelling community in the past?"

"Well I am sure she has over the years. Any one in particular? Or an area or anything that could help me narrow it down?" Mark's eagerness came as a breath of fresh air.

"Dublin, North City, Ballyash?"

"I know it. I have called out there a few times in the last few years. The crowd changes regularly now though. When are we talking about?"

"Up to a year and a half ago."

Mark's jaw dropped. Noelle wasn't working a year and a half ago. She had already retired. Sergeant Martin gave him a moment to let the information sink in, then he pushed things along again.

"I need you to see if she made any record of a family called Connors in Ballyash before she left work so I can see if she is finding new families or if she is still picking off her old cases."

Mark was still stunned.

"I'll look into it and get back to you right away."

O'Connell knocked on the door and handed two copies of Mark's report to the Sergeant, who gave one to Mark. Before he left, Mark gave him Sharon and John's phone number and address.

12

Breda spat her food back in the young nurse's face again at lunch time. Three times a day Breda had spit her liquidated food back on whatever poor unfortunate bitch had the job of spooning it into her ungrateful mouth. This time was once too many; the one Breda had been hoping for. She didn't like acting like a wild animal but she needed to get someone to listen to her and nothing else had worked so far. So when the nurse got a face full of beef and vegetable stew, and instead of pulling a face like usual she threw a tantrum and marched out of the room, Breda knew she had crossed a line. She had won a minor battle and maybe now someone with some sense would come and attempt to communicate with her.

Breda had no idea where she was. In all her time here she hadn't seen one other 'patient' or 'client' as she was sometimes referred to. Her only guess was a mental hospital. She was given injections when she got too 'restless'. She hadn't been given her chair since she had arrived. She spent all her time in bed or on an almost vertical chair that had been wheeled in during the first few days. This place scared Breda. She had never thought she would end up in a home or hospital long-term. Never ever. But now, with the concept looming in front of her, it terrified her. All she had left now were long days with nothing to think of only Tina and how to get to her back. These people knew nothing about her. They had never once mentioned her daughter or the death of her mother. They only looked after her physical wellbeing and not very well. Sometimes they would come in and plonk her on a portable commode. She would be left bare-arsed on the thing any number of times a day. Some days they wouldn't care if she did her business or not. Other days they expressed serious concern at the lack of excrement in the bowl. Then they would prop her back onto the seat and leave her there until her bowels moved and she would be put back into bed or onto the chair.

Breda sat very still after the young nurse stormed out of the room. She waited to hear if there was any commotion that could be taken as a hint that someone else was coming. Someone other than a nurse. But two of the older nurses came in.

"You'll be sent to the mental hospital if you keep this behaviour up!" bit one.

"That's right! You will!" spat the other as they wiped Breda's face, took away her food and put her back in bed. Then one took out a syringe.

Breda was out for the count again.

When she woke up it was the first time that something other than Tina came into her head right away. She wasn't in a mental hospital. The nurse said she would be put into a mental hospital, so this couldn't be one. *Where the hell am I?!* she thought, starting to panic again. She needed out. She needed to draw attention to herself. Fuck the mental hospital! Screw this place! She screamed and shouted and threw her body this way and that. She was a grown woman and these people were holding her against her will! She had a daughter to worry about! They couldn't get away with it. Breda kept it up. Her eyes were watering and her limbs and throat hurt badly but she kept going. She screamed and banged her body off the bed with all of her might. It wasn't working. She grabbed the side rail at the head of the bed and once again flung herself onto the floor. This time instead of making her way to the door Breda grabbed a leg of the aluminium bed and rattled the frame, hard. She was making much more of a racket than she had ever thought possible.

Then her chest felt tight. She was finding it harder and harder to catch her breath between screams. She was seeing black spots when the door opened and three sets of shoes ran by her head. She woke up for a few seconds in the ambulance and found herself reassured by a man sitting far too close to her head. There was an oxygen mask on her face.

Breda spent the night in hospital. She was too weak to even try to talk to anyone. She had heard a doctor giving out that she should have been given her medication in the nursing home. Breda was in a nursing home. Now she would need oxygen at night and something else she couldn't make out. The next morning Breda was put back in an ambulance and was brought back to the facility she now knew to be a nursing home.

She did her best to stay awake on the ride back. She was unbearably curious to see the building where she had been locked away all this time but she couldn't see anything outside the ambulance and with nothing to look at it was hard to keep her eyes open. Still, when she felt the ambulance stop her eagerness to see the nursing home made her eyes open wide. The driver killed the engine and Breda heard his door close. When the back doors opened she was disgusted to see a front door, right at the back of the vehicle. She wouldn't get to see much of the outside grounds, but there was still the inside. Breda hadn't seen anything other than her white, impersonal little room. The man in the back picked up an oxygen tank and put it on top of the blanket that covered Breda's legs; then the two men lifted the stretcher out of the back. Only for a second she managed to catch a glimpse of part of the car park through the gap between the ambulance and the front door. Nothing special there. Then she was pushed through the white-framed automatic doors. The air smelled musky, very different to the air in her white room. She was wheeled past a reception desk where one of the nurses joined in the procession, taking her to her room, chatting to the ambulance driver openly about the trouble Breda had been causing since the day she had arrived.

"She's mentally disabled. Her aunt and her sister set her up in here after she had worn her mother out. Wore her mother out, according to the other pair and I can bloody see how."

"Ah there's no way!" said the ambulance driver.

"You wouldn't be saying that if you were the one she spat her food at day in and day out!" the nurse scoffed.

Breda couldn't help but giggle. She was worn out but she hadn't lost her sense of humour.

"Don't seem so mentally disabled to me; she's laughing at you right now," the driver chuckled, pointing down at Breda's face.

The nurse looked down at Breda lying beneath her.

"It's probably gas."

Most of the doors along the corridor where shut tight but every so often one would be open and she would get a chance to see in as she passed. There were elderly people in the nursing home; she had never even thought of that. Breda now saw them for the first time. They were in their little rooms watching televisions, listening to radios or wandering from one room to the other shouting greetings to one another like they hadn't seen each other in years. Then they wheeled past a big pair of open doors and Breda saw the dining room. It was gigantic, filled with round tables and mismatched kitchen chairs. There must have been fifty places set. Then she was past it and she was being taken through another set of double doors. She saw the word MEDICAL written in white on a red square of plastic, and she was back in white. *That explains it,* she thought. When she was brought around the corner into her room, there, sitting up proud as punch, was her wheelchair. Something was happening. Something had changed. She had never been given her chair here before.

Doctor Ombino had thought about Breda Flood Byrne a million times in the weeks that followed her mother's death. He hadn't seen or heard from her once, not even to renew a prescription. He had thought she would have had a live-in carer with the money she had inherited from her uncle and mother; she could easily afford it. That was what Kathleen's plan had been for her daughter and granddaughter. They would live in her house with the help of private carers. Kathleen had saved every spare cent she had for when she was gone. That, with the money left by James, would have kept both of them happy together. Not to mention the disability and single mothers' allowance Breda was entitled to. But why had she missed her appointments?

Then one day, when Breda was far from the centre of his concentration, Dr Ombino got a phone call that threw him into a tail spin. No one knew where Breda was.

"Hi there. This is Mark Tynan in the North Dublin office of the Department of Family and Children. I was wondering if you have space for a boy who is showing signs of being very disruptive?"

"How bad are we talking? Sorry to be blunt but with the gang we have in at the minute he'd have to be pretty bad to fit in at all."

"Well he is highly manipulative and... eh... the main problem is that.. eh... there is a possibility that he is eh...sexually abusive."

"Oh. This would be the place alright. I'm Tony Bird. I run the centre here. How quick do you need him off your hands?"

"Yesterday preferably."

"I'm no wizard but you send me the paperwork and we'll have him a bed at eight o'clock tomorrow morning. How does that sound for you?"

"That sounds like you're the man I needed to call Tony. Thank you so much."

Mark and Orla went together to meet John and Simon. When Mark had called Sharon to make the arrangements she had warned him that Simon was not happy about being taken away from his sister. Mark had tried to assure her that he would manage but Sharon had insisted that he would need someone else with him. That's where Orla came in. Maybe having a strong, no-nonsense female there would keep him in check, a bit, he hoped. It had worked in the past when kids had been upset; Orla would be firm but kind. She could put them back in line without sounding too harsh and making matters worse.

They were meeting at nine a.m. in a petrol station café on the M50. Orla and Mark were nearly there when they got a call from Sharon to ask if they would mind meeting John in the other car park at the back of the station. Simon was throwing a mad one and John couldn't bring him in; he just pulled around the back to stop Simon from causing a scene. They agreed.

"What the hell?" asked Orla when he had switched off the call.

"This sounds bad Orla. Should we get a squad car?" Mark had gone pale again and Orla knew he was worried about what they were going to find.

"We'll go first, but if he is in a proper state we should get one. Last thing we need is for him to break himself up before he gets down there."

"Would he be ambulance bad?" Mark asked.

"If he is we can deal with that too." Orla sounded so capable that Mark felt better. He wasn't alone in this. Orla would back him up.

The car fell silent as they indicated into the slipway and drove around the building to the back car park. Suddenly out of nowhere something darted out across the road in front of them. Mark jammed on the brakes and the car screeched to a halt. It was Simon Madden and he was running towards the motorway with John running faster than anyone could have imagined after him. But Simon was too nimble. He ran up the grassy verge to the zipping lanes of early morning M50 traffic. Mark had hardly taken off his seat belt and opened the car door when Simon jumped the concrete divide right into oncoming traffic. Orla snapped out of her shock and screamed. They all heard the sound of brakes and tyres under ferocious pressure followed by a deep, low thud. It was too loud. Far too loud. John stopped in his tracks and fell down on his knees.

Sergeant Martin called Garda O'Connell into the office and told him to get out his notebook and take a seat.

"Noelle Flood is still waiting Sergeant," O'Connell reminded him politely.

"She can wait. We have only had her a few hours or so. I checked the book. Sit down." The Sergeant took his usual place behind the big oak desk and took a file out from under a newspaper.

"We seem to have come across something bigger than ourselves. We have an ex social worker doing dodgy adoptions and buying kids off junkies. Nicole Kelly is still missing and now we have an old woman murdered and another little girl taken. Stephanie Connors was living with her mam in a site in North Dublin when they were pestered by Noelle Flood enough that they had to move away from her. Now her kid goes missing and the granny she was living with gets stabbed four times. Then we have Hannah Madden who says Noelle was the friend of parents who were running some sort of paedophile ring that involved another premises and sexual predators, one as young as eleven."

Sergeant Martin looked under pressure. O'Connell had never seen the Sergeant under such pressure.

"One thing at a time Sergeant, that's all we can do. Noelle Flood is next door. We can scare her a bit with Eileen's statement. We have to get something out of her. We can't just let her walk knowing we are cooking up a big pot of shit against her. Paedophiles and multiple kidnappings will have to wait or she'll fly. She has the money and the contacts to disappear by the look of things."

"You're right. We need to be smarter. We need to be her best friends and ask her if she had any dealing with Eileen and Nicole in the past few months. Then we call in the bigwigs and take it from there. We can't risk loosing her."

"Good plan Sergeant. Shall we get to it then?"

"Yes, I believe we shall."

Sergeant Martin knocked lightly on the door of the interview room where Noelle had been penned for quite some time.

"Oh yeah! Bother knocking now!" she muttered.

He pretended not to hear her.

"I'm very sorry about all the drama Mrs Flood. We only had to ask you something small. That idiot out there takes his job a bit too seriously sometimes. Us old timers know how to take it a bit easier don't we? Can I get you a cuppa at all?"

"No you can not after my close encounter with that brute of yours! Ask me your questions and let me get home to my housework," Noelle cut back, not falling for his act for one second and not letting hers slip.

"Okay then, let's get to the point. Have you been in contact with a woman by the name of Eileen Kelly in the past few weeks?" Sergeant Martin faced her dead on and looked her straight in the eye. He saw her flinch at the bareness of his question before she had enough time to shake it off and get back into the dance.

"Who?"

"Eileen Kelly. She was one of your cases when you worked in the North Dublin office of Social Services." He let his voice fall flat.

"Oh yes and little Nicole. The memory isn't great these days. You know I'm seventy-six this year." Noelle batted her spindly eyelashes and put on her best little-old-lady face. She was pulling out the big guns. She could sense danger was a bit closer to her than she would be comfortable with.

"Have you seen Eileen in the past month?"

"I haven't been a social worker for many, many years now Sergeant."

"That's not what I asked."

"What are you implying Sergeant?"

"Nothing at all. I just need to know if you have had any contact with Eileen Kelly in the last month or so. Have you seen her in the street? Or in a supermarket? Anything at all."

Noelle saw a noose and mistook it for a lifeline. Sergeant Martin watched the wheels turn in her brain. She may have been good with words, but Noelle Flood's body language betrayed her. She was a bad liar.

"I do remember seeing her at one point. Maybe in the post office or in Dunnes or somewhere. I'm sorry Sergeant but my memory has failed me once again." She attempted a smile but it came out as a sneer. Sergeant Martin was done playing games.

"Please excuse me for a moment Noelle." He began to move his large body towards the door.

"You know she has issues with drug addiction? Maybe she sold Nicole to traffickers or something?"

He froze.

"I never said anything about Nicole's current problem. What do you know Mrs Flood?" He turned back around just to see the sneer fall. She looked as though her image was carefully cultivated to exude the stereotypical little old lady. Her attempts fell short. She was bad. Sergeant Martin could tell Noelle Flood was a bad motherfucker.

"I merely guessed Sergeant."

"I will be back here in a few minutes and when I come back we are going to cut out the bullshit and get down to business. Do you understand me Noelle?" His face was hard and serious.

"I think I will be heading home soon Sergeant. I just need to make a phone call. I am allowed a phone call aren't I?" She was teasing him. She wanted her solicitor; Noelle was done talking.

"I'll get one of the lads to bring in the portable." Sergeant Martin left.

"We are arresting Noelle Flood on suspected kidnapping. She wants a phone. Get a better statement from Eileen Kelly." O'Connell jumped up from his seat to receive his orders.

Stephanie sat on the bed and tried hard to think of nice things. Nice green fields with the kids. Charlie falling over in the soft grass and Ma in her scarves picking him up, laughing. A picnic on a big red towel with jam sambos and Coke bottles of blackcurrant. Yellow and red of McDonalds. Smiling people, free balloons and the smell of chicken nuggets. Picking wild flowers along the side of the road on the way home from the shops with Nan. There aren't many but if you look hard you'll see them. Once you find one, you find more. Saying Hi to people going up and down from Nan's flat.

The flash of the camera made her jump every time. The net on the skirt was itching her legs but she had to stay still. She made herself think of nicer things; her new school uniform with its nice shirt and pleated knee-length skirt. Her brothers and sisters laughing. Flowery wallpaper. No, not flowery wallpaper. Mister Tom had flowery wallpaper too.

"Can you smile for me hun? We'll be finish soon I promise."

Stephanie's stomach churned. She didn't want this again. Why did she have to let him do this? Why hadn't anyone stopped him? Didn't people know she was getting hurt?

The man was getting frustrated but he knew Stephanie was on the brink of having some sort of breakdown. He didn't need to push her over the edge when so much could still be done with her. He had to think outside the box.

"Would you feel better if you had a friend here?"

Stephanie looked up. This wasn't the first time Mister Tom had brought other little girls into the equation. Stephanie heaved suddenly and threw up on the pale carpet of the pretty pink and white bedroom. Fear gripped her and Mister Tom liked it.

"It's alright. You're alright for a few more minutes. Stay just like that."

He didn't clean her up. He just kept taking pictures. Stephanie was sobbing but very still.

Orla walked into the hospital. Her feet were heavy and she had spent the rest of the day talking to Gardaí and department heads about the accident before managing to slip home to her bed at around eleven. Mark had brought John home to Sharon and together they broke the news to her. They decided not to tell Hannah until a bit later in the day when it was clearer in their minds. If Mark was torn up, he didn't show it. Orla was just glad she hadn't actually seen the car hit him. She had seen him after though. He wasn't all beat up like she had expected. He was perfect. They hadn't moved him so they didn't see where the blood was coming from but he didn't look like he had a scratch on him. He looked as if he had poured red paint on the motorway and lain down. That was all. Orla shook the image out of her head. Today was Tina's day and she wasn't going to let more badness in. Orla hoped she would transition easily.

Before she knew it she was standing at the end of Tina's bed, smiling a smile that could have been a bit fake. Tina was bright this morning. She was sitting up, dressed in a denim skirt, pink tights and a matching pink jumper. She looked so pretty.

"It's your big day! Are you excited Tina?!" she gushed enthusiasm. Tina's smile grew wider and she swung her legs in excitement.

"Yup!" Then she jumped off the bed and got down on all fours on the ground beside it. She reached her tiny arm under as far as she could and pulled out a pink backpack that looked stuffed to the gills. This was the first time Orla had seen Tina wearing anything other than her pyjamas or her uniform. The pride she felt when she saw Tina lately was something she found herself looking forward to.

"I have something for you Tina. It's from Annabelle. She wrote it for you herself."

Fear spread over Tina's face. "Amn't I going there anymore?"

Orla reached into her pocket and took out a white envelope with *TO TINA* written in big bold letters on the front. Annabelle had it dropped off to Emily that morning and Emily had handed it over with a barrage of Post-its when Orla had come in.

"Oh course you are honey. It's a good letter I promise." Orla helped Tina back onto her hospital bed and handed over the envelope. She smiled when she saw Tina's little hands reaching for it curiously.

"What does that bit say?" she asked, pointing to the front. "Oh I know – it says me!" She ran her little finger underneath the words *TO TINA* and her mouth formed the words: "To me." Then she looked up at Orla with her beautiful eyes pleading, "Can you open this bit?"

Orla giggled as she tore open the envelope.

"No problem. If you want help reading it I can do that too."

"Yes please but can I see it?"

"It's your letter you can do what you like with it. It's yours for keeps from Annabelle." Orla handed back the envelope and Tina started to pull the letter out by tugging on one of the corners. Eventually she got it out and unfolded. Her little face crumbled in concentration while she tried to make sense of all the words on the page.

"Can you read it to me Orla? Please?"

"No problem. You hold it up and I'll read it to you." Tina lifted the page so they both could see the words and Orla read.

Dear Tina,

We hope you are feeling better and are looking forward to you coming to stay with us. We are all so happy you are coming and can't wait until you get here. We have a nice bedroom for you. All of the children are really looking forward to meeting you. The girls said they can't wait to have a new best friend.

Can't wait to see you,
love from Annabelle.

She had even drawn a little picture of herself, a stick figure with long flowing hair with a smile in the bottom corner. Orla sat back on the bed so Tina could inspect her letter, probably the first letter she had ever gotten.

"Is that Annabelle?" she asked.

"Yep. She drew a picture of herself for you. Isn't that nice?"

"She's a grown-up woman!" Tina giggled.

"She's not like most grown-up women; she's lots of fun. Wait 'til you see her house! You'll love it!"

"Can we go now?" asked Tina eagerly.

"Yep." Orla got up and helped Tina off the bed. "I just have to find Nina and sign some papers to take you. Do you want to come so we can leave straight after?"

"Yes please."

After saying their thank yous and goodbyes to Nina, Tina and Orla drove to Annabelle's. They listened to a CD on the way. At first Tina didn't look very happy about the pumping music so Orla kept the sound low while she told Tina all about Annabelle's house and the people who lived there. After a little while the song changed and Orla sang away to herself in the front seat. She wanted Tina to see her having some fun and it worked because when Orla took a peep at her in the rear-view mirror, she was bopping away in her booster seat. So she turned the music up and sang louder. Tina laughed and smiled and danced her little heart out all the way to her new home.

They pulled into the long, leafy driveway and Orla turned the music back down.

"We're here."

When they turned a corner and the long two-storey house came into view, they saw a small, pigtailed girl running in through the glossy front door.

"Who's that?" Tina asked as soon as the little girl came into sight.

"I think it was a lookout. I bet she was waiting to see the car so she could go and tell everyone you're here," explained Orla.

Tina had the same look she had when she was watching the bird building its nest through the hospital window. She was in awe. Then the door opened and bodies began to pour out. Orla saw Annabelle come out onto the front step and put a little boy down from her hip. She was smiling and waving in amongst a group of about fifteen children. Annabelle's two other carers, Yvette and Louise, came out too and were coming with some of the older children further down the driveway to meet them. Tina and Orla waved at their welcoming party and pulled up on the gravel in front of everyone, Orla taking extra precautions in case one of the children decided to dart out in front of the car. She was still jittery after Simon but it did her some honest-to-goodness good to see that Annabelle had managed to keep herself in check for Tina after the bad news. She swayed down the steps and Orla got out to greet her. They gave each other a hug.

"It's so good to see you. Only good things today though okay?" Annabelle said sternly to Orla's shoulder. Orla knew it was more for her own sake than for Orla's but she still got the message loud and clear. Annabelle was grieving for Simon and Nicole, and Orla had to keep the atmosphere light for just a little while. When Annabelle let go Orla looked her straight in the eyes and said,

"You are an amazing woman. You have no idea the good that you do." Annabelle's eyes welled up for only a second before she pushed back the tears and only her smile remained.

"Let's get our little monkey out of the car."

Orla said her hellos to the children while the two women walked together around the car to Tina's door. She looked so tiny in the back seat through the window. Annabelle called to the kids to stand back and give her some room.

Tina sat in the car feeling a bit overwhelmed. This house was huge but it wasn't the house that unnerved her. It was all the children. There were so many children here. How was she going to manage around all of these people? Boys too. That would be the hardest thing. Tina had only ever lived with two boys. Kevin and Simon. Neither had been any good. The doctor in the hospital had been nice though. Maybe they would be like him? Tina watched as Orla opened the car door. There was a woman standing behind her. She was beautiful. Orla unhitched Tina's seat belt and helped her out of the car.

Annabelle stepped forward.

"Tina? Welcome to Rosewood House. We are happy to have you with us."

"Thank you for my letter. I never got post before. Can I see my room please?" Orla was delighted to hear Tina talk so much without hesitation. Tina would be alright. Of course she would.

13

"Noelle Flood you are under arrest under Section 176 of the Criminal Justice Act 2006. And that's just to get us started."

Sargent Martin watched as Garda O'Connell charged Noelle. He felt empowered as he watched her being lead from the room. "Time to build up some other charges and find out who the fuck else is involved in this mess." He said out loud as he headed out of the now empty interview room.

Doctor Ombino had not given up hope when he finally got a message that Breda Flood Byrne had been discharged that morning from a hospital in the city. He contacted the hospital and found out that she was a resident of the nursing home.

Minutes later he called and asked if they had a patient by the name of Breda Flood Byrne in their care. The young woman on the other end tutted loudly.

"Yeah, she's here. She can't exactly come to the phone though." The doctor heard her giggling to someone in the background. "Who may I ask is calling?" she continued.

The doctor hung up and got his car keys.

Breda was desperate. It had been so long since she had seen Tina that her body seemed to ache for her. At night her dreams were filled with the last sound Breda had heard her little baby make. The bone-chilling screaming of her sweet, smart girl haunted her night after night, sleep after drug-induced sleep. She had tried to hurt herself again. They just came in and gave her a shot and she was sent to hear her daughter's screams until she could force her eyelids open. When she tried to hurt them, they gave her a shot and again she would be sent to hear her daughter scream. Her wheelchair was taken away. There was no feeding time any more. Breda had been on a drip for a long while. Her hope was fading and she was sure that her mind would be the next thing to give. Already she could feel herself slipping.

Breda had lost the importance of day and night because sleep only came when she fought them or tried to hurt herself and that happened whenever she was strong enough to give it a go. During one of the times when Breda had finally been able to pull herself out of her nightmares, she thought she could hear something familiar in the distance. She listened intently. It took her a little while to comprehend that it was a voice. When she did, Breda realised that it was a voice of a person who she had heard speak a lot.

Doctor Ombino!

Mark couldn't stomach looking through one more of Noelle's files. He had gotten Jean to give up too. Now they were both packing all the files, the scraps of paper, the half-filled out inspection and incident reports, and getting them ready for transport to the Garda station. Mark had already found all of the files and other bits relating to Tina Madden and Nicole Kelly. He had even managed to find a scrap of paper with Stephanie's mother and grandmother's names written in Noelle's hurried scrawl. Slowly the mountain of files got put away one after the other until Jean and Mark were left with sixteen boxes. To Mark everything looked pretty hopeless. He was tired and frustrated.

"Tea?" asked Jean half-heartedly when they were standing leaning against the wall taking in the scene of boxes and debris.

"Please," he replied with about the same amount of enthusiasm.

Jean walked out of the room, formerly known as her office, in the direction of the small kitchenette. Mark stayed with his back leaning against the wall. Neither Stephanie nor Nicole had been seen or heard from. There was now a serious possibility that the children were being held in a holding house for a paedophile ring. And even worse Mark knew Noelle was involved in the endeavour. What if he was right and she had been providing the children all along? What if Stephanie and Nicole were just the latest in a long list of girls? Something else was nagging at Mark. A thought he hadn't let his mind settle on yet. Noelle had another role in the department during her time there. A role Mark had taken over as soon as she left. Every year children are sent alone to travel with traffickers and 'companies' who smuggle people into Ireland. They come in containers, on boats, on fishing vessels to small beaches, in campervans and through airports with false passports and not a word of English. These children get put in facilities for the short term until Immigration can figure out who they are and where they come from. Sometimes this process can take weeks or even months. Social workers are allocated to children that have been placed in their area and they are responsible for the child's education, medical wellbeing and general care. They make sure the child is happy and safe in their placement until a decision is made about what to do with each individual child. Noelle had been the social worker who dealt with the immigration cases in their department before Mark. When she was doing the handover Mark had felt she was being short for a reason. She didn't want him doing it. She didn't want anyone looking into the past files either. She had made it clear that when a case was closed, it was closed, and the files were shredded.

"No point in looking into the past on these cases," she had explained. "They are short and sweet and when they're done, forget about them. We have our own to think about." She had meant Irish children. Mark had been so irritated at the comment that he had totally missed what she was really telling him. Even when she had explained that in so many cases the families of the children expected them to be caught and sent into short term foster care or residential care facilities by Immigration. She had said it was part of the plan. The illegal families in Ireland who the children were supposedly being sent to didn't like to risk collecting the children from Garda-filled ports or airports. Oh no. Instead they waited until they were in care and then they would swipe them back. This was Noelle's excuse for a number of non-national children who went missing each year. Mark had been so happy that Noelle was leaving that he had let it slide. It wasn't until he was placing two boys a while back that he realised that Noelle hadn't notified him when foreign children in their care went missing from facilities. Children had gone missing and nothing had been done about it. That evening he had gone looking for any paperwork that might give him a clue as to the identity of the missing children but there was nothing. Noelle really did get rid of the cases once they were done. It should have been a red flag but when the children continued to go missing long after Noelle left, Mark had assumed Noelle had been right all along. It could have been for a different reason after all. Still, he had tried. He went through the process of reporting them missing and doing some research of his own with the help of information provided by Immigration. But he had never found anything, never even family to take the kids but being illegal they were hardly going to be on the live register. He had kept the files though. He had never gotten rid of one since the day the crazy old woman walked out for good.

Mark jumped when the door of the office swung open. Jean walked in with two cups and handed him one.
"Thanks."
"You're welcome." She walked to the desk and pulled out a chair. "Now it's time for us to talk. Come on. Sit!"
Mark did what he was told. Jean walked around the desk to the other seat and plonked herself down heavily.
"Is it Simon Madden?" she asked forwardly.
"Not really. Although I can't stand to think about what happened for too long," he admitted.
"Is it Noelle?"
And he was off. "Sort of I suppose. But how can we not be pissed off about that? That woman had one job. Protect children. Keep them away from harm. And she had us all fooled

into thinking that was what she was doing. Not only that but she convinced us all that she was doing her job *soooo* well that we shouldn't dare get involved or ask questions and behind our backs she was kidnapping children!" Mark was letting it all out and Jean was happy for him. She sat as still as she could and let him, usually a quiet man, say what he needed to say.

"I mean there were so many signs Jean. So many signs and we – no, sorry, I – just brushed them off. I didn't even think about it too much. I am a fucking idiot Jean and the last thing I should be doing is running this place! I fucked up so bad and now there are little girls and boys, kids Jean, out there somewhere paying for it. I am a disgrace! A total fucking disgrace." Mark put his head in his hands and looked for a second like he was out of steam. A moment later he was on his feet, out the door and marching towards the small record room, with Jean struggling to keep up in her pencil skirt that was a bit too tight for all the activity.

"Mark? What are we doing?" she stuttered, trying not to break the pace or let the rest of the office know that some new drama was unfolding.

"We are giving them the Immigration files."

"What Immigration files?"

"The children we thought had been abducted by family living in the country illegally."

"Noelle kept those on file! I am shocked!"

"Not Noelle, Jean. Me."

Orla had gone back to the office after she had finally dragged herself away from Annabelle's. Emily was standing inside the door waiting when she came in. The young girl's face was full of pity.

"Hi," was all she said to Orla at first, but Orla expected there was more by the way the little redhead was blocking her way in.

"Eh, hi? Do we have a hostess now? A meet and greet sort of thing?" asked Orla in amusement, still merry after the cake and games at Tina's welcome party.

"Are you alright?" asked Emily mournfully.

"Yes Emily I am fine now thanks. I just want to get on with my work."

"I understand." Then in the blink of a ginger-lashed eye, the old Emily was back. "Well Mark and Jean have gone to bring files down to the Guards. It took them two loads each in the two cars but they are down there now helping The Powers That Be go through them. They asked me to get you to follow them there when you got back." She was speaking so fast Orla wasn't even sure she had heard her properly. Then she put her hand on Orla's arm. It made the whole thing even worse. "If there is anything you need me to do, any calls you need made or if there are any messages that you are expecting and want to be informed of, that's no problem. Just write it all down and I'll take care of it and if you need to give me a briefing before you leave that's no problem either. K?"

Orla's head whirred with the speed of it all.

"K," she replied; she just wanted to get to her desk. She had said the magic word that had made Emily step aside and let her in. Her desk looked cold and unused compared to the other ones in the room. She switched on her small desk lamp and opened an A4 pad. After finishing her list for Emily, she gathered up her things, switched off her lamp, and left again.

Mark was being interviewed by two male detectives. One in a very expensive-looking suit and another in a jumper, shirt and slacks combo. To Jean they looked like people who needed to lay off *The Sopranos*. She hoped they wouldn't be too hard on Mark. He did the very best he could every single day in that job. Same as she did except that she got to be out and about in court and in meetings while Mark seemed to be almost anchored to his office more and more as time went on.

Jean hoped Orla would be here soon. Things were looking desperate and Jean expected that a glowing reference from Orla, who knew the most about this case, would show them that Mark was not one of the bad guys. He was not like Noelle. She had already taken the liberty of calling one of the best solicitors in the city who specialised in employment as well as criminal law to give him the heads-up about Mark's situation.

"Jean?"

She looked up and saw Orla walking towards her.

"I'm confused. Emily said you were here to help them go through the files? Where is Mark?"

Jean stood up and Orla had to take a step back to be able to look her in the face. Jean noticed and couldn't help but think once again that if she had been given the gift of Orla's height, that she would have been a model. For sure. Paris Fashion Week, Vogue and New York penthouses. She struggled to get her head back on topic and for a second Orla just stood there looking at her at an angle, confused as hell, waiting for an answer.

"Mark gave them the Immigration files. Supposedly files about emigrant kids that have gone missing; kids who he had written off as being kidnapped back by their families in Ireland. Mark is being questioned about withholding evidence. They think he was keeping the files to himself because he was in on it. I mean, they think Noelle was taking the kids even after she had retired and Mark lied about them being abducted by family members. I need you to talk to them and make they see that there is no way Mark is involved in endangering children. We have to nip this in the bud Orla."

No one came with food for a very long time and the number of people coming in and out of the house grew fewer and fewer. It got really quiet and things were worse than ever before. The only noise that she heard from inside the house was the man shouting every now and again. Nicole thought he might be on the phone but then she would hear the woman shouting back and things would go quiet again. Nicole felt like she had been here for months. She had preferred the big room with the pipe that took your poo and pee away when you poured just a little bit of your water down after it. The bucket stank and the man would only empty it every few days. He crept around the house these days and Nicole didn't know why but the new situation seemed far more scary than anything before. Even when she had gotten hit. All she wanted was to go home to Annabelle or her ma.

Sergeant Martin had been listening in on the questioning of Noelle Flood for nearly four hours when Mark and Jean McCaile arrived with the first load of files. Mark had given him the rest of the notes on Tina and Nicole but when he opened the folder the first thing he saw was a note with Mary Connors' name and her mother's name written on it. They hadn't gotten anything about any of the children from Noelle after her first slip up. Luckily they had the whole thing on tape. She was digging her heels in and it was annoying as anything he had ever come across in his lengthy career. Now they had proof she had known the Connors family, a thing she had denied to high heaven. As well as that O'Connell had located three other traveller families who claimed to have been harassed by the old bitch who was portraying herself as a social worker years after she had retired. They also told him gladly that they had seen her giving the Connors even more abuse than any of the rest of them. These statements alone proved she was lying. Eileen had agreed to give an official statement too.

Sergeant Martin picked up the note with Mrs Connors' and her mother's name on it. He couldn't help but feel excitement at the break and went to hand it over to Detective Griffin who was the new lead investigator on the Noelle Flood, Stephanie Connors and Nicole Kelly cases. Mark and Jean showed up with the second load a few minutes later and he had a few of the lads help them carry the boxes in. Sergeant Martin hadn't expected them to hang around but when he saw Mark trying to make eye contact with him, he gave him the nod and Mark followed him into the office, carrying a plastic box with more files inside. He just put the box on the desk and sat down.

"Are these ones different?" The Sergeant needed to get things moving. He had a million things to do.

"Yeah. They are more missing kids. They came into this country alone, illegally, and after being put in our care, went missing. Every year children go missing like this and we don't even have a way of finding out how many there have been. Noelle Flood was in charge of these cases before she handed them over to me when she retired. She had disposed of all of the case files she dealt with before me and I thought that was the procedure. She had been in the job so long and…" he paused thoughtfully, "…we all learn as we go sometimes."

Sergeant Martin was confused.

"You thought that was procedure? Mr Tynan I am afraid that we need to go back to the beginning on this one."

"When Noelle retired she had to hand over her responsibility of handling the immigration cases to me. Noelle was over that for years. I mean over two decades. So because no one else knew the ins and outs of it, Noelle had to show me how to handle the cases."

"I'm with you." The Sergeant had sat down and was taking out a notebook and pen.

"Well she told me that a lot of the time the children have family living in Ireland who usually abduct them from their placements, like on the way to school or in the garden. Sometimes on a day trip. She told me that when this happens it's out of our hands, that when a child like this goes missing we are to write it off as a family abduction. There have been hundreds, I mean hundreds, of children disappearing and we did nothing about it."

"And you never once looked for any of these children?"

"I did. When I took over the job first there were a few things I found a bit off. Like, for instance, she would destroy the case file as soon as they were marked as being possible family abductions."

"Which she herself would write them off as?"

"Exactly! So I kept all of mine ever since."

"So she didn't keep any of the missing child files?"

"Not even one! I tried my best to look for the first few, I swear. I even reported them missing. It should be in your records somewhere but I told you that the families were likely to have taken them back. It's just, time went on and children kept going missing. I thought Noelle must have been right. They must have been abducted by family because there was no trace of them. At all!"

"So you knew more children had gone missing when Noelle was in charge and you didn't report them? And the ones you did report you claimed had been taken by family?"

"Yes. I thought it was my job."

"Mark this doesn't look good," Sergeant Martin said, slowly shaking his head.

"I swear to God I had no idea. I swear."

"It's up to the detectives now I'm afraid."

"Did she give you a written set of instructions at the time?" asked the older detective. Mark had learned his name was Detective Yeats.

"No I just went to her desk a few times over the space of a week or so and she showed me what to do."

"And let's go over how she was at the time of these conversations."

Mark exhaled. He was a bit relieved that it wasn't Orla in the hard plastic seat. She would go crazy if she had to repeat herself this many times. She would eventually take their heads off if they kept getting her to go over and over the same things again and again.

"She just seemed like it was such a big deal explaining the process to me. She made me feel like I was stupid not to know what to do but as I said, since I started there Noelle had been over the immigration cases and no one else really knew what was going on with it so she had no choice but to show me."

"She seemed bothered how?" asked the suited detective, Detective Griffin.

"Just huffing and puffing and rolling her eyes when I asked a question. And when she was telling me to get rid of the files when a case was closed she was very serious, like if I didn't follow her instructions that I would be totally out of order. It was the most important part of the job as far as Noelle was concerned."

So far they had only touched on the immigration cases but Mark was not naive enough to expect them to leave it at that. They were going to make sure he wasn't involved in any of Noelle's other suspected ventures and they were going to be tough. They had already given him a list of charges he would be saddled with if he couldn't prove that he had no idea that there was a possibility that these children were being distributed to sex offenders and traffickers, pimps and professional paedophiles.

"You wrote in your most recent statement that there is another house somewhere where children are being held?" asked Detective Griffin.

"Yes. Hannah Madden told me she had heard about it while she lived at home with her parents. She said that Tina Madden had in fact been there and been abused there. Tina also said there were other children there," Mark explained, happy to see they were taking the house seriously.

"We have a detective interviewing Hannah and Tina Madden over the next day or so. What do you expect to hear from them?"

"I expect that you will hear exactly what I heard from Hannah anyway. I hear Tina can take a while to warm up to people, but Orla managed it. They are such good kids and Hannah is determined to help us – well you – any way she can."

"So you never heard of this house before you spoke to Hannah?"

"No. Never. But I have a feeling that Patricia and Kevin Madden are there. If you look for the house you will find them too."

"We have that one under control Mr Tynan."

The detectives walked out.

Sergeant Martin stood outside the interview room and waited for the two bigwigs. When they come out and the door was tightly shut behind them he spoke.

"We've gotten a delivery. The evidence found in the 1225 High Park search, round one and two combined, has just come in. The techs are waiting in my office to debrief us."

"Good. All in its own good time as they say," responded Detective Yeats.

"I don't think Tynan is involved. He is as green as grass that fella. We scared the shit out of him and he hasn't budged," added Detective Griffin, shaking his head.

"I didn't think he would be, but you never know with this crowd. Who would have thought that sweet old Noelle Flood would be kidnapping kids?"

"We have that settled on then?" asked Sergeant Martin.

"Oh hell yes. Proving it is another thing. We are getting a warrant to search her house. I have a feeling that there is a biscuit tin or jewellery box stashed away somewhere. There is no way she did all this without holding onto something and if she is still active, which we are pretty sure she is, then there could be current evidence that she didn't have a chance to dispose of." Yeats sighed loudly. "That's if she didn't clear the place after your man called down the first time."

Sergeant Martin felt a pang of guilt. If he had just waited until she came out, however long it had taken to get Noelle into custody that first night, then maybe they would have found something in her house. Now there was a possibility the sly cunt had gotten rid of more evidence. O'Connell should never have been sent there by himself. She was a suspect in a kidnapping. They had a witness now though, Eileen Kelly, to say she had gotten money from Noelle Flood for her daughter. But Noelle Flood was right, Eileen Kelly was a junkie and it made him doubt her serious allegation in the presence of the two detectives.

He straightened his spine. The other two men were looking at him, waiting for him to do or say something. He obliged.

"Let's not keep them waiting then. You know the way. Come on."

"Should we get someone to release Mark Tynan?"

"Nah he's grand for another bit. It'll make him stay on the straight and narrow," replied Sergeant Martin, but still he called over his shoulder before he was in the door of his office. "Let Mr Tynan know that someone will be with him in a while. We just have to see a man about a dog."

Orla had asked if she could give a statement about Mark's activities at work. When the Guard asked if she had any further information about any on-going cases she just started gushing about how good a man Mark was and how he would never hurt children. She could give them a million instances when Mark had gone above and beyond to ensure the safety of children.

The Garda just raised his eyebrows sympathetically and told her in his thick Cork accent that she would have to take a seat. Mark was a big lad and he could handle a few questions. Everyone knew Mark in the station by now. He had been in and out all the time over the past few weeks. But still the Garda's over-familiarity with Mark and his flippant, patronising way of talking about him being questioned pissed Orla off. She cut him a look that could skin a rabbit.

"Sorry?" he offered.

Orla turned and walked back to Jean who was sitting up watching the exchange.

"Hopeless. Fucking hopeless," Orla told her, a bit too loudly for Jean's liking, before throwing herself in the seat next to her noisily. "He'll be okay though. They haven't charged him with anything yet. He'll probably be released after they hear what he has to say."

Jean turned towards her.

"Orla this could be bad. Loads of children are missing. Mark knew and he didn't report them. He doesn't even know how many. This is really serious and I can't see how he will be able to just walk away from it."

"It can't be that bad Jean. It can't be! Noelle freaking trained him!" she screeched.

Jean's soft, worried face got hard.

"Orla I will ask you to calm down and lower your tone please. We are in a Garda station in a professional capacity."

Orla felt her blood boil. Before she knew it she was on her feet, lecturing the room.

"Those lazy bastards are questioning Mark while Patricia and Kevin Madden get a head start! They could kill those girls if they have them! We lost one this week Jean, we didn't need them to lose us another one!" Orla walked out. Jean just sat with her mouth open in disbelief.

Fuck them all. How come no one had found Nicole and Stephanie?! How come they hadn't started looking for the other house? She thought. They already knew what Hannah was going to say thanks to Mark and now they were stalling and it left a sour taste in Orla's mouth. If they weren't going to do anything she fucking would, she kicked a public bin as hard as she could just to free herself from the heat of her anger. After leaving her victim still standing Orla strode to her car, took her keys out of her pocket and pressed the unlock button before getting in and speeding off.

At first she drove in the direction of her soon-to-be-vacant apartment but the boxes reminded her of when she had been moving in; David had helped her. When she had started packing and the spacious apartment began to fill with boxes, she felt a familiar feeling that made her think he could just walk back in at any moment. But he never would.

What am I doing thinking about that wishy washy fucktard when we have two children missing?! Orla was disgusted with herself for letting David hijack her thoughts when she had real problems to deal with. She stopped as a set of traffic lights turned to amber then red. She didn't want to go home. Home was depressing. Orla needed to do something. She needed action.

Then her eye caught something. There was an entrance to a factory up ahead on her left. When the lights turned green she hit the accelerator with a bit too much vigour and flew up the hundred yards to the factory where she turned the

BMW around and went back in the direction she had come. She was going to get something done about these kids, right now! She knew Tina was in Annabelle's. She had only left there two hours ago. They would still be home.

14

It was definitely him. There was only one person in the world Breda knew with that accent; that deep African mixed with posh Dublin. Breda was an expert at getting onto the floor from her bed by now; she didn't even think twice once she recognised Doctor Ombino's raised voice. She pushed herself along the floor until she was able to lean up against the door and bang her torso violently against the varnished wood. She heard his next words clear as day. He was in the part of the nursing home called 'Medical' too. He wasn't far away.

"Breda? Is that Breda making that noise?" He projected his voice down the shiny white corridor. Breda saw hope and banged her head and torso as hard as she could take. She could hear people trying to calm him down; she couldn't make out who they were.

"I will be back here and I will be getting her a much more suitable level of care! I will be back here!"

Breda stopped instantly and tried to make her ears hear more.

"Breda I will be back! I am not leaving you! I will be back!"

No! This was her chance to get out of here! This was her chance to see Tina! She just wanted to see her baby.

Breda felt all of the air leave her lungs before she heard a loud sob. It was her own. She let her heaving body fall away from the door and felt her limbs shake as she lay on the floor.

"Tina. All I want is Tina! Let me out of here. Please. Please. Please let me out of here." She was lost in her own hopelessness. She knew the nurses were coming in but she didn't care. They called the porter to come help get Breda back in bed and he came in too. Still Breda didn't protest beyond her sobs.

"Tina, Tina, Tina!"

Breda didn't notice the older nurse stop fussing with her blankets.

"What did that man say her daughter's name was?"

"Tina. Why?" replied the porter.

The older nurse looked at him in horror.

"I think she is saying her name!"

"No. Her family said she didn't remember anything! You told me that yourself!"

The large man looked down at Breda who was still sobbing in her bed. The nurse leaned over her and tried to look her in the eyes.

"Breda?" she said quietly. "Breda can you hear me?"

Breda was far away now. Breda couldn't hear her.

"Let's give her a little something to calm her down," said the nurse eventually.

"Can you hear me lovie?"

Tina screaming and something else.

"Breda? Can you open your eyes for me lovie?"

The screaming quietened slowly, but the other voice didn't.

"Breda?" Someone was shaking her.

"Oh wake the fuck up will ya!" another voice hissed. The punch in the leg made Breda wince but it wasn't enough to drag her out of sleep fully.

"Let's just get her dressed Pat. We don't want to be heard talking to her like that here. Come on, give me a hand."

The Garda Crime Scene Investigators were waiting patiently but as soon as the three men entered the room the more superior of the two was on his feet with his arm extended. "Detectives, Sergeant Martin. Good to see you. We found nothing you didn't in the main body of the house."

"But..." probed the eager Sergeant.

"But we found a false top in a chest of drawers in the room we have affectionately call 'the porno room'. The stacks of pornography you found there was general stuff. The kind you could get in any adult store anywhere in Ireland. Some of them were illegal copies but still the content wasn't anything too outrageous. In the chest of drawers though..." He paused to shake his head and take a breath. "...was another story. We found these."

He reached down and lifted up a small bag and put on the table.

"I will ask you to wear gloves if you wouldn't mind."

Sergeant Martin and the two detectives looked at each other before they took gloves from a box on the table and put them on. Then they reached into the bag and took out three small orange photograph albums, the kind you get free when you get pictures developed. These ones were old and well used.

"There are two more in the bag. Five in total. We also found a bag containing some of the rigouts in the pictures. It was shoved behind the piping in the bathroom."

Sergeant Martin felt sick.

"We found two boxes of disposable cameras in that chest of drawers. We are developing them now. No doubt what we're going to find there."

"We'll have to make sure we find out where the hell they were getting them developed," said the older detective.

Sergeant Martin opened the cardboard cover and saw the first girl. That was all he needed to see. He flicked through the rest of them quickly. There were so many girls and a few boys in the pictures from all corners of the world as far as he could tell.

"Have we found any pictures of our current missing girls?"

"Yes. Take a look at this."

The man reached into the bag and took out another album. Near the back there was a pink fluorescent marker sticking out. He opened it on the page and handed the album to Detective Yeats.

"Oh God. The rest of the fucking book is her!" Sergeant Martin exclaimed.

It was Stephanie Connors.

"We also found this." The guard was handing them the final album opened on a page. It was Tina Madden.

"We need to find that second house now!"

Orla drove at speed through the streets of North Dublin, cutting corners and jumping lights. She indicated around slow drivers and even gave a few people the finger on her way. When she pulled up at Annabelle's, she realised it was a miracle that she hadn't been pulled over. Adrenalin was making her crazy and she knew she would have to calm down before she spoke to Tina. The front door opened and Annabelle stepped out with the same little boy from Tina's party clinging to her for dear life. She took a few steps towards the car and saw Orla's face. She took the little boy down from her chest and spoke to him happily. Then he toddled back inside and pushed the door closed after him. Annabelle walked around Orla's car for the second time that day and got into the passenger seat.

"Did they find Nicole?" she asked.

Orla shook her head. "No and they are chasing their arses rather then actually looking for them. They are waiting until they get a first-hand account of the other house existing."

"But the two Guards are coming to talk to Tina tomorrow. There are two little girls who have been gone ages now! Even I know you need to find missing kids fast! Seriously, I learned that from SVU! They have to know better than that!" Annabelle couldn't believe their stupidity.

"Now they are wasting time questioning Mark rather than getting it out of Noelle or looking into who owns the houses in the area or knocking on doors. Something at least!" Orla was grateful that she wasn't the only one who saw the madness in the situation. She took a breath and lowered her voice before she continued. "Tina knows where the house is. Hannah Madden said that Tina was brought there all the time." She turned to look Annabelle in the eye.

Annabelle knew what Orla wanted to do.

"Will it be traumatising?"

"I have a better chance than strangers."

Annabelle looked more serious than Orla had ever seen her look before.

"I know that but will it hurt her?"

"I don't think so. Not if I only talk about the house itself and not what happened there."

Annabelle couldn't believe what she was considering. She shook her head meaningfully.

"Even that might bring it all back for her. I won't let her go through anything that I think is too much Orla. I don't give a fuck who tries. Even the Guards tomorrow. I honestly don't give a shite. It won't happen if Tina gets too upset." She turned and faced Orla.

"Annabelle, I would never put Tina through anything terrible. I am mad about her, you have to know that. But the reality is that tomorrow two strangers will be asking her far more intrusive questions than I want to ask her today." Orla let the fact sink through Annabelle's objections before she kept going. "If they put her over the edge it could take months to find out where the house is. I am promising you now that I will only ask her about the house itself. The structure and no more. I swear."

Annabelle broke eye contact with Orla and sat back in the leather seat.

"You're right and I know you are but if anyone finds out we asked her, then we're screwed and I won't ask her to lie. I'm sorry, but no. We have to wait until tomorrow." Annabelle opened the car door and got out. Orla stared after her. Then she started the engine and drove away.

When she turned back to the house, Annabelle saw a small figure at the upstairs hall window. It was Tina. She had seen Orla and now she would be worried she was in trouble. Annabelle had seen it so many times. Children who had suffered abuse could be so anxious that they read signs where there were none. She could already tell Tina was one of these children.

Annabelle walked into the house and closed the door behind her. Now she would have to go and explain to Tina how Orla calls over for other things too, not just her. She exhaled loudly and started up the stairs.

"Tina honey? Are you up here?" She went to Tina's bedroom but it was empty. Annabelle checked a few more bedrooms while she made her way through the floor. She knocked on the bathroom door but it swung open and the toilet was empty, surprisingly. There was only one room left, the homework room. At first glance Annabelle couldn't see anyone in there, only desks, chairs and bookshelves, but a small noise in the far corner gave away Tina's position.

"Tina? Honey? Are you in here?" Annabelle asked softly, closing the door behind her. After a few seconds she got a response.

"Yeah. I'm here." Tina sounded upset. Not angry but sad without the crying.

Annabelle walked around the room to where the little voice came from. Tina was in the corner holding her knees to her chest. She looked so scared that Annabelle didn't want to approach her too quickly. She took long slow steps until she was beside the little girl then she sat down on the floor and held her knees too.

"Are you alright?"

"Yeah."

"Did you get scared when you saw Orla coming back?"

Tina nodded.

"You don't have to worry honey. Orla is one of my friends so she comes here all the time over tonnes of stuff," Annabelle told her, trying not to lie.

"Am I still allowed to stay here then?"

"Of course you are staying here honey. I only just got to meet you, I'm not letting you go anywhere yet!"

Tina fell silent for a moment. This was all so new to her. No one had ever wanted her in their house before. No one nice anyway.

"Why do you want me here?" Tina asked, looking at the floorboard in front of her new sequined shoes.

Annabelle didn't know what to make of the question. She knew there was more to it but for now she just took it at face value.

"Because I want to get to know you and I want you to learn that there are good people in the world and that you are one of them, most of all I want you to be safe."

Tina liked the sound of that. She looked up into Annabelle's face.

"And you are one of them too?"

Annabelle felt so much respect for this little girl. After everything she had been through, she still had hope that people could be good.

"Yes I am. We all have our faults but I am a good person."

"What's your faults?" asked Tina quietly.

"I try to help people too much and forget to mind myself sometimes. And I leave lights on by accident after I leave rooms. The other kids are always running around after me turning them off." Annabelle giggled. "But you? You are a sweet little girl and I can see that. I will never, ever do anything to hurt you."

"You know what Orla knows don't you? About where I lived before?" Tina asked, worrying.

"Yes I do, and it has nothing to do with why I like you. I like you because you were brave enough to come here to stay with all of us. I like you because you fit in so well and you speak so nicely to everyone. I know how strong you are and I like you because you make my smile a bit wider." Annabelle moved so she was sitting in front of Tina.

"But you know the bad stuff don't you?"

"Yes honey, I do. And I want you to know that I will not speak about it unless you want to. Never ever." Annabelle felt a lump in her throat. She felt such empathy for the tiny girl. They were sick bastards and Annabelle would have given anything for ten minutes in a room with each of them. Tina had small wet tears rolling down her cheeks.

"Bad people can't come here can they Annabelle?" she asked seriously.

"No they can not! We have a Garda station only two miles up the road and there are always at least two staff on at all times of day and night. No bad people can come here," Annabelle said rigidly. In the back of her mind the name Nicole was repeating itself over and over.

"Promise me." Her face made Annabelle uneasy. Was this a test? Did she know about Nicole? It took all of her strength to say the next two words and keep the doubt out of her eyes.

"I promise."

"I have a secret." Tina's eyes were back on her spot on the floor.

"What kind of secret Honey? Don't worry, I'm on your side no matter what you tell me." Annabelle was so scared of what she might hear. She knew Tina Madden's case inside out, so she knew it could have been anything.

"Pat isn't my ma. My ma was a retard in a wheelchair who didn't even want me."

Annabelle had this one.

"I know Patricia wasn't your mam but your mam wasn't a retard. That word isn't very nice. She had a disability and I am sure she wanted you. She lived with your granny and you for a long time you know. I am sure she loved you and your granny loved you. Who told you that silly stuff?" Annabelle didn't expect all this so soon but she could handle it. *What if I ask her? Just about the house.*

"Pat told me. That's all," Tina said, avoiding Annabelle's eyes.

"Do you remember her? Your real mam I mean?" asked Annabelle.

"Yeah I remember. She just lies there doing nothing but making noise. Pat says it's because she hates me so much that she screams her head off when I am there."

Pat says? Pat and Breda had been together recently?

"Honey was your real mam in Pat's house?"

"Yeah but now she is in the other house."

Annabelle could feel hear heart beating.

"What other house Tina? Can you tell me about the other house?"

Tina turned away.

"I don't want to talk about it."

Annabelle thought about Orla's plan again. She spoke slowly and encouragingly.

"How about this, we don't talk about anything that happened in the house. We won't talk about any of the people there or anything. What if we talk about the building? Just the building and where it is? Can we do that?"

"You want to know where the house is?" asked Tina, sitting up straight.

"Well you know I told you about the lady coming tomorrow to talk to you so we can catch the baddies?"

"Yeah," Tina mumbled, unimpressed.

"Well she will be asking you about the house too so if you want we can wait until tomorrow. Or if you're not able then, we will wait until you are ready okay?" She spoke like Tina was so much older than she was. Most abused kids grew up before their time but this was a new low.

"I need to tell someone where the house is."

"Why Tina?"

"Because the other girls are still there and I think about them all the time." Tina began to cry uncontrollably. Annabelle was so startled that she jumped on the child's first heavy heave. Then she composed herself and scooted closer to Tina and put an arm across her back.

"We are going to find them honey. I swear. Orla and a load of policemen are looking for them right now. That isn't your problem. That is a very grown-up problem."

"If I tell you where the house is can you go and bring them here?"

"If you tell me where it is I can get them out of there honey, I know that for sure, but I don't know if everyone could come here. Some of them might have to go to other places just as nice as here," Annabelle tried.

"Promise they will be as nice as here?" asked Tina, almost threateningly.

"I promise. And you can visit them."

"And Hannah?"

"Oh honey of course you can see Hannah. We just didn't know if you would want to."

"I want to." Tina breathed in. "It's called 1226. It only takes a second to get there. From home I mean. I mean from Kevin and Pat's house. It's a house down from it in the ring." Her tiny back straightened and her shoulders lifted from relief.

"Oh you brave, good girl! Would you like to come with me while I ring Orla? Or would you like to keep talking for another while?"

"I want to go and play with the girls downstairs."

Annabelle stood up and held out her hand to Tina.

"I believe a big fat bar of chocolate each is in order first. What do you think little missy?"

Tina smiled, and let Annabelle pull her up from the floor by the hands.

"Yes."

It was the quickest chocolate bar on the planet. Annabelle ate fast so she could ring Orla sooner. Tina ate her bar fast because she had found a new love, chocolate. After faces had been washed, Annabelle brought Tina into the playroom and got her involved in a game with some of the younger girls and made her escape.

"Orla?"

"Yes?"

"It's Annabelle. I have something for you. 1226. It's one house down from the Madden's. She brought it up and wanted to talk."

"No way! What number did you say?"

"1226."

"I am so sorry about earlier. I just felt so…helpless."

"Well now is the time to do something. And it is forgotten. Tina told me and I rang you. You have to ring the Gardaí. Now. There are other children and Breda."

Orla hung up. She was already parked outside 1225 High Park.

"Mr Tynan. I want to let you know that you are no longer under any suspicion regarding any of the crimes mentioned previously. You have proven yourself in interview."

The older Detective Griffin was looking up at Yeats from his seat across the table from Mark. He seemed amused by the younger man's amateur dramatics. Yeats was marching back and forth in the far too small space while explaining the situation to Mark. He had a small bag in his hands and a box under his arm. Mark suspected there was going to be more to this.

"Fantastic. Now can we get back to looking for the child abductors please?" Mark was getting pretty close to being fed up.

Griffin spoke.

"We have found something in the residence of Kevin and Patricia Madden that we would really appreciate you taking a look at. I have to warn you, some of the content is a bit hard to digest."

"What are we talking about here?" Mark was suspicious but grateful for the information.

"Photographs, Mr Tynan. We want you to look at pictures of children we found in the Madden home. We believe it was some sort of catalogue. We need to see if you recognise any of the children."

"Orla Flynn took over Noelle's files when she retired. She would definitely be the one to ask. If you need me to I will though," he offered.

"How about you take a look? You dealt with Immigration; a lot of these kiddies are not Irish. We'll get in contact with Orla Flynn about the others after that. Can you use gloves please? There is a notepad and pencil there if you need to take notes of names or any information you remember about any of the children in the pictures. Just knock if you need anything."

With that they left him to it.

It was a long, upsetting hour for Mark in the interview room alone with all those scared faces. The Guards hadn't managed to get in contact with Orla, so before they let him go they asked Mark if he would ask her to come in and mentioned something about her being there briefly earlier. His head was spinning when he stepped out into the waiting room and saw Jean rushing towards him.

"Are you okay?"

"Yeah. Just tired and a bit worn down. Where's Orla? She isn't answering her phone to the Gardaí." Mark hadn't even guessed there was anything wrong.

"Well she had a bit of a meltdown in here a few hours ago and stormed out. I just let her go. I think the weight of the work load at the moment is getting to her."

"Well it's hardly been same old, same old has it? It would get to a Buddhist monk Jean! Did she say where she was going or anything?" Mark asked, unimpressed by Jean's hard line.

"No."

"Fine." Mark took out his phone and switched it on while they walked out the automatic doors and into the car park. The phone vibrated and Mark put it to his ear.

"It's a voice message from Orla."

15

Orla got out of her car and looked up at 1225 High Park, then she turned her head right and left looking at the other houses in the ring. Her hands felt cold and her spine was stiff when she looked at the battered front door of 1226. She went to the front window and tried to look in but all the windows were covered. She checked the side of the house and saw a small black gate half hanging off the wall leading into the back of the house. She squeezed herself past it and found herself in a small overgrown garden; overgrown apart from the path worn in the grass from the back alley behind the houses to the back door of 1226.

Orla heard something. It sounded like something heavy falling, a saucepan or a tin tray, and she was sure it had come from inside.

"You fucking eejit!"

She stepped back around the corner to the side of the house and stood as still as she could. There were definitely people in 1226 and they must have had a damn good reason to cover their windows like that.

Orla knew whose voice she had heard. She knew it. That had been Patricia. Orla felt her fear being replaced by hatred.

She made her way slowly back to the corner where she had heard the voice from. There was some shuffling around but other than that it all seemed still. Orla didn't really know what she had been expecting, but this wasn't it. All these houses looked so rough, surely someone would be concerned if they knew people were actually living in them. According to Patricia on their first encounter they even had neighbours, something that hadn't slipped Orla's mind when she parked the car in the street and walked openly to the house. Her anger just stopped her from caring. The same anger that had stopped her calling the Gardaí when Annabelle had called her with the address. Why she left Mark the voicemail instead. She knew she had to go back to the car. If they were hiding out here they would be paranoid and seeing her car could make them do something drastic. Even being on the property had made Orla come to her senses. She realised how much more danger she had put the children in. She couldn't press down her ego and call the Gardaí. She hated them as much as she hated Patricia and Kevin Madden at this point. No, Mark always checked his phone. He had been there over two hours when she left the Garda station. He wouldn't be in there much longer.

Orla turned back down the walkway and slowly squeezed herself back through the broken gate. She felt her pocket for her keys as soon as she reached the road. Suddenly her phone rang, loudly. The shock of it made her stop for the briefest of moments as her head computed how close a call that had really been. If her phone had rung ten seconds earlier, she would still have been at the bottom of the walkway right beside Patricia Madden. Her hands were shaking violently when she took the phone out of her pocket and pressed the hang up button and shoved it back into her pocket. When she got to the car she got in and started the engine before she had even closed and locked the doors. She put the car into first gear and drove back slowly and parked right beside the only way in and out of the small group of dilapidated houses. She had a perfect view of all of the houses from there; 1225 with its yellow and black tape, 1226 with its boarded-up windows and secrets. She took out her mobile again. She had another three missed calls. It was an hour since she left the voice mail and all the calls were from the Garda station. *They know where the house is and they are not here. They ring me instead.* Orla had no idea that they needed her to ID victims in photographs; she presumed they had gotten the message and either didn't believe it or hadn't bothered coming there yet. Then the phone rang again.

MARK CALLING

"Mark? Did you get my message?"

"Orla, where the hell are you? Are you at that house?! Tell me now!" Mark shouted down the line.

"Relax. I haven't done anything."

"Yeah, like you didn't ring the fucking Garda station as soon as you found out! You leave me a message that you know I won't get for ages! Now listen to me. Get your ass into your car and drive away! Pull up on the side of the road somewhere, call me and I'll come meet you. They know the address and they are on their way. Now just get into your car and call me when you are down the road a bit. Okay?"

"Okay," Orla agreed. She felt like she was in a dream. She felt light-headed and angry all at once. It felt like such an odd combination. *What if they get out the back?* The idea came from thin air but all of a sudden Orla felt an overwhelming urge to sneak into the alley she had seen behind the houses. If they made a run for it she could scream and yell until the thick Guards came around the back. They probably wouldn't even surround the house before they knocked on the front door. They would be there soon. She had to make a decision.

Orla looked left and right and scanned the row for any eyes before she opened the car door. Before she knew she had even made a decision she was running across the grassy green in the direction of 1225, the Madden's house. She got to the side of the house, but unlike 1226 the gate cutting the front from the back garden was high and locked. She took off her boots and pushed them through the bars at the bottom of the gate, then she climbed over it. At the other side she jogged through the long grass and nettles in her stockinged feet, leaving her boots abandoned on the weedy concrete. There was a rotting wooden fence dividing the house from the alleyway with a 'practical' little gap at one end. Orla knew why the gap was there and it made her shudder. She crept along the fence until she came to it and glanced down the back alley in the direction of 1226, then back in the other direction. It was eerily empty. She listened hard for footsteps or doors opening or closing but there was no noise to hear. The place was dead. After checking the alley again Orla stepped through the gap into the open. Keeping as close to the back wall as she could, she moved towards the back garden of 1226 steadily.

Nearly there. Nearly there, she repeated over and over in her head, eyes focused on the end of the wall. There was only a small hedge at the back of 1226 and another little gap where Orla had first seen the back alley. Before she could stop herself, Orla was at the end of the wall peering around the corner at the back of the filthy-looking house.

Nicole didn't really feel hungry anymore. Her tummy had been sick for the past few days and it was stopping her from giving in to sleep. The bucket was filled to the brim and she was sure they must be able to smell it in the rest of the house. She was so embarrassed by how the room looked and smelled that she had assumed it was the reason why she was only getting bits and pieces to eat.

She lay on the floor and rubbed her palms over her stomach, lifting her knees up every now and then to ease the pain. For the last few hours there had been a dreadful sound coming from somewhere else in the house. Like someone in pain who had their mouth covered up. It reminded Nicole of her ma in not nice times and she wished it would stop. If she had a choice between having her stomach ache stop or the noise stop, she would pick the noise.

Then it happened. She heard the man come up the stairs and unlock a room. He closed the door and that was when the sound stopped. Nicole didn't worry about him coming in anymore. He didn't do anything other then empty the bucket, refill the water bottle and sometimes give her food. But after she heard him go into that room, heard the sound stop the way it did, she was very scared of him again. From now on if he came in she would curl up in the corner and be as quiet as possible. Then she managed to doze off.

Nicole was woken up some time later by another noise, this time at her door. Immediately she remembered her last thought and pushed herself into the corner of the mattress. The door opened slowly and the man walked in. He hardly looked at her as he crossed the room and picked up the bucket. Then he backed out of the room, put the bucket down in the hall and caught her eyes looking out at him from behind her knees. His look was a warning that she recognised. He closed the door softly and locked it. Nicole didn't move until she was positive he was gone then she lay back down again.

Kevin padded down the stairs and into the kitchen. Pat was looking rough as fuck, leaning over beans she was making on the hob and smoking a fag, not minding where the ashes went. He walked straight by her and looked through the small hole he had drilled in the back door. All looked clear so he unlocked it, walked out and closed it behind him. Halfway down the garden path he cut across through the grass and started dumping the contents of the bucket out on the lawn. When it was empty he turned back around to walk back to the house but something caught his eye. He thought he had just seen a head looking around the wall from the alley. For a second he didn't know what to do. It might have been nothing, but he was sure he had seen someone. If it was someone should he go back inside?

In a split second he placed the bucket down carefully and ran quietly along the wall to the hedge. He felt his breath deepen as he moved along its rough surface towards its end. When he got there, he looked around the corner down the alley. He was right! In a leap he cleared the low hedge and saw shock spring into a neatly dressed woman's face. She was only two feet away and he caught her easily. She was a big girl, tall and strong looking. Kevin slammed her face first into the wall as hard as he could to take some of the strength out of her. When he straightened her up from the blow he pinned her there against the wall. Blood began to trickle from her nose down her upper lip.

"Who the fuck are you?!" he demanded, inches from her face.

"I lost my dog," she stammered.

"And you thought it would be in my fucking garden? Come on! Now!" He dragged her off the wall and back towards the house. He forced her though the hedge and threw her on the grass where he had emptied the bucket. She began to sniffle.

"Shut the fuck up!" he hissed, bending close to her ear.

Orla kept very still. So this was Kevin Madden. He was your average scumbag; built a bit bigger maybe but he had all the traits of a forty-something-year-old scumbag. When she had seen the door open she had been terrified but now she wasn't. She had gone through so many emotions in the past few hours, she didn't know what she was. He was carrying a bucket and didn't seem all that worried for a man on the run. He started to pour something on the grass; a nasty-looking substance. It took a few moments before she realised what it was.

Then the man turned around and Orla pulled her head back in quickly. *Did he see me?* she thought in a panic. She stood as still as she could. She couldn't hear anything. There was no noise. Nothing happened...

Next thing she knew Kevin Madden was right in front of her after jumping the hedge. She didn't even have a chance to run. Orla felt his fingers dig into her arms. She felt him throw her into the wall and she definitely felt the wall do some damage to her nose. She was stunned. When he asked who she was she said she had lost her dog. She wanted to buy her brain some time after the blow. He pulled her in the direction of the house. Her nose was making her eyes water. Then he shoved her down onto the filth in the grass. Orla groaned when she saw where she had landed.

Kevin bent down to her face and whispered threateningly; Orla had heard worse. Then he started to walk away. She pulled herself up and saw him bending down over a bundle of knotted ropes. There was solid concrete block on the grass beside him. As tempting as it was, Orla went for a piece of two by four instead. Once, hard, on the back of the head. The only noise was the impact because she knelt on the back of his head when he fell.

"Come with me you fucking prick!" She had him by two pressure points, one in his shoulder and one in behind his ear, so she found it easy to make him stand and walk back though the gap in the hedge down the alley out of sight from the house.

"Kneel down," she ordered and he did as he was told.

"Lie face down." He tried to struggle but Orla tightened her grip on his shoulder and he dropped forward without any more problems. She kneeled as heavily as she could on the middle of his back, let go of his ear but kept her firm grip on the delicate muscle of his shoulder. Orla reached into her pocket for her phone and pressed 1 for it to dial Mark's number.

"Two minutes Orla! We'll be there in two minutes! Have you left?"

"Not exactly. Back alley behind house. Come now." And she hung up, put the phone away and focused all of her attention on making Kevin keep his fucking mouth shut. It was not long until she could make out the sirens.

Mark wished Jean would do more to keep up with the squad cars ahead of them. If there was ever a time to drive fast this was it, and Jean just didn't seem to get that. *Orla would have*, he thought as they pulled into High Park. When they came out of the trees they saw Orla's car parked up like there was not a thing in the world wrong. Mark found himself very worried about Orla. He had told her to drive away and park. What had happened to make her go in? Why was she in the back alley? Was she alright?

The five Garda cars had pulled up outside the Madden's home first. He saw two jump a gate at the side of 1225 and another two run down the side of 1226. Mark jumped out of the car and tried to run towards 1226 but Sergeant Martin held him back.

"Orla called me! She's in the back alley."

"Wait now Mr Tynan. They know what to do."

So he was forced to stand and wait on the green and let the real men do their jobs. The two detectives strolled around the back of the house as soon as the rest were inside. A minute later Garda O'Connell came from the back with a man who could only be Kevin Madden, handcuffed. Then right behind them came Orla. Her face looked awful and a bit bloody, her trousers were badly stained and she wasn't wearing shoes but she was alive and walking. Another Garda was walking alongside her asking questions. Mark knew she was ready to thump him so he went towards her.

"He attacked me, don't worry. I didn't go to the nightclub looking for a fight," she explained.

"Yeah. Save it for them." He smiled and gestured to the Guard who was still looking in Orla's direction with concern written all over his little face. Jean stood back at the car taking in the scene. An ambulance pulled in and now a medic was tugging Orla into the back of the thing.

"Just give me some tissues and I'll go to the hospital a bit later." She brushed them off. Everyone was now standing and waiting to hear what was happening inside. A radio crackled.

"We need a stretcher." The crew from the first ambulance ran to the house.

Orla and Mark exchanged a glance. The front door of 1226 was opened up and the crew disappeared inside. Then a female Garda walked out the front door with two little girls, each holding one of her hands. Orla felt tears falling down her face and Mark walked towards them in disbelief. The girl on the right was Nicole Kelly. She looked worn down but it was her and she was still alive too. The girl on the left was a girl who looked Eastern European who neither of them had seen before. Another medic came and whisked them into the back of a second ambulance. They waited for Stephanie to be brought out next but she didn't come. Next came Patricia Madden's fat ugly face, shouting and roaring and doing her best to throw off the two guards who were restraining her. She was brought out just in time to see her husband being driven towards the lane to the main road. Mark and Orla watched with their mouths open as she kicked and threw her head around trying to avoid being put in the back of the squad car. Everything seemed to fall quiet for a few minutes. The ambulance left with the two girls and the squad car finally drove off with Patricia thrashing around in the back seat. Mark turned back around to the house.

"Who is that?"

Orla and Sergeant Martin turned in time to see someone being carried out on the stretcher. They could only see the top of the person's head and from that angle Orla thought it was an adult male. The hair was short and choppy. Then the stretcher was moved parallel to them.

"I believe we have just found Breda Flood Byrne," said Sergeant Martin quietly. "Orla we'll need a statement from you about what happened before we arrived."

"Okay," she replied, mesmerised by the figure being moved into the back of the stretcher.

A guard came through the front door and jogged up to Sergeant Martin.

"The big wigs are looking for you sir."

"I believe it's time for my close-up. Excuse me."

Sergeant Martin stepped over the threshold into hell. The house smelled so bad that he found himself involuntarily taking out his hanky and holding it over his mouth and nose.

"No Stephanie Connors," called detective Griffin.

"How can that be? She was in the pictures," Sergeant Martin replied. "They're keeping her somewhere else perhaps?"

"Yes they are. We found this." Detective Griffin held out his hand. He was holding a red, hardback notebook that had definitely seen better days. He flipped it open with his gloved hand and held it out so the Sergeant could read the tiny writing inside. There were three columns on each page. On the left was a long list of names; in the middle there were more names; and in the last dates marked out and in. At first he couldn't comprehend what he was looking at. Then he had it.

"Open it on the last entry."

Griffin obliged and held the book out again on the last page.

Tom w.   Stephanie.   Date out and no date in.

"We need to get back into the cars."

"I'll get Yeats and some boys," responded the detective.

The Sergeant had to leave 1226 before he even had a chance to look around. Mark and Orla watched him turn around and come out of the house, taking a very large mobile phone from his pocket and making a call. Then Detectives Yeats and Griffin walked out of the house too and started to make their way towards them.

"We'll need a social worker. We have evidence that Stephanie Connors is being held at a different address," Griffin told them quickly.

"Where?"

"We'll call you when we have it. Stay put 'til then."

The three men went to one of the two remaining squad cars and got in. Four other Gardaí came out and walked right past them to another car. Mark knew there were now only one squad cars and two Gardaí left at the house. This was big. Stephanie Connors hadn't come out of the house, and now all the guards were high tailing it off?

He thought out loud, "They're gone to get Stephanie."

Stephanie knew there was going to be a party. Mister Tom had brought back big bottles of Coke and lollipops and big glass bottles of drink from work the evening before. She saw them when he let her out of the bedroom. Now she was sitting on the bed watching a kids' programme with little boys and girls playing hurling and winning prizes. Stephanie was never very good at hurling. She could never hit the ball. Still, she would have loved to have a go at the game. Get herself an iPod or a stereo because everyone who played got something. So if she was playing she would get something too, even though there was no way she would have been able to get the sliotar into the red plastic goals. Then she could bring her nan home a present too.

For the twenty minutes the show was on, Stephanie managed to put the party at the back of her mind, but now, with the credits rolling, she wondered how much time she had left before he was home. How long until the other men arrived? Would there be more girls tonight? Probably. Usually one or two of the other men brought someone. Stephanie felt the coldness go from her scalp down her neck and into her spine. She got up from the bed and walked into the small pink ensuite. She turned the big knob on the shower and let it run. For a few minutes she just stood there and watched the white stream hitting the ugly pink tiles. Then she took off her socks and stepped under it. She felt her clothes drink up the water like they were thirsty and her hair soak through. The water made her feel cleaner. She sat down on the plastic shower tray, closed her eyes and let the water do its job.

She didn't hear a thing other than the water. So when she saw a dark figure in her bedroom through the open bathroom door, she thought it was Mister Tom home from work and up to unlock the door. Usually she didn't want him to see her in the shower, she didn't like to encourage him, but today was different. She just sat there and looked at the figure through the water that was running in and out of her eyes.

Detectives Yeats pulled the car into the address given to him by Sergeant Martin. The second car pulled in behind them followed by another car that had joined them on the road from Pearse Street. The Sergeant had been on the phone with his contact during the journey over to make sure he had the right address, but now he was sitting forward in the passenger seat with his seatbelt off. Justice Thomas White was in session for the next ten minutes, he wanted to get into that house as soon as he could.

They had the front door broken with one good shoulder by one of the bigger team members and they flooded the house. They were in the kitchen and in the sitting room; in the bathroom and in the first bedroom. Then Detective Yeats' hand fell on the only locked door in the whole place, the second bedroom. He could hear a shower running.

"Lads!" he called down the stairs, before turning sharply and shouldering in the door. The room was definitely odd. Green and pink floral wallpaper and an old-fashioned white and lace duvet cover with matching curtains. He turned to his left and saw the door of the ensuite was open wide. He could see the shower. He could see the drained little girl sitting under the water with her clothes on.

He froze and didn't know if he should go to her. Would she be scared of him and think he was like the other men? He didn't have long to straighten himself out because Sergeant Martin walked into the bedroom behind him and strode right over to the small bathroom.

"Stephanie? Is that you? We are the Gardaí and we've come to get you out of here. Are you alright?" In the blink of an eye he had the shower off, gotten a big white towel from somewhere and was wrapping Stephanie up in it.

"You're alright now. Good girl. You're alright now," he said over and over to the drenched bundle in his arms as he carried her out.

Yeats saw the other men standing behind him and told them to continue the search just in case. There was a big white wardrobe at one end of the room and for some reason Yeats found himself drawn to it. He opened the big double doors and stood back. There were some ridiculous dress-up clothes hanging up neatly on white silk-covered hangers. Things with big skirts and princess dresses galore. *Sick fuck.*

Then he saw it. Along the bottom of the wardrobe there was album after photograph album, one after the other, all expensive looking and in two neat rows, one on top of the other. On top of them were matching CD cases.

16

After pulling Orla's boots back through the side gate of 1225, Mark and Orla were in her car on their way to the address Sargent Martin had called them with. This was inter-agency cooperation at its best, which made Orla very happy. They were finally doing something. Jean had gone back to the office to report back to the department.

"You stink Orla Flynn," Mark spat out of the blue, driving her car with ease.

"Eh what the hell? Why?" She was cleaning up her face the best she could with some baby wipes and a first aid kit.

"No you really, really stink." He wrinkled up his nose.

"Oh. That. It's my ass," she laughed, sticking a big plaster over the bridge of her nose. "I interrupted Kevin Madden while he was dumping out some shit from a bucket. He pushed me into it afterwards and I landed on my ass. I didn't think the shit in the bucket was actual real life shit in a bucket."

Mark was laughing away when Orla glanced over at him in the driver's seat of her BMW. He wasn't so bad looking when he laughed. But his laughter was cut short by the shrill ringing of his mobile phone.

"Mark. It's Sergeant Martin here. We need you to hold back until I call you again. Justice Thomas White will be home very shortly and we want to nab him while we are here."

"No problem. We'll be in the carpark up the road from the house. Just call us and we'll be two minutes away."

"We have her by the way. I'll be calling a bus as soon as we have him. She is okay for now but she seems a bit… disturbed. We'll need to get her checked out."

When Mark hung up he had an awful image of Stephanie being locked in the back of a squad car alone while this guy was paraded in front of her.

"Okay we have to wait. I want to get to the girls in Crumlin now though. Do you mind if I head over and get you to meet the Guards, get Stephanie and follow us over?"

"Nope, I wouldn't mind the few minutes to change my clothes. You hop out and grab a taxi."

Mark indicated and jumped out of the car.

"See you later," she called as he jumped out, leaving his phone on the front seat.

Orla moved over to the driver's side and felt something under her bum.

"Okay." He caught her eye for just a second longer than he had to and Orla felt a bit weird about it but there was too much going on for her to give it much thought and she pulled off and kept going.

Sergeant Martin was looking after the girl and the detectives were putting the plan into action. All of the vehicles were pulled around the corner and two Gardaí were hiding in neighbours' gardens waiting to give everyone the green light when they saw his green Excellence coming. They were lucky; most people were tucked up in their houses and hadn't noticed a thing. There was still a chance that he would notice the crack in the front door around the lock but they would just have to take that chance.

Sergeant Martin had Stephanie rub the towel onto her hair as quick as she could and then he wrapped her back up and put his big Garda fleece on over it. He got her to rub her hands together and rub her legs as quick as she could. He had the car running and the heating on full whack so she wouldn't be cold. She was stony-faced through the whole thing. He had tried to chat to her but she hadn't responded once. Fifteen minutes later the radio came on and one of the lookouts reported that the car had driven into the estate. Two minutes later the other lookout reported that he had just passed her.

Detective Yeats was positioned behind the next door neighbour's front garden wall. His heart beat fast when he heard the second call on the radio. This was a judge and he got the chance to shit all over him. Yeats couldn't help himself.

He was happy to be picking up someone more white collar; especially someone as nasty as this one. He saw the green car passing slowly and indicating into his driveway. The car came to a halt in front of the garage door. Yeats could see the man inside gathering a few things together and reaching for the door handle. His head almost touched the roof of the car. He watched the car door open and a long thin man unfold himself out onto the drive. He must have been six foot six, with hair that didn't quite make it to the top of his head, just ran around the sides in a fuzzy mess. His glasses were a bit too big and his suit looked creased. Yeats pressed the button on the side of his walkie talkie and gave the order to go.

Sirens filled the air and Thomas White stopped dead in his tracks half way to the front door. Detective Yeats ran up the driveway towards him. Thomas White was holding a briefcase and a plastic shopping bag.

"On the ground please Mr White."

Cars pulled up in time to see him spread himself out on the tarmac. Yeats knelt close to his head and pulled his hands around his back to cuff him. Thomas White twisted his body until the two men were face to face.

"I am a small cog and if you give me leniency I will give you the larger wheel," he whispered.

"You held the girl in the house you live in? Not very smart for a judge. Oh and you will tell us everything." Yeats whispered back threateningly, before hoisting the man up with more effort than he really needed to use.

"Careful now," warned the paedophile.

"Fuck you." Yeats replied under his breath, just loud enough for Judge White to hear.

Orla drove up to the house but got directed to the bottom of the road. She found the Sergeant standing outside the squad car waiting to wave her down. Orla realised she was really watching how she was driving when she pulled in behind the car. Sergeant Martin walked up to the driver's door and opened it for her.

"I have a little someone for you. It's Stephanie Connors. She was sitting in a shower with all her clothes on. Locked into a bedroom with a bathroom attached to it. She isn't talking. The ambulance is on its way."

"I will look after her don't worry. Will I leave the car here? I don't really want to move her from your car to mine and then to the ambulance," Orla explained, getting out of the car and going to the boot.

"I will probably take a walk up to the house to see what's happening up there for our investigation so just leave the key in the visor for me."

Orla saw that he wanted to say something else. She wasn't going to interrupt him so she just stood there waiting for it. There was a silence for just a second before Sergeant Martin spoke again.

"You're not in trouble. Earlier I sounded like I was hinting that you were in trouble." He was embarrassed. Just a bit, but Orla could see it. Still, a part of her was relieved at hearing she wasn't in the firing line after leaving the voicemail for Mark rather than calling the Station directly, and maybe for going to 1226.

"Thank you Sergeant," she said honestly.

"I think we can do things a bit better the next time round though. What do you think?" It sounded like a warning but Orla couldn't be too sure.

"Definitely."

Sergeant Martin's forehead furrowed and he leaned forward, inspecting her bruised face.

"That's some shiner you're going to have. You need to get that nose seen to."

"Oh, it's a mess. And I'm expecting two lovely shiners to match." She smiled and tried to lighten the tone a bit. "Don't worry. This auld face has seen worse."

"I really hope not Orla. So you go on with her and I will see you in my office at nine a.m. Oh, and Mary Connors will be meeting you at the hospital.

"No problem. Thanks again Sergeant." Orla knew she would have to go in to give her statement, but she was glad that it wasn't going to be as awful as it would have been if they hadn't had this conversation.

Orla finally reached into the boot and took out a change of clothes for Stephanie before she went and opened the door of Sergeant Martin's car. Taking off her jacket she got into the back of the car beside Stephanie.

"Hi. I'm Orla. Your mam has been looking for you. She asked us to come find you as soon as she knew you were missing."

Stephanie turned her head. Her ma. Her lovely batty ma.

"Can I see her?"

"Yes. She's coming to meet us at the hospital. Do you miss her much?"

"Yeah. Can I go home with her?"

"If the doctors say you are good to go then you can. You are such an important little girl Stephanie. I am so happy we found you."

Orla saw blue and red out of the corner of her eye. The ambulance had arrived.

"Come on Stephanie. Time to go."

The crime scene investigators found one particular set of fingerprints in Mary Connors' mother's flat that interested them. They were bloody, and perfectly preserved on the handle on the inside of the kitchen door. As soon as they had Thomas White and Kevin Madden in the door Detective Griffin made sure they took two copies of both men's fingerprints and rushed them through forensics. The investigators had been called to 1226 and to the judge's house. They were blitzing the place. Patricia, Kevin and Thomas were waiting for the detectives in each of the three interview rooms. Yeats thought they should go into Kevin Madden first, put him up against the women, Noelle and Patricia, but Griffin wanted to get down and dirty with Patricia first. He wanted to go in from the Breda perspective. How could she let her own sister get into such a state? Why did she hate her so much?

They would be questioning Noelle again too. She was being held on remand for her trial but everyone was really waiting to saddle her with the other charges she would undoubtedly accumulate. They settled on Thomas White first. Yeats went to the office and got a copy of the Noelle Flood file with some of the court orders signed by Justice Thomas White inside.

White's hands were visibly shaking as he held the polystyrene cup to his mouth. His eyes were wide with fear and two dark patches had appeared under the arms of his beige jumper. His back was straight and his eyes kept darting towards the door.

"Here we have the small cog. Isn't that right Mr White?" Yeats mocked, walking through the door followed closely by Griffin.

"I was confused. I didn't know what I was saying," Thomas White mumbled.

"Oh right. So you took the girl yourself then?" Griffin threw back.

"I didn't say that."

"What are you saying then?" asked Yeats, now sitting across the table from him.

Thomas White leaned forward and put his elbows on the table, letting his head fall lower than his angular shoulders.

"I am saying I didn't take her. Look, I amn't even calling my solicitor yet." He lifted his head and looked Yeats in the eyes. "I want to comply fully but there is no big wheel. There are just sick, pathetic, weak people."

Yeats had already pressed record on the tape player down beside him. He leaned towards it.

"Interview one. Justice Thomas White, Detectives Yeats and Griffin 5.20pm." He straightened himself back up and spoke to Thomas White.

"I think you need to start from the beginning Mister White. When did you first start dealing with Noelle Flood?"

The ambulance took longer to get to the hospital than Orla had expected. Stephanie wasn't in any immediate danger medically so they took their sweet time. After about ten minutes when Stephanie was calm and resting, Orla took Mark's mobile phone out of her pocket and flicked through it. *No harm, no foul,* she thought to herself mischievously. She had found it when she was changing her clothes in the car but she hadn't looked at it yet. She opened his inbox and clicked down through the names of the senders.

Mam

Mam

Sean

Laura? Orla opened the message. Laura was Mark's long-term girlfriend, had been for years. Nearly fifteen years in fact. Orla had thought they were married until Jean had corrected her a year ago.

Fine. Bye, she read. *Nothing telling there,* she thought, exiting the message.

Laura. Orla entered the next message but she felt a pang of guilt when she read it. Too much guilt to be called a pang. Enough guilt to make her exit Mark's messages and put the phone back in her pocket, embarrassed. But it was too late. She had seen it and now she knew. *My stuff is gone and I put my key through the letter box. I hope you and your career have a fantastic life together. Let me know if you want the plants back. Goodbye asshole.*

She had never thought of Mark as a single man before and now that she had, she wasn't fully sure it was a bad thing. He wasn't as tall as anyone she had considered before. She could do flats. Maybe. Orla realised what she was thinking and was horrified at herself. *Good Jesus Christ are you sick girl?!* Then she quickly turned her attention back to Stephanie who was just basking in every mile that passed dividing her from the people who had had kept her.

"Is Nicole okay?" she asked quietly.

"Yes we have her too. She will be in the hospital we are going to. And another girl," Orla told her.

"Is it Tina?" asked Stephanie.

Orla had to remind herself that Tina was once held in the same house as Stephanie and Nicole. Stephanie had known Tina back then.

"No. Tina got out of hospital this morning. She has moved into a big house with my friend Annabelle." Orla changed her tone slightly. "Stephanie? Do you know who the other girl is?"

"No I thought there was only a few of us in the house. We usually met other girls at parties."

"How many girls do you think you have seen?"

"Loads and loads and loads. There were a lot of parties." Stephanie turned away from Orla and her annoying questions. She just wanted to see her ma. She didn't care about the booze or anything. She just wanted to see her ma, see Nicole and go home to the van.

Patricia Madden was screaming her head off in the interview room. It was pissing everyone off but most of them just gritted their teeth and got on with their work. Sergeant Martin came marching out of his office and bellowed for an explanation.

"She wants another fag, Sergeant, and she seems to want it now." Griffin and Yeats were writing up their interview with Thomas White who was to remain in custody. They heard the ruckus and decided it was time to interview Patricia.

"Sorry about that Sergeant. We'll be going into her now," apologised Griffin.

"Don't worry about it. We have all had our share of screamers. Let her at it. I will be receiving a call from Mark Tynan as soon as the doctors have seen to the girls and Breda."

"Good, good."

They all looked at Patricia Madden through the small window in the door. Then Sergeant Martin turned and left the detectives to it. He was trying to decode the log book found in 1226 by using the register of sex offenders.

The two detectives decided not to tell Kevin and Patricia Madden about the death of their son until they had gotten through the preliminary interviews. Even without telling her she would be difficult to deal with. Patricia stopped shouting as soon as the men walked into the room. Her beady eyes looked them both up and down in disgust. She saw herself as so below clean, fresh-smelling people, that she hated them to the core.

"We have just had a very long and interesting chat with Thomas White."

"Fuck you," she spat.

"He says you and your husband steal kiddies and give them out to perverts." Griffin put on the pressure.

"He is a fucking liar."

"He is a judge, for a few more days anyway. Who do you think a jury will believe?" Yeats asked her.

"He likes little girls. No one will believe a word that comes out of his cunting mouth. So fuck you."

"We are searching 1226 High Park as we speak. What do you expect we'll find there?"

"Fuck all."

"Like what?"

"Fuck you. I want a fucking lawyer. Now!"

The detectives looked at each other and went to leave. Just before the door closed behind them Patricia shouted,

"And a fag! I want a lawyer and a fag!"

Kevin Madden was sitting quietly in Interview Room Three looking at the glossy table top blankly. Yeats had gone to get Noelle brought to the station from the women's prison so Griffin went in alone first.

"Did you kill a little old lady so you could kidnap her granddaughter Mr Madden?" he asked as he was coming through the door.

Kevin Madden raised his eyes.

Detective Griffin continued. "It's just that we found a lovely big bloody set of fingerprints on the kitchen door handle and seeing as the results of their comparison to yours will be back any minute now, I was just wondering if you wanted to tell me anything."

Kevin just stared blankly back at him while he pressed the record button.

"It will look better for you in court if you confess, you know that. But only if it was you of course. Only if you went to the little helpless old woman's house and murdered her. If you didn't do it of course you shouldn't tell me you did." Griffin spoke quickly. He wanted some of his words to stand out. It would be up to Kevin Madden to choose which ones they were. He saw Kevin's eyes drop back down to the table top. He looked like a little boy. His hands were between his knees and his shoulders were slumped.

"Were you made do it?"

"I did it." The words came clear as day. Griffin smiled to himself.

"Did what Kevin?" asked the detective sitting forward.

"I killed the old woman. And I took her granddaughter."

"What else did you do?"

"I helped my wife run a house where we held kids for her aunt and her paedophile friends."

Detective Griffin's jaw dropped.

"Excuse me?"

Kevin Madden exhaled loudly.

"Patricia and I ran a house for her aunt Noelle. Noelle had kids. She sold them mainly or rented them out to men."

"Noelle Flood?"

"Yes."

"And what was Noelle's involvement in the killing?"

"She set it up. Gave me an address and two photographs. Told me to go to the flats and wait at the bottom of the stairs 'til I see the girl coming out and going past me. Then I had to go up and kill the woman in a room that wasn't the hall. Then I had to wait in the hall for the girl to come back and tell her that her granny was sick and I was sent to bring her to the hospital. I had to say I worked there. Then I had to bring her next door. No one saw me, but it was very close." Kevin still stared at the table. He hadn't blinked for some time. It made Griffin uneasy. So uneasy that he was happy to see Yeats who slipped in and took a seat quietly in the corner.

"What else did you do for Noelle?"

"We let her have her meetings in ours. We kidnapped kids for her. Usually at school or on the way to school. Usually foreign kids, some knackers and some normal too though."

"Who do you mean 'we'?"

"Me and Patricia. We have a van Noelle gave us. We keep it in a car park. The keys are in the house."

"Your house?"

"No, the holding house."

"And what was your role in this holding house?"

"Feed them, empty their shit and piss. Keep them quiet. I have to keep the place together." He cut himself off for a moment too long. Griffin jumped in.

"What else Kevin?"

"I gave the men tours and I kept the book."

Griffin needed to keep him talking.

"Kevin? Can you tell us the names of the people in that book?"

"I'll tell you everything I know."

The results from the fingerprints came back from forensics quicker than anyone could have hoped. It was a match. Kevin Madden had definitely killed Stephanie Connors' grandmother. He had also translated the fifty-two coded names of the men utilising Noelle's services in the log book and told the detectives as much as he could about the girls he had cared for during the nine years he had been working for Noelle Flood. He couldn't even hazard a guess at the number that had come and gone in those years. He had no idea where the majority of the girls had ended up. As soon as Yeats mentioned Tina Madden, Kevin clammed up. He wouldn't go there no matter how hard they tried. He just said the same thing over and over.

"Ask my wife."

He told them how Noelle had snapped up 1226 when it went on the market six years previously. Before that she had another house near Crumlin but Noelle had him do it up before she sold it after getting the new, better premises so close to the Madden's own home. Kevin even went as far as describing in detail fifteen of the child abductions he and his wife had undertaken for Noelle and how much they got for each one. He didn't like hurting the children though. He just wanted them to stay healthy and stay quiet. That was all.

"My wife would hit them. Punch them in the face and kick them. She was worse with our own. Not Simon as much but the young one went through hell with the cunt. And Tina ...." that's where he stopped every time. He would not speak about Tina no matter how many times they approached the subject. What Kevin Madden didn't know was that the detectives had been on the phone to Breda's doctor, who was thrilled to have her back in his care. Breda Flood Byrne had never willingly had sexual intercourse he told them. She had been raped in hospital. Now they wanted Kevin Madden's DNA. Tina could have been a plan to gain control of Kathleen and Breda. Maybe Patricia had organised it.

Eventually the sample was taken and the detectives wrapped the interview with the intention of picking up where they left off later when the results were in and they would have more to put pressure on him with. They charged him with kidnapping and first degree murder as well as child endangerment and sent him to wait for the special sitting of the court to find out if they would be held or if bail would be an option. Everyone knew bail wasn't likely to be on the cards. Not in a case as big as this and with charges as serious as the ones being dished out left right and centre.

With Kevin and Thomas's statements, and with the other evidence obtained, Patricia, Kevin and Noelle were all looking at long-term stints in the Irish prison system.

Orla walked beside the wheelchair that the porter had put Stephanie in. They were being whisked to X-ray then to MRI. Orla was thrilled when they finally stopped at a bed in a ward and she got to see Stephanie settled and ready for her mam to arrive. Eventually Orla found Mark in the waiting room. The girls were resting and he said he didn't know where else to go. Orla laughed, grabbed his coat by the cuff and led him to the family room on the ward.

They sat down and she took his phone out of her pocket and handed it back guiltily. He squinted his eyes at her when he took it.

"You read my messages didn't you."

"No, I swear I didn't." Orla lied like an angel. "But there was something I was wondering."

"Go on."

Orla took a breath.

"Is Annabelle still looking for someone to work with her in Rosewood?"

"Yes. Why?"

"Do you think I have the qualifications to apply and be taken seriously?"

"Absolutely. Without a doubt. Orla where are you going with this?" Mark asked, flabbergasted.

"I want to quit. As soon as possible. I can't do this any more after all the drama and I have to quit. Do something more positive." Orla let it all out on the table. Mark looked on with sadness. When she was done, Mark spoke.

"I'll make the calls. Annabelle will be thrilled."

"I'm sorry but I want to go find Breda Flood Byrne. You can deal with the girls from here can't you?" Orla asked, keeping the conversation to the matter at hand. Mark's reply came out meek.

"Go for it. I'll call you."

Orla went to leave but stopped at the door and looked back at him long and hard. "I really hope you do."

Then feeling like an idiot she went to call around to see which of the adult hospitals Breda had been brought to.

Orla found Breda easily. She was in the care of Doctor Ombino and had already improved with the IV of drugs and muscle relaxers he had immediately started when she arrived.

"I tried my best to find her. I went to a nursing home a few years ago and she was there. When I came back her sister had come and taken her. She hadn't got medication in years and years. It put her back massively in her treatment." The doctor's dark eyes were full of concern for Breda. Orla wanted to hug him.

"There is something else. I knew Kathleen, Breda's mother, since Breda was a little girl. She put a very specific plan in place for Breda for after Kathleen passed. That plan went out the window. Breda was supposed to get her mother's house. Kathleen had savings; she wanted Breda to have a live-in carer with her daughter Tina. She had the money and she wanted to make sure her family got to stay together. The nursing home told me Patricia and Noelle, her sister and aunt, had access to all Breda's money. They used it to try to lock her up in the home." The doctor was flustered and so was Orla. She couldn't believe what she was hearing. She instantly took out her phone and rang Jean McCaile. She agreed to meet her as soon as Orla called her to say she was out of the hospital.

Jean would get Breda what she was entitled to. No doubt about it.

Orla put her phone back in her pocket.

"Sorry, but where is her daughter? I think she should see her daughter," Doctor Ombino asked gently.

"She is with a very dear friend of mine. I'll have her brought over now but if I have my way, Breda and Tina will be with me forever."

Orla stood outside the door of the room where Breda was resting. She felt like she knew this woman. She was scared to meet her and have her ideals blown. This was a woman who had been torn away from her daughter. A woman who had been held prisoner and deprived of the medication that gave her comfort. Her wheelchair had been taken. Her ability to support herself and her daughter taken. Putting her hand on the handle was the first step. She pushed it open and walked inside. Her eyes landed on Breda who was sleeping soundly in the neat white bed. She looked so frail that Orla could make out the small trails that were her veins under the thin skin of her forehead. Her thick black lashes fluttered in a dream and a flash of anger crossed the sleeping woman's face.

Doctor Ombino had told Orla about the Breda he had known four years ago. She was determined to care for her daughter. She had done everything in her power to make her mother's life easier. She hadn't complained when her mother had to buy her clothes for their functionality rather than to Breda's taste. She had never even once missed any appointments for her physio, speech therapist or any of her doctors. She organised extra sessions weekly so she could communicate. And she could communicate. Breda had gotten to the point where she had been able to be understood by people who knew her. That broke Orla's heart. The fact that Breda and her mother worked so hard, all so Breda could one day live alone with her daughter just to have their dreams ripped apart. All their hard work went down the drain. Breda was back to square one, Tina was taken; both had been prisoners. Noelle Flood had done this to her own niece. Patricia Madden had done this to her only sister. Orla didn't have any siblings but she had longed for them her whole life. She would give her right arm for a sister to spoil rotten.

She walked up to Breda's bedside and looked at her face in awe. *You're still here. You brave woman, you are still here.* Tina needed to be here. She needed to understand who this woman was.

"I'll be right back," she whispered and padded back out of the room, closing the door behind her. She took out her phone again and dialled.

"Hi Annabelle. I have Tina's mam here with me in hospital. I think she needs to see her daughter."

Orla waited in the corridor until Annabelle showed up with a sleepy Tina in her jammies, a long coat and wellies. It was only half eight but Orla knew Annabelle's bedtime rules, it was half an hour past Tina's bedtime. *Under eight, bed at eight,* she murmured to herself, walking towards Tina.

"I want to see my real mam," Tina told Orla when she reached them.

Annabelle jumped in.

"We had a little chat before and we finished that chat off in the car. Tina knows the real story about her mammy now. Don't you honey?"

"Yes Annabelle."

Doctor Ombino appeared at the nurses' desk. He saw them all and started towards them.

"This is Breda's – your mam's – doctor. He has been treating her since she was a little girl. He remembers you Tina. From before," Orla explained to both Annabelle and Tina at the same time.

"Orla. Will you introduce me to your friends?" asked the doctor when he stopped in front of them with a smile.

Orla gestured to Tina first.

"Doctor Ombino, meet my very good friend Tina." Orla saw Tina smile at being called her very good friend. The little girl reached her hand up and took Orla's in gratitude.

"Tina, this is Doctor Ombino. He is probably the kindest man in the world and he is working really hard to make your mam feel better," Orla finished.

"It is very nice to meet you again Tina. You have grown up so much since I saw you before. You were only a teeny tiny little thing back then. Do you remember? I had a big jar of red lollipops and we all had them in the office. Even me." His lips stretched wide over his teeth and he chuckled through his smile. "Actually, I believe I have something for you in here." He reached into his pocket and took out a giant red lollipop and gave it to Tina. She looked at the doctor, then at the lollipop, then to Annabelle.

"Go ahead honey. The doctor is our friend now. We trust him very much," Annabelle told her softly. Tina took the sweet from the big brown hand.

"What do we say?" prompted Annabelle.

"Thank you," replied Tina, happily working on tearing the wrapper off.

"Hi I'm Annabelle. I have been looking after this little monkey." Annabelle shook the doctor's hand.

"I am pleased to meet you. Thank you for everything you are doing for Tina. It would mean so much to Breda and to Kathleen, her grandmother," the doctor gushed. "Breda loves her daughter very much. This would mean the world to her." The doctor glanced at his watch. "I need to wake her because she is due down in X-ray in fifteen minutes. How about you three wait here and I will come get you when she is awake. She will be a bit groggy though. It has been quite a while since she got her medications and it will take some time for her to get used to them building back up in her system again. Okay?"

"Okay," Orla and Annabelle chorused together. Then they navigated Tina and her lollipop to a row of chairs lined up along the wall halfway to the nurses' desk. She sat down with the lollipop consuming her thoughts.

Orla glanced at Annabelle. She was staring at Tina.

"You okay?" she asked.

"Yeah. I'm just wondering how healthy it is for her to eat that in here." Annabelle screwed up her face at the thought.

Orla laughed.

"Well the doctor saw her open it and he didn't say anything so I think we might be safe." They settled into silence for a few seconds before Annabelle broke it abruptly.

"Mark called me."

Orla felt her face flush.

"And?"

"And you want to work with us? Leave social work?" Annabelle looked at her.

"Yes. That's exactly what I want to do. I want to help you expand and I want to work with you full-time," Orla replied honestly.

Annabelle's serious face changed into a smile.

"Excellent. I just wanted to make sure it's what you really want." She turned back to make sure Tina wasn't listening. "I'm pretty excited now."

"Me too. But there is one more thing. I want you to consider something. Just consider it. Tina's mam had a lot of money taken from her. If we build a room for her and have her hire her own carer as well as me, is there any chance we can have Breda and Tina live with us permanently?"

Annabelle screwed up her forehead.

"We aren't state-run here Orla. We run on corporate donations. We can do what the hell we want once we stay within the state guidelines. They choose to give us grants we apply for, or not most of the time, so yes we could do it but I have to think about all this Orla. It's all a bit much for me to take in. I am the only permanent person living in the house. One of the other girls stay each night too but that's not the same."

Orla's head dropped.

"I understand. It's just that if they can't live there, then they will be living with me. That lady has no kind family left. All she has is Patricia and Noelle and I won't let them take her daughter away or lock her up again."

Doctor Ombino interrupted them by clearing his throat. Both women turned sharply and looked at him.

"I am sorry ladies but Breda is ready for her visitors. She is very excited to see Tina safe and away from those nasty people."

Epilogue

Breda woke up with Tina dressed and ready for school beside her bed. She smiled at her only child and how smart she looked while pulling herself up into a seated position quite easily.

"Is my hair alright?" Tina asked, catching herself in her mother's dressing table mirror and leaning over the wheelchair to get a closer look. Breda nodded and in a voice stronger and clearer than ever before said,

"Yes, you're only lovely."

"Thanks Mam. Can I use your straightener?" she asked, coming back to the side of her mam's bed.

"Not a hope. Not 'til your sixteen," Breda replied, rubbing the sleep from her eyes.

"'K. I'm going to the house to get the bus with everyone. Helen is in the kitchen sticking you on a cup of tea. I'd say you have another five minutes' peace before she's in shifting you out of bed," Tina giggled. "And Orla is here already. She said you have to come on up to the house and keep her company. I think she is sick of the belly already. Jesus it's only nine months, she needs to just deal with it."

Breda was laughing at her busy twelve-year-old. They were best buds but Breda didn't depend on her daughter for anything other than love and the odd bit of company when the pre-teen's busy schedule allowed it. Soon after Tina and Breda had been saved, Doctor Ombino had organised her to begin a type of treatment that had only been in the earliest stages of trials when Breda had first applied for it. It had worked wonders and Breda had the use of the majority of her upper body muscles, including her face and mouth. She could speak up now and she made use of it. Being in the chair was nothing to her any more. She had help but she was independent and it was all because of Orla and Annabelle. They were family to her now. They were her real true sisters. She had outside help too. A lady called Helen who was happy to help Breda get dressed in the mornings and undressed in the evenings. Breda liked to have her dignity after her degrading ordeal.

Not to mention Jean McCaile! Jean McCaile who had gotten Breda her inheritance back, all of it. What was in Noelle Flood's bank account massively overshadowed the money Breda was owed and Noelle had given it back without very much fuss once she established that Breda didn't mind if they had to do it in a civil case. Thankfully it didn't come to that and Breda now lived in her own apartment with her daughter, attached to the end of the new extension of Annabelle's house. It was beautiful and the perfect place for Breda to have therapy and physio. She was a pretty busy woman these days and it made her heart feel full for the first time since she was a toddler. Tina had transformed herself. She had friends and visitors. Tina had her very best friend in the world, Hannah, who was around lot of the time. Tina loved to spend time caring for the small children in the house too. Annabelle loved Tina. Orla loved Tina. Breda loved Tina. Life was good.

Orla waddled into the kitchen.

"Sorry I'm late!" she called into the hurricane of school preparations. Five little people ran at her legs.

"Morning!" they all shouted, not exactly in unison, giving her a big hug all at once.

"Morning guys. Say morning to the baby or it will be kicking me all day." The little boy and four girls cupped their hands around their mouths and whispered their good mornings to the baby taking over Orla's middle.

"Okay, you need to be ready to go in twenty minutes so chop chop! Finish getting dressed. I'm getting the breakfasts going." Orla got to it. She took out twenty-two bowls and twenty-two spoons and ten boxes of non-sugary cereal. The school bus would be there in twenty minutes but it would leave when the last child got on board and no earlier. Annabelle always gave them a few extra 'just in case' minutes by getting up just a little bit earlier than they had to. The bus usually pulled out half an hour before school even started.

Orla filled two eight-slice toasters and wondered to herself where Annabelle picked up such accommodating things. Five juices were put out at each end of the huge kitchen table along with three tubs of butter and four litre jugs of milk. The masses began to arrive and sit and only then did Annabelle swan in with a handful of school bags.

"Morning Orla!" Annabelle called, an oasis in the midst of the chaos.

"Morning zoo keeper!" Orla called back with a wink.

"Morning elephant!" called one of the kids from the table where the older ones were helping the younger ones butter their toast and pour out their milk on top of their colourful bowls of cereal. Everyone laughed, including Orla and Annabelle. Annabelle was loading lunch boxes from the fridge into school bags.

"By the time the baby is born you will be able to handle it with your eyes closed."

"Mark seems to think so anyway. He keeps going on about what good parents we'll be. It gets a bit old after so long you know?" Orla wiped up a spill and handed out more orange juice. "Haylee eat more than that. A half a slice of toast does not a breakfast make." The pigtailed pre-teen rolled her eyes and picked up another half slice of toast.

"Better than nothing. Good woman."

Annabelle was now busy lining up shoes and lunch-filled school bags along the wall.

"Oh I understand how that would be annoying. Tell him to get a grip," she laughed. "Sure a few days of seeing how down and dirty parenting is, and he will be well and truly knocked back to planet earth."

The back door opened and Tina walked into the kitchen.

"Morning all," she called.

"Morning Tina," the room chorused.

"Morning again Honey," said Orla as she leaned down and received a kiss on the cheek. Tina walked around the table and

Annabelle paused for a good morning hug before running off to do some hair. They had to wake the babies after they got the school-goers on the bus and down the lane.